Adolescent Summers

Cameron James

SRL PUBLISHING

SRL Publishing Ltd
London

www.srlpublishing.co.uk

First published worldwide by SRL Publishing in 2024

SRL PUBLISHING
THINKING DIFFERENTLY, DELIVERING CHANGE

ISBN: 9781915073396

3 5 7 9 10 8 6 4 2

A CIP catalogue record for this book is available from the British Library

SRL Publishing is a climate positive publisher offsetting more carbon emissions than it emits.

This book is for Kit Connor, and anyone who has ever experienced something similar.

Content warnings:
Swearing, alcohol, sex, transphobia, car accident

Series 10

Day 1

There was something familiar about this set. The lights, the furniture, the smell of hairspray. Sometimes coming back to this set felt more like coming home than *going* home.

It was like that song from an Andrew Lloyd Webber musical. The one about the old timely movie star.

Sunset Boulevard.

She sang *that* line, those in particular lines.

I know my way around here.

The cardboard trees, the painted scenes, the sound here.

It didn't matter how much I'd changed; this place never did. It was a comfort. Or was it? Maybe it was *actually* terrifying how frozen in history this set was.

My deadname being blacked out with a sharpie on my script proved that maybe this was a recurring nightmare rather than a fond memory.

I gave it to Brooklyn the moment he was within armlength of me. I looked towards him as he huffed a swear word, the script hanging at his side as he searched the props table.

He soon found a sharpie and wrote *OZ* in huge letters across the front page. I exhaled, thumping my chest three times, he winked back at me.

Before the *Sunset Boulevard* lady sang *those* lines, she sings.

I don't know why I'm frightened.

And okay, I don't know the actual story of *Sunset Boulevard*, we hadn't been to see it so I didn't know if she *should* be frightened, I just didn't know but I knew that there was every reason for me to be.

It had been eighteen months since we closed production on this set. The end of series nine, when my character *finally* got to kiss Brooklyn's. A fandom dream come true; things looked like they were finally settling into place for all our characters. We all knew we were going into the last series; we were only contracted for ten. None of us were renewing our contract, we were in the end game now.

A week after production closed, so did the world.

We were supposed to be back on set a month later, four weeks off then back for series ten.

Now, we were stood with masks on, *after* sticking a swab down our throats and were being told not to go near each other. Even though Brooklyn and I had been sleeping in the same bed for two years and Quincy lived with us.

I jumped when arms wrapped around me and then I relaxed back into them, sighing and leaning my head back to look up.

"Current mood?" Brooklyn asked the top of my head.

"You know that emoji, with the wiggly mouth and one eye bigger than the other."

He hummed acknowledging me. "The one no-one really knows what it means."

"That one," I agreed headbutting his chest. "Yours?"

"Scared," he whispered.

"Hey." I turn to him.

"It's stupid. Just haven't been around here for a long time, and I'll flip shit if anyone does wrong by you."

"I love you," I told him, "but let me put you on standby. We're not going straight in for attack remember."

"I didn't agree to that," Quincy sang as they passed.

I turned to look at them. "You can do *whatever* you wish. I do not own you."

Quincy rose two fingers at us.

"Script reading," they told us. I nodded as Brooklyn sighed.

"Let's do this." I tapped Brooklyn's chest, he leant towards me, kissing me even though we were both still wearing our masks. I laughed, shaking my head as I removed my mask from one ear. He was practically beaming when he did the same.

"I got you."

"I believe you."

He kissed me.

I gasped before he'd fully moved away.

"What?" he widened his eyes at me, I smirked.

"Social distancing." I stated. He rolled his eyes, pushing me away but not committing fully as he pulled me back by the arm.

Series 1

Day 1

I already regretted telling my mum I could do this alone. Who was I kidding? I hadn't even done my few adverts without my mum. This was a television series, and not just a pilot. A ten-year, ten-series contract.

I was *barely* ten years old. This series was about to take over my life and I'd told my mum she could wait outside.

I was officially an idiot, and this was the scariest thing I'd ever done. I had been the last to get my screentest. It had gone well, I *think*. I had done three before this, they'd all gone well, too.

The lady doing the test had told me to head to the script reading room, apparently *everyone* had beaten me there. The silence, however, was like there was no one there. Everyone else looked as, if not more, awkward as I did. I hadn't done *any* auditions or screentests with these kids.

There were three others, two boys and a girl. Another girl. They were all around my age.

I had known there'd be other kids. Of course, there would, the books that inspired the show - that I'd binge read before today, were about four kids who went on adventures and solved mysteries. *Secret Seven*, meets *The Magic Key*, meets *Narnia* kind of thing.

It was pretty good.

I knew I was playing Izzy, the strong courageous character, with a sharp wit, who climbed trees, and scraped their knee, who was *one of the boys*.

I tried to guess who the others were playing.

The other girl, a very young-looking black girl, with her hair in space buns, some of the curls of her hair dropping over her face. She must've been Ally, the main female protagonist, who was a ball of sunshine, with far too much optimism. Dakota. She was Dakota.

The Japanese boy, their hair long and shaggy with a sweeping fringe. They were Todd. The dork, who did all the research, and knew all the facts. The Willow if you will. Quincy. They were Quincy.

And the tall white boy, who looked a little older than us, with short cropped blonde hair and freckles all over his face. They were definitely Kevin, the main character, the male protagonist, the main event. Charming, affectionate, compassionate and attractive. Brooklyn. He was Brooklyn.

He scared the living daylights out of me.

I choose to sit beside Dakota.

"Welcome to day one," the lady with bright red hair said who I'd been told was our chaperone, Eliza. She had a coffee cup and a nose ring. I don't know which one I was more intrigued by. "I know we're all a little bit nervous, heck so am I, so we're going to read through our script then go through that door and eat doughnuts and play some games."

I laughed as did Dakota.

"Are you ready for your first script?" Eliza asked as if she was trying to pump up a pre-concert crowd. "We're starting with episode five. Weird, weird, I know but that's just how we do things around here."

"Why are we starting with episode five?" Brooklyn asked, his head tilted like a golden retriever, the question would've probably come off as rude if Brooklyn didn't have the charm of a million charm bracelets.

"Because episode five has a flash back to everyone meeting."

"Smart," Quincy added. "I totally appreciate how smart that is."

"Thank you, Quincy," Eliza proclaimed then passed me a script. It wasn't as thick as I'd expected although I suppose that'd make sense. This wasn't a feature length movie after all. My name was written on the top in a black sharpie, highlighted in green.

ADOLESCENT SUMMERS
SERIES 1
EPISODE 5

"Whoa," I said out loud. I stuttered, swallowing deeply because the *entire* room had turned to look at me. "What? This just got real."

Brooklyn laughed, smiling widely at me, his teeth were a little crooked. It was endearing.

"This just got real," he agreed.

Series 10

Day 1

"Good morning, team," Eliza declared placing a tray of coffee cups into the centre of the table. "There's been a lot of changes around here this time around." She smiled at me affectionately before she picked up a cup, turning it in her hand and passing it to me.

Oz.

"Thank you," I whispered then I swallowed deeply. "Thank you Eliza."

She winked at me.

"And this hair, I love it." she declared to Quincy. They laughed, removing their mask to drink from their cup. Their hair was currently purple. "As much as I love it though, you know it'll have to go."

Quincy rolled their eyes. "We can do *literal* magic in this show, but I can't have purple hair."

"Just wait until Brooklyn learns about his nose ring," Eliza said, then winced and turned towards Brooklyn's whine. "It looks amazing, just... Kevin doesn't have a nose ring."

"Kevin doesn't have any fun," Brooklyn muttered; I choked on the sip of my drink.

"You've turned twenty-one since we last saw each other too, huh?" she nodded to me. "You were what?

Eighteen?"

"I was. Weeks away from my nineteenth." I pointed at Brooklyn, "he's twenty-three."

Eliza rose her hand, shaking her head as if she didn't believe such slander.

"You're getting old, my love," she rose Brooklyn's chin. "I don't know if we've got anywhere near enough makeup to make you look like a teenager."

"Words hurt, Eliza." He genuinely looked hurt for all of a second before he grinned at her. He reminded me of a kid who wanted praise for acting good.

"Look at you."

We all turned together. Dakota stood in the doorway; her arms open wide as she took in the room. Freya stood behind her, laughing and shaking her head.

"Oz, darling," Dakota continued, I blushed hiding my face from her, especially as her warmth towards me was unexpected. We hadn't had a proper conversation in maybe four years. She didn't let me hide too much before she came up behind me wrapping her arms around me. "You look incredible, I've only seen you on Brook's Tiktok." She stroked over my chin, lifting my head to inspect my face. "We need to talk," she turned to look at Freya. "She can drink now. Let's go out and drink and chat."

"I miss when you were kids," Eliza mumbled, then waved her hands at us. "You cannot go out and drink tonight. You have to show up early because Elaina is coming in tomorrow."

"The author," we chorused; Eliza laughed shaking her head.

"It's not going to be the *best* meeting."

"What I'm hearing is, drink to make it better?" Quincy rose their hand; Eliza shook her head pointing at them.

"No."

"Is this because of me?" I asked. Eliza winced. "Ah so that means *yes*. Fantastic. Do I need to be present for the recasting?"

"Oz," Eliza shunned as Brooklyn reached for me, lightly stroking the back of my neck as he laughed. "She has a lot of…" she paused looking up towards the ceiling, "…feelings about this series. She wants to make sure everybody is on the same page."

"Are we on the same page?" I asked. Eliza looked down towards me, she looked sympathetic for all of a moment before something else took her over.

"We are on the same page, Oz."

I swallowed, nodding, that had affected me far more than I'd thought it would.

"I have always been and will always be on your side. Okay? You're not kids anymore, but you're my kids and I will protect you *all* to the best of my ability." She looked around us all, "*every* single one of you." She pointed at Quincy, "but you have to give as well as receive, so *your* hair will be dyed back natural by the end of the week." To Brooklyn, "either take it out or we'll buy a bar for you to put in." To Dakota, "you will *not* go out drinking tonight."

"Fine," Dakota mumbled rolling her eyes at me. I pulled my tongue back.

"You will all be here; nine thirty sharp and you will *all* use those spectacular acting skills of yours to bullshit your way through the meeting. Deal?" She held her coffee out in front of her.

I glanced at Brooklyn; he was fiddling with his nose ring looking a little gloomy, but he nodded, tipping his cup towards Eliza's. I met them in the middle. Freya's followed without any real hesitation. Dakota rolled her eyes but nodded, knocking the straw of hers against ours.

We all glanced at Quincy.

They scoffed. "I have *many* feelings that are mostly negative." They stood. "But I guess we're a team." They knocked their cup against ours.

"Look at you," Dakota gasped *again* when Eliza had left us. I let her look at me, opening my arms so she could examine me fully. "Literally, darling, you could've told me."

"It wasn't nearly as simple as that," I whispered, then cleared my throat. "Lockdown kind of helped, I guess, bet you never thought anyone would say that."

"You just disappeared sunshine. You were in Brook's and Quincy's TikTok's so much, then you disappeared and when you came back you were…"

"Oz," I aided; she lifted my chin nodding as she hummed.

"How have they taken it?" she nodded vaguely in the direction of the office.

I laughed sarcastically. "They're pretending it's okay. I know it'll go south so fast tomorrow."

"You don't know that for sure," she said. I rose my eyebrow at her. "Well, *fine*, but we all love you." I laughed, although I didn't actually mean to.

"What made you choose Oz?" she asked instead of addressing my rudeness. I closed my eyes.

"It's lame," I assured her. She shrugged at me, a huge gesture that reached her ears. "You know…" I sighed, "you know that moment Dorothy opens the door, and her life is full of colour. The entire thing just fills the screen and it's so bright, no-one knew it could be so bright.

"You go into the film thinking it's just going to be black and white all the way through, beginning to end, *then* you get this taste of colour, and you realise life can be so much more." I bit my lip.

"You stepped into Oz?"

I nodded looking down at my shoes.

"What does that make Brooklyn?"

I snorted. "The scarecrow."

She crowed before turning in a gasp, clapping her hands over her mouth as she looked towards Brooklyn.

Series 9

Day 176

Brooklyn was practically dancing as he stood in the doorway of *The Clubhouse* set. He was excited, that I knew, he'd been practically ecstatic when we'd gotten the script and he read Kevin and Izzy kiss.

He'd practically crowed finally and had been like a child on Skittles as we prepared to film this scene. The last scene, of the last episode, on the last day of filming, the last thing we were shooting of series nine.

He'd filmed his episode six breakup with Ally this morning and had been told off far too many times for smiling during what was supposed to be a sad scene. Now, Dakota stood watching us film with a *big* ass smile on her face. Quincy at her side, looking far too amused and Freya sat crossed legged on the floor beside them ripping apart a pretzel.

I want a pretzel.

"Do you want a pretzel?"

"So much," Brooklyn groaned. "Let's get a pretzel after this."

I pointed at him, nodding hugely obviously disgruntling my braids as our hair stylist miraculously appeared in front of me, and squirted my hair with a spray bottle. I flinched, she laughed softly, stroking my hair flat before twirling a bit that didn't quite reach the plait in her finger and letting it fall down my cheek.

"Places," Jordan called as he took his seat, he turned his cap around on his head, so the peak was at the back, then he checked out our positions. "Let's go kids."

I took a seat in front of the computer that had a typewriter as a keyboard and didn't fully work, or at least, didn't work enough to distract us during scenes.

Brooklyn was scripted to make a dramatic entrance. He'd been practicing said dramatic entrance all damn week which was why we had to retake *his* entrance eight times because he fell, or because he couldn't stop giggling, because he ran into the set, because he made *me* laugh, because he came in too fast, because he came in too slow.

The eighth take was when Jordan got pissed with Brooklyn and told him in no uncertain terms that he was to do the entrance right this take otherwise he'd regret it.

Brooklyn finally got through the damn two-dimensional door.

"Izzy."

I waved my hand at him.

"One sec, I've got to do this whilst I remember it."

"Izzy," he pushed. I turned to look at him, frowning.

"What's wrong, Kev? What's happened?"

"Stand up," he told me. I pushed the chair back. "No, no wait, stay sitting down," he growled sounding frustrated. "How do people do this? How does anyone do this? They make it look so easy; you've seen it right…"

"What?"

"Boy meets girl, boy *fucks* up, redeems himself in some big unnecessary romantic action…"

"Kevin," I interrupted him, standing from the seat,

we both ignored as it rolled backwards a bit further than we expected.

"This is my big romantic action," he *shouted* at me, opening his arms wide as if he was saying ta-da.

"Ally."

"I broke up with Ally. We've been broken up for weeks, Iz."

"She didn't say. I couldn't do that to Ally. I couldn't..."

"Izzy, please."

"Kevin," I gasped. "I can't. You can't tease me with this."

"I'm not teasing," he shook his head raising his hands in surrender. "I swear."

"No, you don't understand." I sighed. "I've wanted this since the day we met. I've loved you for so long Kevin, you can't, you can't kiss me right now, then walk away and never come back."

"I'd never."

"Are you under a spell right now?"

"No," he laughed.

"Cursed, or have you drunk a potion?"

"The only potion I could've drank is a truth teller."

"Kevin," I swooned, then I shook my head. "Kevin, stop."

"You know there's one sure fire way to break a spell."

"This isn't a fairy-tale..." I paused, "*this* time."

"True loves kiss."

"Kevin," I shunned, he grinned at me with all his teeth. I looked away to laugh.

He turned my head back, his fingers threading through my hair, twirling *that* one piece of stubborn hair.

"I would like to kiss you."

I pursed my lips, biting deeply into the bottom lip.

"Can I kiss you?" he whispered. I swallowed and met his eyes. Brooklyn's eyes, not Kevin's, *not* the character he was playing, not him acting but Brooklyn. My Brooklyn.

"Yes," I whispered.

"Cut," Jordan called. We swore together. Brooklyn knocking his head against mine. "Hold that position for me," he requested before whispering to someone else.

"I can't believe I didn't get to kiss you then," he whispered as he continued to fiddle with my hair. I knocked my head back against him.

"I can't believe you broke up with Ally," I teased, he laughed, turning his head, searching out Dakota, who was now also sat on the floor watching us.

"I ship you two far more than Kevin and Ally," she proclaimed, making a heart with her fingers and raising it to us.

"To be fair, they have far more chemistry than you two did," Quincy murmured.

"Agreed," I rose my fist. Quincy snorted as they raised their fist back.

"Places," Jordan requested, "from Brooklyn's last line and, lights…"

I looked back at Brooklyn as he pushed my hair behind my ear, then pulled it back out.

"For continuity," he whispered. I sniggered then swallowed my laughter down.

"Action."

"Can I kiss you?" he whispered, well, he stage-whispered, his nose stroking against mine as I made him wait, I *really* made him wait. I saw it on his face as he yearned for me to reply whilst also trying to figure out if I'd forgotten my line.

"Yes," I told him. His entire face lit up. His fingers tangling in my hair before he came to me. He didn't pull me forward, instead, he took a step closer, he tilted my head backwards and then he kissed me. Brooklyn kissed me, with such a Brooklyn kiss that there was *no* way it was Kevin and Izzy, there was no way it was acting - I loved the guy, but he wasn't *that* good of an actor.

"And swell of music… cut."

He almost didn't stop.

I pulled away, smiling at him as he opened his eyes and grinned at me.

"Wow, that was good acting," he gasped at me, and I *squawked*.

Series 10

Day 2

"I'm going to cut to the chase," Elaina said with a laugh she sometimes did that meant this isn't remotely funny. We'd heard the laugh at least once every meeting we'd had with her presence, usually because one of us had gone off piece. Even though sometimes it was the writers that had led us astray from the original plot. She didn't appreciate being told that.

"Izzy isn't a boy," she smiled at me.

I grinned right back. "Ah, but see, I am," I told her. Quincy choked on their water as Brooklyn turned away from me, his shoulders shaking.

Elaina smiled at me as if she wished her hitman, that I was sure she'd have, would pull the trigger and end me right now.

"You understand the dilemma here," she continued. "The last book is when Kevin and Izzy really take off. Love conquers all."

"I haven't read it," I hissed back at her. "Just haven't *quite* had the time, but I don't see why Izzy can't transition or…"

"You could wear a wig."

"No."

"You want him to play a girl with that Adams apple?" Brooklyn laughed.

"You never heard of drag, darling," Quincy sang back to him.

"No, no, although I totally respect drag as an art form, I am *not* doing Izzy in drag."

"Come on, we can negotiate this."

"Negotiate? That sounds like a conversation that should be had with the writers," I mocked.

"Or at very least Oz's mother," Quincy commented. I bit my lip as Elaina rubbed her forehead as if she had a migraine coming on - it wouldn't be the first time she'd referred to us as a migraine.

"Kevin and Izzy can still be in a relationship," Brooklyn commented raising his finger as if he was in class. Elaina turned to him with a look of resignation.

"I wouldn't want you to be uncomfortable Brooklyn," she said.

"I am literally his boyfriend," he told her. "I've been his boyfriend for like, five years."

"Hence the on-screen chemistry," Dakota commented. I grinned at her, she winked back. "Somehow, it felt like I was cheating with Brook whenever we did a scene."

"Even though Oz was *literally* watching cheering you on?" Quincy smirked

"I'm very supportive of my boyfriend." I informed them, nodding.

"I feel like we're drifting off topic," Elaina said.

"I feel like this is a conversation meant for the writers, *not* us."

"No, Dakota." She pushed Dakota's name out through gritted teeth.

"What exactly do you want Oz to do?" Quincy queried as Elaina glanced towards them. "I mean, he's a boy, he can't just put that on pause because we have however many weeks of filming, can't you figure out something? This show is *literally* magic. He could take a potion or, cast a spell, some shit like that to become a boy because Izzy isn't comfortable."

"That's *not* in the book."

"It wouldn't be the first time we strayed from the book," Brooklyn *helpfully* pointed out. She rolled her eyes. "Quincy's entire relationship with AJ wasn't in the books but was loved by the fans. Dakota's whole storyline where she travelled isn't in the books. Kevin's disappearance *isn't* in the books."

"Your voice was breaking," Elaina reminded him.

Brooklyn tapped my head. "Now Oz's voice is breaking," he almost cooed. I hit his hand away.

"So, what I'm hearing is, you're unwilling?" she asked me.

I frowned back at her. "Unwilling to, what?"

"Co-operate with me?"

"Oh, I guess, yes."

"Why couldn't you have *waited* until we'd finished filming exactly?" she asked. I rose my eyebrow at her, putting my hand on Quincy's arm so they didn't start scrapping for me.

"Elaina, the world was ending. What else was I supposed to do?"

Lockdown 1

Day 56

Quincy hadn't made their way downstairs yet. AJ had, I'd seen AJ this morning and he seemed quite content as he wished me a good morning and went into our garden to read.

Brooklyn was also up but I'd lost him to Bud, who he'd very happily dressed in a little bowtie to take on his walk.

I decided my best bet was to infiltrate Quincy's bedroom, so I did just that. They were awake at least, on their bed playing on their Switch. They didn't even look my way when I walked into their bedroom.

"Hello, darling," they finally said then they looked at me, their eyebrow quirked. "I thought you were AJ, *but* hello darling to you, too."

I laughed then swallowed deeply.

"I bought something, and I'd like your help with it."

"Does this something aid Brooklyn in any way?"

"No," I snorted, then I gasped. "It is not a sex toy. He's got a new puppy; do you *think* we're having sex?"

"Hence the sex toy," They waved at me as if saying *duh*, I shook my head.

"What is it, darling?"

I passed them the box.

"All of it?" they asked.

I nodded. "Will you do it for me?"

"Of course, of course I will."

We watched each other for a long minute. I frowned at them.

"Aren't you going to ask why?"

They shrugged as they picked at the Sellotape on the box.

"Are you ready to tell me?"

"No," I offered.

"Bathroom." They cleared their throat as they got off their bed, "you have a *lot* of hair. I have carpet."

"Valid," I said as I turned on the bed and waited for them to pass to follow.

"Would you like to sit in the bath?"

"You ask me the best questions; I won't lie to you," I laughed as I pulled my t-shirt off and hung it over the radiator. I climbed into the bath, sitting with my back to Quincy then taking a breath and closing my eyes.

I didn't open them when I felt Quincy thread their fingers through the loose strands of hair.

"I'm going to cut at the plait," they said.

I exhaled. "Do it."

"Do you want it after a warning or…?"

"No, no count downs. Just, cut."

"Just cut?" they repeated.

"Gone, get gone," I confirmed. They laughed softly, I opened my eyes.

"Something like that?" they asked as they dangled my plait over my face. I took it from them, holding my breath.

"Shit."

They squeezed my shoulders, shaking me from side to side as I traced over the plait.

"Oh, god," I took a deep breath. "Shave it off,

please."

They turned on the razor and I watched as my hair fell off in curls, littering the bottom of the bath, so much hair even after they'd removed the plait.

I started to think it'd never stop falling until they turned the razor off.

"I've just got to say…" they whispered into my ear, "you really suit this."

I turned my head to look at them. They smiled at me; it was gentle *but* somewhat playful.

"I'm trans," I whispered. They climbed into the bath with me wrapping their legs around mine as I continued to stroke over my severed plait. "I… I'm trans. I kept trying to wait, I kept pushing the thought away, we were still filming and I didn't want to cause trouble, but we've been locked in here for weeks and I don't know how much longer I can be alone without… cracking."

"Well, congratulations on cracking your egg, darling," they whispered, taking my hand in theirs.

"Brooklyn doesn't know," I said in a breath. "I… he doesn't know yet and he should, what if me transitioning makes him not want to be with me, what if…"

"Brooklyn loves you," they grabbed a little tighter. "Brooklyn adores you. I'm not going to force you to speak to him, I never would, but he'd listen, and you guys will figure it all out."

"He, him," I told them, they nodded. "I've figured that out. He, him."

"Have you changed your name?" they whispered.

I swallowed. "Maybe. No, no, not really, I don't…"

"Talk to me darling."

"Can I… Can I write it? I don't want to speak it into existence yet."

"Of course," they whispered. I nodded lifting my hips to get at my phone. I paused opening our text thread and then I typed it.

Their phone pinged, vibrating the entire bath before they got their phone from their pocket. They grinned almost immediately.

"I love it," they whispered. I dived into their chest, hugging them around their middle. I felt them kiss the top of my head, then they laughed.

"That felt really nice," they whispered rubbing their cheeks against my hair.

We both jumped when the bathroom door opened. Brooklyn stopped his hands already undoing his pants.

"Oh," he bit his lip, then locked his eyes onto me. "*Oh*," he repeated, a little bit more enthusiastically then reached for me, running his fingers over my head.

"What *are* you doing?" I gasped, he laughed childishly.

"I love the feeling, it's all fuzzy," he gasped, then scratched his fingers over my head. I rolled my eyes lightly at Quincy, they grinned right back. "Now…" he scratched again; it made me shiver. "I need to pee, *and* I'm going to. If you're still in here, that's a *you* problem."

"Oh, don't set the challenge if you can't follow through," Quincy purred. Brooklyn smirked back shrugging at me as he undid his jeans.

"You think he's shy; we've *all* seen him do sex scenes before," I said.

"That's a good point," he almost cackled. "Still haven't had my turn, have I?" he kissed towards Brooklyn, who blew a kiss right back.

"I'm looking forward to any potential Kevin and Izzy sex scenes come the next series," Brooklyn teased. I laughed then groaned.

"Oh, I didn't think about that," I moaned. Brooklyn laughed then stumbled as Bud ran into his shins.

Series 10

Day 5

Dakota was a stunning actress. I'd known that since we were kids, she carried us all, Brooklyn included, and when we'd had special guest stars, actors with paygrades higher than the year I was born, she excelled.

Now, she sat opposite me on her on set bed, hugging an excessively hairy cushion and was crying. Sobbing but not making a sound, the tears running down her cheeks too fast to wipe away. They felt real.

They weren't real. I knew that because between takes she laughed and joked and wiped her face as if nothing was happening. But in this moment, they felt so real. Why had they made her character cry?

"I'm a boy, Ally," I told her, the words complicated. This scene didn't feel like a coming out scene, I hadn't had a coming out scene. "I don't know how to explain it to you, but I'm a boy."

"Izzy," she replied shaking her head then she gasped. "Can we still call you Izzy?"

"I…" I paused. "I guess so." I let out a breath, "I don't know Ally, but it's me, I'm still me."

She stood from her bed, discarding the cushion as she walked towards me.

"You're my best friend," she whispered, then her

tears practically dried up. Her face hardened. "You're still you, no matter what."

"Cut."

We turned together, frowning at Jordan as he chewed on the end of a pencil, apparently ruminating on something.

"I thought that was quite good," I told Dakota.

She laughed nodding, agreeing with me. "Scene feels weird, though."

"You feel it, too? I thought I was just being overly critical."

"I don't understand why I'm crying, and so heavily at that."

"At least you're not suddenly in love with me."

She smirked at me. "Ah, any penis will do," she teased.

Jordan cleared his throat. "Reset please, from Dakota's line." He let his pen tell us, his head not rising from the script. I rolled my eyes but reset all the same.

"And…" he drew out, "action."

"You're still you, no matter what," she stated with some intensity. I almost took a step back.

"I…"

"We'll sort this out, we'll—"

"—Cut."

"That must've been your fault," I said. She almost choked on her laugh.

"Dakota please find the alternation to the script," Jordan requested. I sighed turning on the spot and finding Brooklyn.

He grinned at me, as he leant on the edge of the set. He was wearing a ruffled shirt and patterned waistcoat, a pocket watch strung over his pocket because, for the first half of the tenth season, Kevin found himself lost in the past. Flung back to the nineteenth century with India,

Freya's character, in tow.

We, on this end, were attempting to retrieve the two of them, we had the advantage with having Todd on our side; they were the smart one amongst us.

We didn't seem to be doing very well, however, and India was a twopence away from being taken above a ship that'll inevitably be seized by pirates whilst Kevin lived a life of luxury having been taken in by an Aristocrat.

I didn't know how we were going to get them back. I hadn't had that script yet.

"Reset, from…" Jordan looked up at me, waving his hand in a circular motion towards me.

"O-Z," I told him. "Two letters, you got this."

"From Izzy's line."

"So close," I mocked, then glanced at Dakota. She looked positively livid.

"Izzy's line, and…" he actually looked at us this time, "action."

"I…"

"We'll fix this," Dakota said. I *did* take a step back that time.

"What?" I asked, even though that definitely wasn't in the script. Any and all lines I had that followed that one had completely left my head. Dakota looked up at me.

"Whatever it takes Izzy. We…" she paused, shaking her head ever so slightly, so I dropped my eye line, "…will fix this. We'll bring you back, you'll be a girl again for when Kevin returns."

I opened my mouth, but no sound came out. I turned away from her, rubbing my hand over my mouth and catching Brooklyn's eyes. He shook his head, his expression hurt before thumping his chest three times.

I swallowed, nodding to him then turning back

towards Dakota. *Well* Ally, because these were not Dakota's words. Never.

Just like how my next words were not my own, they were Izzy's.

"I know we will," I swallowed past all my instincts that told me to *not* say the next words: "I know you'll help fix me."

Series 6

Day 150

Brooklyn shushed me. His finger on his lips, his eyes sparkling under the torch light. I remained quiet, grinning as he pushed back the draped sheet, and stepped inside.

I bit my lip.

This could be it; this could finally be the moment I'd been waiting for. It had all the potential. The blanket fort that we'd crafted together with music playing in the background. The fairy lights we'd strung up inside, the popcorn bowl we'd popped together. Some canned mixers we'd found in Home Bargains, even though I was sixteen, and he wasn't *quite* eighteen yet.

A simple Google search would've revealed Brooklyn's age but he was served anyway because it was Brooklyn. It was gorgeous, cute, charismatic Brooklyn who I *think* liked me back.

Well I hoped he did at least, otherwise this would be dreadfully embarrassing. I wouldn't be able to handle that embarrassment. I'd have to resign.

My mum wasn't home, and she definitely wasn't meant to come home. Not until tomorrow morning, after we'd both left for set.

So, tonight was Brooklyn and I, a blanket fort, fairy lights and popcorn and the potential of a first kiss.

Oh, God, I hoped I'd read the room right.

I followed Brooklyn into the blanket fort. He grinned at me as he sat with the popcorn bowl between his legs.

"I didn't realise how much I missed popcorn when I had braces," he said, as I sat beside him. I took a handful of popcorn.

"Popcorn?"

"I know," he laughed. "I know, but I didn't miss sweets, or too much chocolate or whatever. Popcorn though, that was a killer." He rose a kernel between us, holding it delicately between his thumb and first finger.

He smiled at me, wide and full of teeth. They were no longer crooked, but his smile was still as endearing.

There was the Brooklyn smile. The one he did to the producers, to Jordan, to Eliza, the one that let him get away with so much shit. A cheeky turn to it, a bit of tongue sticking out.

There was the TV personality smile that was full of white perfectly straight teeth, and never quite reaching his eyes but looked the part on press releases.

And there was the smile I believed he only did for me. I didn't care if I was delusional, I liked believing he only did it for me. He bit his bottom lip, crinkled his nose, his eyes soft, his head tilted ever so slightly. It was relaxed, considerate, and *real*.

In a world where everything we did was a farce, we truly sought out the real. It'd taken me a while to identify that smile as real, as unreserved and relaxed.

He ate the popcorn, just about swallowing it down before he began to laugh, clapping his hand over his mouth and rocking back and forth because everything Brooklyn did, he did it with his full body.

"Okay, okay, okay," he waved both of his hands at me before reaching for the remote. "One, two, or three?"

"What?"

"Pick a number." He nudged me with the remote, I shook my shoulders.

"Two."

"Ooh, Disney Plus."

Ah, I got it.

"One to six."

I looked at the screen. "Four," I whispered; he smirked a slight inclination in the corners of his mouth.

"Marvel," he rose his eyebrow at me.

I laughed taking the remote from him. "You pick a number."

"Between?"

"One and…" I scanned the screen, "twenty."

"Fifteen."

"Doctor Strange," I nodded. "Good choice."

The credits rolled up and he still hadn't made any kind of move to kiss me. So maybe I *had* completely misread his signals. Maybe we were just mates, maybe it'd been that way all along and Brooklyn saw us as friends, saw us as…

"You'll miss the post-credit if you keep staring at me," he mumbled without looking away from the TV.

"I'm not staring," I whispered. I totally was staring and now I was totally blushing. He looked back at me a confused expression on his face, so I sat up, crossing my legs and facing him head on.

"Did I misread this?"

"Which?" he asked slowly, frowning at the screen as if searching for something I could've possibly misread.

"Us."

"I didn't think there was anything to misread between us," he cleared his throat. "I… why?"

"I just thought…" I shook my head. "I thought you liked me."

"I do," he laughed, with no reservations about

himself. "I do like you."

"Then why haven't you… I don't know… made any move to…. Kiss me?"

He rose an eyebrow at me. "You want me to kiss you?"

I shrugged one shoulder.

"Then why didn't *you* kiss *me*?"

"What?"

"If you wanted to kiss *me*, why didn't you?"

"I thought I had to wait, I thought I had to let *you* kiss me."

He shook his head, his eyebrows burrowed as he laughed.

"Why? Is there some kiss edict I missed?"

"Do you *want* me to kiss you?"

He nodded thoughtfully, then pushed himself up onto his knees. He bounced gently.

"Yes. I'd really like that, actually."

"I've…" I began then I swallowed deeply, "never kissed someone." I frowned. "For real. I mean, *Izzy* has kissed a whole host of people, but I've never cared."

He opened his arms to me. "Take your time."

"You kissed lots of people, and I'm not even including Dakota."

"I…" he grinned. "Yes, I've kissed some boys. Mostly out in clubs though, nothing excessive. Nothing meaningful. A few girls, too, but I'm always a little *apprehensive* in case they're a fan and they're just…" he swallowed. "Anyway… you don't have to wait for me to kiss you."

"You're older than me," I mumbled as a lame excuse.

He smirked lightly then pursed his lips. "Well, I'm not going to kiss you."

"Harsh," I said.

"Be brave," he whispered. I bit my lip then knelt like

he was. I pressed against him, inhaling sharply when I felt him against me.

His body, the knot in his joggers, his breaths. Every single one of his breaths.

I met his eyes, smiling as he just watched me.

I moved towards him, a jerk of an action.

I headbutted him.

He barked out a laugh, covering his nose and shaking his head at me.

"Tactile, I see, weaken the enemy." He rose his fist above his head. I grabbed his cheeks, pulling him towards me and kissed him.

He laughed into my mouth. I could've sworn I felt the smile on his lips, as his fingers slipped around the nape of my neck.

He took a breath, short and sweet before leaning his forehead against mine.

I opened my eyes, watching him as he smiled, as he licked his lips, as he took breaths.

He didn't open his eyes before he kissed me again. Parting my lips and touching his tongue to mine.

I decided then that I never wanted another day to pass where I wasn't kissing him.

Series 10

Day 5

Quincy grinned at me, their tongue between their teeth before nodding up towards the roof.

I bit my lip, pausing purely for effect because I was definitely going to follow them.

I rose my eyebrow at them. They took it as it was intended and started up. I watched them go until I heard Brooklyn coming up from downstairs.

He paused, leaning on the banister, examining me.

"What?" I asked finally, he grinned at me shaking his head.

"I was just, enjoying you…" he told me, walking a few more steps until he was exactly my height, three steps below me. "You've changed a lot this month."

"Yeah?"

He nodded, long slow nods. "Your shoulders are squarer, your Adams apple more prominent."

I rose my fingers to my neck, swallowing to feel it.

I felt it.

"Your stubble is… well, have I ever told you I like stubble?"

I grinned, looking away from him to laugh.

"Your voice has dropped. I'm in awe of what

testosterone is doing to you."

I nodded, smiling as I stepped closer to him so I could kiss him without either of us having to stretch in either direction.

"Quincy has lit a joint," I said against his lips. He licked his own, then pecked me gently.

"Why exactly are we still standing here, Oswald?"

I choked. "Oswald?"

He grinned at me, taking the last three steps. "I don't know, it felt like a full-name moment."

"Oswald isn't my full name."

"It should be," he whispered then passed me. "I'm changing my pants. I'll follow you up."

So, up I went. The roof was accessible through a staircase that escaped through a skylight in the loft. The loft was a converted room, that, if we had another roommate, they would live in.

The loft where Dakota and Freya stayed when we partied too late.

The window to the roof was open. Quincy was sat on the eves of the roof, like a nonbinary Jack Frost, watching what was happening in the city below. I wasn't quite brave enough, so I sat closer to the chimney.

Our roof was mostly flat, the smallest of inclines that didn't affect our balance all too much. It was a three storey drop – four, maybe? Does the roof count as the fourth storey? Regardless, I wasn't brave enough to sit on the eves, even though there was a little ledge that Quincy was resting their feet on.

They were well aware I was behind them, apparently, as they reached backwards without looking at me, offering me the freshly lit joint.

They turned when I took it. "Are you okay?" they asked, I let the smoke out through my nose.

"Now? Yeah?" I teased; Quincy rose their eyebrow.

"No," I added. They stood without any hesitation, turning and walking so they could sit closer to me.

Our knees knocked when they sat back down, I passed the joint back.

"We'll fight for you," they told me. "Tooth, and fucking nail."

"I…" I looked back at them, nodding because I believed the next words that were coming out of my mouth. "…know you will."

They passed the joint back. I inhaled deeply. Blowing the smoke out as Brooklyn pushed himself through the roof, whilst talking to someone below him.

He turned towards the smoke, grinning at me then reaching out for the joint with his super long noodle arms. I passed it over.

He inhaled deeply whilst continuing out of the roof.

AJ followed him up.

Brooklyn grinned at me, tipping my chin back, and releasing the smoke into my mouth.

"You know what I'm waiting to happen?" AJ mused as he took the joint from Brooklyn's outstretched hand. "A helicopter to go over that belongs to Disney Channel or some shit, and you all get exposed for getting high on your roof."

"Disney Channel?" Quincy questioned. "Queen, we do not work for Disney Channel."

"I wish I had been a Disney Channel kid," I mused, as I tried not to focus on the burning at the back of my throat.

"I almost was," Brooklyn muttered. "I'll be a Disney adult," he added, taking the joint back. Quincy knocked his shoe against Brooklyn's socked foot.

"Explain?"

"There's been a lot of interest in… Me." His smile was awkward before he swallowed. "Voice work for the new Pixar film. Main character. I've already said yes, to be honest. I also did some cameo pieces for DreamWorks and Sony over lockdown, some of them took off."

"You're going to be a Pixar character?!" AJ laughed.

Brooklyn nodded, "No details released, not yet, but the contract is signed."

"And our prison guards allowed that?" Quincy mused as they retrieved the joint.

"Not necessarily," Brooklyn said slowly. I knocked my head against his shoulder. He wrapped his arm around me, his hand rubbing my bicep. "But my agent advised I don't wait, I just go. She said, it's the last season, what are they going to do? Fire me?"

"Hey, I might still be fired," I offered, in what I wanted to be a jokey tone, but it came out flat. I took the joint when it was offered back to me.

"They literally can't fire you," AJ told me. I shook my head, brushing him off. "No, Oz, literally. They cannot fire you legally because you've transitioned. You're a protected characteristic, and there's nothing in your contract that states you were not allowed to transition."

"They haven't got a leg to stand on, Oz," Quincy said. "We've fought this battle before, on a smaller scale, yes, but we've fought this, and we will fight again."

"Your fight got you an onscreen boyfriend," Brooklyn said whilst taking the joint from my hand. He lay back onto the roof as he smoked the end of the joint then put it out on the roof tile.

"And a real life one," Quincy agreed as they examined AJ. "This guy just won't leave me alone."

"I'd have let you go ages ago, but our Only Fans just makes so much money."

"I knew he was only here for the money."

"It's why I'm still with Brooklyn," I shrugged,

glancing behind me as he rose his fist.

"Hear, hear." He closed his eyes, a quiet smile on his face. A *stoned* smile. He was so *very* easy to get stoned.

"Don't you remember how Todd's on-screen boyfriend ended?"

I made a gun with my fingers, aiming it at AJ. He reacted to me pulling the imaginary tigger,

"And *then*, I fucking got over him in the series break and got with Freya."

"Aw, Todd and India stans," AJ mocked.

Quincy rolled their eyes. "Are we even still together?"

"I think so," I winced at them.

They laughed shaking their head. "I'll leave her stuck in the past, it's fine."

"Excuse me, get me out of the past so I can have an onscreen fuck with Oz," Brooklyn said without opening his eyes. I rose my eyebrow at him, he didn't even flinch.

"Can you imagine the fucking praise them bigots will get for showing a queer sex scene, between a main cis character and a trans boy," AJ mused.

"Boy?" I repeated.

"Doesn't it piss you off?"

"The awards, the accolades. It fucking pisses me off," I assured him. "The so-called diversity they're hiding behind. Honestly, it was a factor in me coming out."

"Really?" Quincy whispered.

"I think I've known this since I was, thirteen? That's the earliest I can think, or the earliest I can remember. I knew I liked boys; I've always known that and it's weird because I never doubted that..."

"Being born a girl?" AJ asked.

"Isn't it *weird*. I never worried about my sexuality because *apparently* it was..."

"Normal," Quincy offered.

"I didn't even flinch when I started to listen to myself

because, it's fine, I like boys, but maybe I'm *also* a boy."

"Thirteen," Quincy repeated. I hummed as they obviously thought. "I came out when we were fourteen, did I…?"

"Not you," I interrupted. "You coming out as nonbinary didn't *influence* me, not really, but how *they* treated you, what they did. That scared me."

"That scared me, and I'm just bi," Brooklyn said. I looked at him as he sat up. "Genuinely, I was thinking I only want to fuck boys *and* girls, nothing more, and it scared the *shit* out of me."

I squeezed his thigh. "It stopped me coming out because I figured *exactly* this would happen. But, day off tomorrow, so I don't even have to think about *them*."

"I don't have a day off," Brooklyn muttered. "I'm going to a grand ball tomorrow, wherein I'll get myself into a sticky situation in a Lady's chamber."

"You're cheating on me tomorrow?" I teased.

He gasped. "Oz, no, I love you."

"You're stoned," I whispered.

"No. I think we get to the future before I get punished."

Quincy snorted, shaking their head as I sighed, knocking against Brooklyn.

"Good. That's good," I whispered. Brooklyn smiled softly, then gasped as Bud whined from below us.

"My dog," he said as AJ peeked down the ladder, he laughed.

"Why is he wearing a hoodie?"

"In case he gets cold," Brooklyn said. I turned to Quincy.

"In case he gets cold," we repeated together.

Series 5

Day 17

Quincy was definitely ignoring me, and they weren't even attempting to hide that fact, so I followed their eye line.

A boy. *Of course.*

A boy I'd never seen before, a boy who was obviously an extra who'd wandered away from their holding room.

A granted very cute boy. I said this to Quincy.

"He's gorgeous," Quincy confirmed. "I wonder who he belongs to." They turned their head to look back at me, "I just had my I-Can-Hear-the-Bells moment."

"Your… what?"

"Hello. *Hairspray.* Tracy sees Link, she can hear the wedding bells."

I bit my lip. Primarily so I wouldn't laugh at their dramatics.

"The wedding bells?"

"The fucking wedding bells," they slapped their knees enthusiastically. I clapped my hand over my mouth when I laughed. They elbowed me in the side.

"Quincy."

We both looked up at Eliza as she approached us, script in hand, an uncapped pen behind her ear.

"Come meet AJ," she beckoned. They rose their eyebrow at me then stood, quickening their pace to catch up to Eliza.

I ran after them.

"Who's AJ?" Quincy asked when they'd matched Eliza's pace.

"Todd's love interest," she explained. Quincy turned to look at me over their shoulder, their expression surprised.

"And AJ is?" they prodded, Eliza frowned at them. "I'm playing for pronouns here?"

"He, is right there."

"He," I repeated, as Quincy gasped.

"Todd is getting a male love interest?" they turned, grinning pleased at AJ, the boy who wasn't an extra, who was exactly where he was meant to be. "What on earth did I do to deserve this?"

"The writers wanted to show some diversity."

"Make the Japanese boy gay, I see," I mocked.

"Bisexual," Eliza corrected, then she sighed.

"You don't seem… happy by this?"

"It's a diversity stunt. Just be careful, okay?" She squeezed Quincy's elbow. "And, you know, act like you love him, make sure your acting is next level."

"Oh, no acting needed, Eliza." They rose their hand, then turned it into a wave. "AJ? I believe?"

"Quincy," AJ replied, an ever so slight blush on his cheeks. Quincy looked at me over their shoulder. "You're they, them, right?"

Quincy gasped. "I love him," they proclaimed; I smirked as they turned back to him.

"I am, darling. How did you know that?"

"Twitter, mostly. Followed you for a long time. Dare I say, I'm a fan."

Quincy smirked as AJ took a step closer.

"I'm a fan of Quincy, *not* Todd, for the record."

Quincy smirked. "I'm a fan of AJ."

"I'm a fan of not watching flirting," I offered. I saw Quincy roll their eyes even though they weren't actually facing me.

"Shut up, I have to sit next to you as you flirt with Brooklyn."

"You and Brooklyn…." AJ interjected so I glanced up at him. "You guys, are a thing?"

"No," I gasped. "Shhh."

"Oh, you fancy Brooklyn?"

"Oh my god, shut up. You're the worst," I informed Quincy, they smirked before waving me off.

"Did you know you were coming in as my *love interest?*"

"I knew I was coming in as *a* love interest, yours, no. But…" AJ exhaled, "I couldn't be happier. What does she…"

"Eliza."

"Mean *this is a stunt?*"

"Oh," Quincy sighed. "I came out as nonbinary last year, you probably know that. Our lords and masters didn't take it all too well because *apparently* a fourteen-year-old being nonbinary could take down the whole production."

"Oh, yeah," AJ gasped. "I remember reading something about how they'd taken it badly, and they were discussing recasting you?"

"I seem to remember they were planning on killing Todd," I offered.

"They're obviously trying to redeem themselves for being shit to a kid," they scrunched their nose, then shrugged one shoulder at AJ.

"You're in for a hell of a ride AJ," I whispered. "For the record, *they* didn't mean for that to come out. It was a leak, and they panicked, like, a lot."

"A lot." Quincy's smile was bright, *so* bright and so out of place.

I jumped when arms draped over me, then a head hit the back of mine.

I knew it was Brooklyn when he sighed. Was that weird?

"I am so tired," he told me,

"AJ, I assume you know Brooklyn," Quincy teased. Brooklyn rose his head, extending his arm pass me to shake AJ's hand.

"Who's AJ?" he asked.

"Todd's boo," I mocked.

"That's not fair, I'm the main character I should have my gay phase first." He pulled his tongue at Quincy, who pulled theirs straight back.

Series 10

Day 7

I'd been summoned to the break room. I didn't know who *had* summoned me, but my presence was required so I went.

I was either going to be fired or silenced and I knew which one I preferred.

I was surprised when I saw Eliza in the break room, a pile of scripts on the table in front of her, two coffee cups to her right.

She tapped the seat beside her.

I sat on it without being told twice. She turned the cup to me; *Oz* was written on with a smiley face in the O. I pulled it towards me, taking a breath then drinking from it.

"I've been reviewing the script changes today," she told me; I didn't look at her. "I've also received the scripts for next week, so I wanted to read over them before *Jordan* decided to change anything on the fly again."

We looked at each other.

"I'm so sorry for what he did to you the other day."

I swallowed.

"That was not discussed beforehand, not with me at

least, and it was dreadfully out of order." She scoffed, probably at herself.

"It felt pretty shitty, too," I said.

She sighed. "Why didn't you call me, Oz?"

"I got high." I narrowed my eyes at her, she almost smirked at me.

"That's why it took Brooklyn *numerous* takes to get his lines right yesterday?"

"Presumably," I laughed then I sighed. "I don't know how to feel about this, honestly. It was a shock, it *hurt* a lot, but I wasn't surprised."

"I think that makes it worse."

"I agree."

"Okay, stand up," she ordered, standing herself, I frowned up at her. "Stand, Oz."

I did. She wrapped her arms around me, hugging me tight.

I thought about collapsing, about breaking down and sobbing, letting myself feel the pain that was buried deep but I didn't. In fact, I refused to, but I did give her a slightly tighter squeeze.

"I'm sorry," I whispered.

"What for, darling?"

"All this. I should've just… waited."

"No, no, never think that, Oz, never." She sighed, lifting my chin with her fingers. "I've known you since you were ten years old, and *honestly* I've never seen you glow as much as this. There was a little spark with Brooklyn and I thought, *maybe* but now, Oz, darling you're a supernova."

I inhaled sharply, *don't cry.*

"Never apologise for doing what you need to do, never *ever* apologise for self-care."

"Sorry," I repeated, she tapped my shoulder gently. "I mean, sorry for being sorry for…" I cackled, "oh my god."

She hugged me again, swaying us side to side. I exhaled.

"What are we filming next week?" I whispered.

"Oh."

"Oh?" I repeated. "I don't like that oh, that oh had something behind it."

She turned whilst keeping her arm around my shoulders. She picked up the script, flicking through it as if she knew what page she was heading to.

She held the script to me.

I frowned at her. She tapped the script as if saying, *read it.*

Kevin, *Kevin*, Kevin lines, and then Izzy. So, we get him back from the past then, *good.*

"Kevin and Izzy…" I met her eyes. "Have sex. As in, on screen? As in, not fade to black? As in, *me* Oz, having sex with Brooklyn, on screen, for people to stream, *forever.*"

"Correct."

"Fuck."

"Now, like I do with *every* single one of you when your first on screen sex scene has come up. Let's chat."

"What about?"

"You're not contractionary required to film sex scenes."

I frowned at her,

"When you signed that contract, when you were ten there was no clause to say you'll perform sex scenes. You can say to me *right* now that you don't want to do it. You can read the script at home then tell me that, you can perform this sex scene then come and be like *Eliza I'll be honest, I'm never doing that shit again.* Okay? You've always got an opt out option."

"Brooklyn, Dakota, and Quincy too?"

"Even Freya. It doesn't matter how many you film, you can always say enough is enough."

"Okay," I exhaled. "If I were to go ahead with this scene?"

She nodded, retrieving a piece of paper.

"Then a few boundaries. I do this with everyone, okay, but I feel this should be extra delicate with yourself, *and* with yourself and Brooklyn being in a relationship we…" she cleared her throat, "*I*… want to make sure everything is safe and consensual between the two of you."

"I appreciate that."

She smiled at me, a soft smile that was definitely caring. I didn't doubt even a little that she cared.

"What are your personal boundaries, Oz?"

I rose my eyebrow at her, she waved her hand at me.

"I mean onscreen, please do not start telling me your kinks."

I snorted, swallowing it down in hope that I wouldn't giggle.

"A big, *big* no is my chest," I told her, she hummed as she wrote on her sheet. "I… I'm paying for the surgery, but it can't really be until we finish filming, and I'm currently still binding. Brooklyn knows, Brooklyn is well aware that I don't want him anywhere near my chest, or anything like that – *honestly*, it's always been that way with us, he's always known my chest was a no-go zone."

"So, you're happy to be in your binder? On screen?"

"Very happy to," I assured her. "Representation and all." I rose my first, *like* Brooklyn. She did it back whilst continuing to write.

"You're binding safely?"

"I am," I told her. "Quincy helped me out with all that."

She nodded.

"Any other?"

"None that immediately come to mind."

"You're happy with being naked from the waist down?"

I shrugged gently.

"Yes, I guess so."

"And I expect yourself and Brooklyn to come up with a safe word, that you will share with myself, Jordan, and the rest of the team. Which if at any point you're uncomfortable, or want to take a break, or do not wish to proceed you say."

"Understood."

"Any questions?"

"Yes," I said slowly, she nodded to me. "I know I've watched Brooklyn do it before, but… how is it done? Like, I assume Brook and I won't *really* have sex or anything?"

"No. So you two will meet with our Intimacy Co-ordinator."

"Amy?" I asked, smiling beside myself because Brooklyn liked Amy, *really* liked Amy. He kept attempting to get her to come out for a drink with us, she was only a handful of years older than him, and granted *very* pretty.

"Amy," she agreed. "She'll choreograph your sex scene, and establish where you can touch each other, throughout. As I say that bit is quite important especially with yourself and Brooklyn, because although you're of course extremely comfortable with each other, you may be uncomfortable with certain *things* becoming should I say public knowledge."

"Right," I said.

"You'll both wear a modesty pouch, which is just like a stick-on thong. There'll be no genital contact. We'll give you a block of time to film on a closed set. No one else will be scheduled in to film, there will not be any other filming happening in the studio. It'll likely be a very late shoot. After a day full."

"I assume there'll be grooming time," I rose my eyebrow at her.

She nodded. "As always."

"Right."

"Is this a green light? For now?"

"For now. Yes. I'll read it through, and talk to Brooklyn, and really think about it."

"Make sure it's your decision, Oz, please don't feel pressured into *anything* and talk to each other. Not just Brooklyn. They've all filmed on-screen sex scenes, all in different ways."

"I will. I'll…" I swallowed, "I will."

Series 7

Day 101

Brooklyn ran up the small staircase towards the front door. His hands lying flat on the royal blue painted door, the number thirty-one in gold.

He turned to me so quick, I worried for a moment that he might fly down the stairs.

"Keys?" he asked, clapping his hands together. I laughed lifting my hip and nodding towards it,

"Pocket," I said. He jumped the stairs, then held his hands up to me, wiggling his fingers.

"May I?"

"You may, or take the box?" I offered, the all things considered *very* light box I was holding. He bit his tongue, reaching into my pocket. I squirmed when I felt his fingers against my thigh. He sniggered lightly, his eyes meeting mine.

"Now we live together, we can do *that* whenever we want," he whispered, then threw the keys up. He caught them then spun on his heels to run back up the stairs.

"Why are you bright red?"

"Shit," I jumped. Quincy smirked at me before hoisting their box a little higher. I shook my head.

"Nothing, *nothing*." I knocked against them. "We have

a house," I said, they knocked back against me. "We are seventeen years old, and we have a three bedroomed townhouse, in London."

"We *are* seventeen." They repeated with a laugh, Brooklyn snorted as he put the key into the lock.

"I'm nineteen," he said as he pushed the door open, "but it's still pretty cool to be nineteen and owning a house." He sighed contently, taking a big breath of the hallway in. Then he ran away like an excited cocker spaniel.

"So, we're going to need a sex rule, right?" Quincy said, I stopped on the steps up to the door. I turned back to them. "That's why you were blushing." They grinned following me in, I sighed.

"We've only done it *once*," I whispered, even though I fully believed Brooklyn wouldn't be sensitive about that kind of information.

"Ah, and never again? I see."

"That's not what I meant," I laughed.

"I *mean* because once I'm eighteen, we're definitely making an *Only Fans*." They grinned behind them as AJ came through the door.

"I *want* to…" I swallowed, "doesn't matter. We should definitely have a housewarming or something."

Quincy nodded pointing down the hallway, so I looked.

"Party. Yes?"

"Yes," Brooklyn proclaimed. "Let's have a party, tonight. Let's do it, you guys put the boxes upstairs. I'll call around." He grinned before walking towards me. He cupped my chin, "and you my lovely partner, you can choose our bedroom." He kissed me, soft and loving.

"What? Full reign, no specifications?"

"No way. I know you'll choose the perfect room, no doubt in my mind."

"Not if I get there first," Quincy called back as they began up the stairs.

The house was alive. Music pulsing through every smart speaker we had situated around. People filled every room. Drinks were flowing and we'd invited our new neighbours on either side, to ensure we didn't piss them off on night one.

I had *never* taken as many selfies in my life.

I was stopped every time I started to walk. Someone grabbing my arm, or pulling me back, holding a phone in front of my face.

Brooklyn and Quincy were getting cameras shoved in their faces too, but it was okay. We were okay.

We might have been a little drunk, *we* as a collective that was, the entire house. Maybe even the entire street because of the alcohol fumes that were radiating from our house.

I took a seat in the little box garden that was surprisingly empty. There were bulb-like lights strung from fence to fence in a zig-zag style. There was a few overgrown plants that *might* have been fake. Big leaves of plants I'm sure didn't actually exist in this country.

I sat on a swinging bench, controlling the swing with my feet so it didn't move too quickly. I couldn't decide whether it was actually comfortable or not.

It flung backwards when Quincy fell into the seat next to me. I just about managed to cross my legs before I was thrown from the seat.

They leant their head on my shoulder, closing their eyes.

"I found you," they whispered.

"Was I lost?" I asked. "Did I get lost?"

"To me, *yes*. To Brooklyn too, he doesn't know where you are."

"Oh no."

"Why are you afraid of sex?"

"Why am I what?" I repeated, Quincy lifted their head to look straight at me, they frowned ever so slightly.

"Are you asexual? Because that is okay. In fact, that's completely valid and I fully support that."

"What's asexual?"

"In the most simplistic of terms, no sexual attraction. You don't wish to have sex."

"I'm *not* asexual."

"Then… are you not ready?"

"I am," I swallowed. "I mean, Brooklyn didn't force me, I fully consented to *doing it* with him and…"

"So, I return to my original question?"

"It's embarrassing," I murmured, they nudged me. "I… I don't know, I don't talk about… s…"

"Sex," they offered. I knew I was blushing although I may've been flushed from the alcohol. Yeah, *totally* the latter. Sure. "Say the word, it gets far less scary when you *say* it."

I swallowed, shaking my head so they sighed,

"Okay," they hummed. "AJ and I have sex. We enjoy sex. We *talk* about everything to do with sex."

I sighed lightly, rubbing my forehead because I was *definitely* sobering up.

"I don't like him touching my…" I looked at Quincy all over, running my eyes over his body. "Chest," I sighed, "and he *really* likes it. I think. I don't know what it is, it's stupid, unnecessary. It's not worth mentioning but then I get anxious, or I panic that's where he's going when we're kissing or *whatever*."

"Tell him."

"No great wisdom, just that?"

"Just that. It's Brooklyn…"

"Yeah, exactly it's Brooklyn. He's perfect. He's

confident and gorgeous and…"

"So, you've spoken to him about that then? You've sat down and he's told you that *he* thinks he's perfect."

"No."

They gasped dramatically. I put my finger to my lips, shushing them so they swung us a bit quicker.

"Talk to Brooklyn. Get it all out in the open."

"I'm not making an *Only Fans*," I joked, they grinned. "Are you allowed to do that? In the contract and all."

"At this point, darling, I don't give a fuck. They were going to kill me off, *then* they straight up killed my boyfriend off. I'm done following their rules. AJ already has one. A really popular one that he's had since he was eighteen himself but he's not pressuring me to join his channel, no way.

"We talked about it, because we talk about sex all the time. Since the first time we slept together, we talk through everything, make sure each other are comfortable."

"Brooklyn makes sure I'm comfortable," I nodded. "He always asks, he always takes a pause for consent."

"Then start telling him the truth."

I nodded slowly then sighed.

"Does this officially make me a party pooper?"

They laughed.

"It was getting a bit loud in there and there's only so many times I can smile for pictures."

"True that," I laughed.

"I should've gotten some weed," they sighed dramatically as we swung and swung.

Until the undeniable opening bars of *YMCA* where we stood together, and far too quickly so the swing went at double speed, hitting us both in the back of the knees, so we stumbled forward grabbing onto each other's hand and breaking into a run.

We got into the living room as everybody's arms rose into a Y. My hands were taken before I could get into the M. I tilted my head back, smiling at Brooklyn as he moved my hands for me until he could spin me around, so I was facing him.

I'd never slept with Brooklyn. In the *literal* sense. I'd never spent the night, I'd never even napped beside him, either his dad was coming home, or my mum was kicking him out because boys shouldn't stay the night with their partner.

It was a marvel she'd actually let me leave the house to move in with him.

Now I sat on *our* bed, that he'd made at some point – because I definitely wasn't in one of his t-shirts and a pair of shorts, *watching* as he changed. He was stood with his pyjama pants on but had been distracted by his phone pinging.

Ping after ping of notifications and messages. Presumably from the party guests who we'd kicked out at 1AM because we'd had enough, and we wanted to go to bed.

We weren't drunk. I wasn't at least. I *really* didn't think he was. I did, however, really want to sleep with him. In the sexy sense and I didn't know if he was up for that.

He looked at me, his eyebrow raising. I swallowed.

"I don't like it when you touch my chest," I word-vomited at him. He looked surprised, but he shook it off quite quickly, placing his phone on the bedside table and kneeling opposite me.

"Okay," he nodded. "Ever, or like during sex?"

"Ever," I said without thinking. "Yeah, *ever* honestly, I don't even like touching my chest, and it makes me anxious when *you* do, so I *request* you don't touch my chest."

"Done," he nodded. "Thank you for telling me." He smiled, his genuine smiled so of course, I frowned back at him. "What?"

"I just wasn't really expecting you to be so… understanding."

"That's sad," he nodded. "Yeah, I think that's sad. I love you, I will *literally* do anything to make sure you're comfortable with me, *especially* when we're just being us because I'd hate to think you feel anxious about me being around you."

"You love me?" I whispered. I saw his expression widen in surprise but he softened it quite quickly – the teen acting sensation he was.

"Yes. I love you," he laughed. "I love you," he said a little louder. "You're like my favourite person ever. I want to spend every day, every hour with you and when I'm not with you I'm thinking *God* I'm going to tell you that when I see you again.

"I want to make sure you're comfortable and that you get enough sleep, and that you drink so much water, that you're so *fucking* hydrated. I love you with all my heart and if you tell me something makes you uncomfortable, I will make an active effort not to do it. I will mess up though, I can guarantee that, I will forget, or do it by accident and I'm already sorry for this but I ask you to please understand I'm not doing this on purpose."

"You're pretty cool, you know."

He grinned, his nose crinkling, his tongue peeking out between his teeth.

"I…" I sighed, but it was definitely amused. "I'd really quite like to have…" I closed my eyes, it was just a *fucking* word, "sex with you."

"Oh, good," he nodded. "I'd definitely like to have sex with you." He tugged on the bottom of his t-shirt that I was wearing, "*and* can I just say, the idea of having sex with you, *whilst* you're wearing my t-shirt is *one* of the hottest things I can think of."

"You're lame."

"Excuse me, you said I was cool not even a minute ago."

I mumbled, kneeling up a little closer to him, then wrapping my arms around his neck, pulling him towards me so I could kiss him.

Series 10

Day 12

My knock was hesitant. I figured they probably didn't even hear it over the music that was coming from the room.

So, I chickened out, moping my way out of there, thanking them silently for not hearing me.

"Come in."

Shit.

I sighed, turning to look back at the door as the music lowered.

"Hello?" laughter followed. I laughed with them, sighing and opening their bedroom door.

Quincy smiled at me from where they were sat cross-legged on their bed in pyjama pants and a vest, still scrolling through their phone. AJ was under the duvet, leaning back against the headboard smiling at me as if he had a secret he wanted me to ask about but would never tell me.

"Are you okay, Oz?" Quincy asked.

"I want to ask after some advice," I told them, sighing. They tapped the bed opposite them. I watched AJ lift his legs, crossing them so I could sit, so I did.

"About what?"

"I've been informed that I have an on-screen sex scene in the next script," I swallowed. "I've never had one on-screen ever and like, it's with Brook, it's supposed to be easy."

"No way, honey," Quincy sighed glancing at AJ. "No way, there's a big difference between sex and performance." They waved their hand at me. "I assume you and Brooklyn do have sex… still have sex."

"We…" I laughed, "yes, we have sex."

"For a while, too, yeah?" AJ asked.

"Like duration?" I asked, frowning. He shook his head as Quincy laughed.

"I like how you think, Ozzy."

I smirked at him.

"I mean, you guys have been for a while. You guys have been together for years, right?"

"Yeah, we've been having sex since I was seventeen. What's that got to do with anything?"

"It's a good start that you trust him. You know Brooklyn well; he knows you and your body. He wouldn't do anything to make you feel uncomfortable."

"Like you guys?" I asked.

"AJ wasn't my onscreen sex scene. We had a few fade-to-blacks, or dry humping with our clothes on."

"They were the hottest," AJ teased.

"I went all the way with Freya, and it was a completely different experience. Just make sure you're talking all the time with Brooklyn, but with Eliza, too."

"You guys are always communicating?" I looked between them, they laughed.

"Yeah, of course. We actually get paid more for talking to each other sometimes."

"People like consent," AJ said.

"Brooklyn's done loads of on-screen," Quincy said.

"Hence why I'm not asking him, because I should

just be chill, right?"

"Why? I'm pretty certain he also gets nervous. What did he do the first time he had an on-screen?"

"He had sex with me the night before."

"Like, first time?"

"Yeah. He said he didn't want to have fake sex with Dakota before he had with me."

"I love Brooklyn," AJ sighed touching his chest and leaning back almost headbutting the headboard. "Quincy's right, it'll help that you feel comfortable with him. If anything, it'll just help you relax into it a little."

I exhaled deeply.

"But not too much," Quincy teased. "That's the benefit of doing *OnlyFans*. You can actually enjoy it."

"How haven't you been fired yet?" I tilted my head.

Quincy bit their tongue. "I ask myself that question every day."

"So," I said as I leant back against our bedroom door, clicking it shut. Brooklyn glanced up at me, his eyebrow raised curiously as he took one of his Air Pods out.

"So?" he repeated to prove he could hear me before taking his pods out.

"Tomorrow's a big day on set," I said, smiling at him. He nodded taking his other Pod out and putting them on the bedside table, "and if I'm being fully honest with you, I'm nervous."

"That makes…"

I rose my finger to my mouth, he silenced immediately.

"There's nothing that'll ease these nerves. I know that but I would like to… I guess, uphold tradition."

He frowned, tilting his head at me so I smiled at him.

"The night before your first on-screen sex scene. We had sex for the first time."

"Do you want to have sex for the first time again?"

"Yes, Brooklyn," I laughed. He grinned at me, putting his phone beside his Air Pods. "I trust you," I told him as I walked towards the bed. "I really do and I know you won't do anything that'd make me uncomfortable tomorrow."

"Never," he whispered, stretching his legs out tapping my knee with his foot.

"I, too, won't do anything that'd make you uncomfortable. Ever. We're a team, okay? You tell me if you don't want to do something, and we'll stop instantly."

"And if you tell me we stop, too."

"I know," I nodded. "I know that so deeply that I don't even have to question if it's true."

"I love you," he said through his grin so I kissed it but he was technically too far away, so I fell into him, and he began to laugh, dragging me towards him until I was firmly placed between his legs. "How do you want to do this?"

I hummed.

"Can you start with your fingers?" I whispered. He nodded almost immediately, his fingers stroking over my thigh, circling around the particularly sensitive parts of my body that he knew made me shiver. His grin was playful, his tongue between his teeth before he kissed my cheek, then buried his face into my neck. Kissing and sucking so I tilted my head giving him more space, closing my eyes as I let my hands stroke up his back to his hair.

His fingers slipped into my pants. Stroking me through my underwear in a way that if he didn't get inside me soon, I would end him.

He snorted against my neck, it was disgustingly attractive as he lifted his head, grinning at me. I knocked my forehead against his.

"I swear..." I all but growled at him, he gasped mocking me, so I growled again then gasped back at him when his fingers slipped inside me. "Brooklyn."

"Yes, darling?" he whispered, I squeezed his hair a little tighter.

"You're a fucking tease."

He wiggled his eyebrows at me because he was still a giant dork.

I cuddled down onto him, catching his smirk as he pushed up to meet me, I didn't quite know how long I could keep this up, so instead I tugged on his waistband, lowering his pyjamas just enough to get at his dick.

"That's not..." a deep breath, "fair. I was..." he moaned lightly, "teasing you."

"Game, set, and match," I whispered directly into his ear. I felt his dick twitch in my hand, as I tried to suppress a full body shiver which came out as a moan.

Now it was a game of chicken, and we both knew it. The way my thumb circled the tip of his dick, the way his fingers were angled perfectly over and over, the way I pushed against his balls with his hand that was buried inside me, the way he touched my clit, as if he was doing it mistakenly, as if it was a finger slip. The fucker.

He gave first.

"Stop, stop, stop, Oz." he gasped, his head falling onto my shoulder. "I'm going to come, stop."

I unexpectedly laughed. His sigh was deep as he examined me, throbbing in my hand. I stroked the underside of his dick softly as I reached for our drawers. I searched out a condom, biting deeply into my lip, as he stroked me as softly as I did him.

I pulled out what I thought was a condom, we both moaned together when we saw it was a screen wipe.

"Fucks sake," I muttered. He laughed, biting my

shoulder as I all but pulled the drawer out before finding a condom. I held it to him. "We need to store these better," I told him before opening it, dropping the packet onto his stomach. He picked it up.

"Oh, *pleasure me*," he read. I laughed as I rolled the condom down his dick.

"You're the one who bought the *surprise me* forty-pack."

"It was almost the one hundred and twenty pack," he told me. I glanced up at him as he grinned at me. "But they weren't in stock."

I sighed, laughing mildly as I shook my head.

"I think you'll find these are ribbed for your pleasure."

"Shut up," I gasped. He laughed, holding my face in his hands and kissing my nose.

"I love you," he whispered into my mouth.

"I love you," I nodded, kissing him. "With all my heart." I knocked our heads together, "but Brooklyn?"

"Yes?"

"Please fuck me."

He smirked, sliding his hands down to my waist, until he could push me up onto my knees. I barely gave him time to consider it before I lowered myself onto him.

I groaned, burying my head into Brooklyn's chest at the thudding on the door. He laughed, sighing and rubbing his forehead before pulling the duvet up high enough to at least make him suitable.

"What?" I shouted at the door. I heard Quincy's laugh from the other side.

"Can I come in? Or do you want me to pay on the door?"

Brooklyn sighed, sitting himself up and knocking me off his chest.

"One hundred online, two fifty on the door."

Quincy snorted as they walked in.

"You think I have that kind of money?" they scoffed, grinning at us both. I laughed covering my face as Brooklyn shook his head. "We're ordering dessert, would you like some post-intercourse dessert?"

"Yes," I sighed. "Yes I would."

Brooklyn looked at me over his shoulder.

"Wouldn't you?"

He rolled his eyes. "Oreo milkshake."

"Oz?"

"Cookie dough," I said.

Quincy nodded blowing kisses to us both. "It'll be about twenty-five minutes, enough time for a round two."

"Go away," I squawked. They smirked raising two fingers to us before leaving. I rolled onto my side; Brooklyn lay down to face me. He kissed the tip of my nose.

"We need to put some boundaries in place with your best friend," he whispered.

"Boundaries are a really thin line, when they'll literally watch us film a sex scene tomorrow."

"That's a good point."

Series 2

Day 1

If I'd been old enough to have a Twitter account, I'm pretty sure it'd have blown up. Brooklyn's had, at least. He'd made an account on his thirteenth birthday, a month after filming had ended, and then I had text after text from him as the numbers rose. After the pilot, he had *five thousand* followers.

Episode two, twenty thousand.

By the midway point of the series, episode five, he had the little blue tick. Verified, Brooklyn Sampson had the little blue tick and one million followers.

Episode eight, two-point-two million.

Episode ten, the final episode, he had five million, and a selfie he uploaded of us all on the last day of filming series one had gotten over thirty million likes and retweets. We were trending, not just the show, not just *Adolescent Summers* – that was *now* an undeniable success but our names. Brooklyn Sampson, Dakota Chidubem, Quincy Ikeda, and *my* name. We were famous.

I'd sat beside him, as he scrolled through his feed, showing me fanart and fan-made videos, all the love and dedication to our characters who they barely knew. Who they'd been with for ten episodes.

But that wasn't right. The books had been out for years, Brooklyn had said he read one in junior school. We belonged to them people, we *were* those characters. We'd brought their favourite stories to life.

And that was a whole lot of responsibility I wasn't quite expecting. Not at eleven years old.

So, Brooklyn not turning up to the first day of filming series two was… weird.

"It's weird, right?" I asked Dakota. She side-eyed me, frowning ever so slightly but he also humoured me.

"Yes, it's weird but maybe he just isn't scheduled in today."

"Why wouldn't he be scheduled in the first day of filming?"

She shrugged dramatically at me, the gesture huge. "Maybe he's been fired."

I rolled my eyes at her.

"Text him," she shrugged, grinning at me. "Ask him where he is."

"I can't do that," I whispered.

"And why not?"

I shrugged, mumbling nothings at her but the fact of the matter was I couldn't possibly just *text* Brooklyn. He needed to initiate the conversation because what if he didn't want an eleven (but like *so* very close to twelve) year old to text him. He had just turned fourteen, he had so many better things to do, so many cooler friends.

"I heard he's sick."

I turned to Quincy, as they approached us, reading their script with disinterest. "Eliza said he'll be with us soon, when he's feeling better."

"Oh," I whispered.

"Nothing…" they grinned at me, "…contagious."

"Actors to makeup, please," Eliza called. We all turned towards her as she beckoned us, a smile on her face and a tray with cups in. "Sprite," she beckoned Quincy towards her, taking the cup from the tray and holding it up to them. They grinned at me ever so slightly before walking towards her, taking the drink and stabbing it with the straw.

Dakota followed, taking her coke and going with Quincy through to the makeup chair.

I approached Eliza warily.

"What's up, darling?"

"Is Brooklyn sick?"

She tilted her head at me and sighed, sounding sympathetic.

"He'll be fine, don't you worry. All we're going to do is film all the scenes Kevin doesn't feature in, then when he comes back *which* he will, we'll film all his scenes."

"He will come back."

"Of course, it's nothing serious." She squeezed my shoulder. "Here," she passed my drink. "Go get your makeup on. Brooklyn'll be fine."

His dad answered the door. He appeared confused as he examined me, stood on their doorstep, then he turned towards the stairs.

"Brooklyn."

I looked down at my shoes.

"Someone at the door for you," he added, his eyes casting over me again before walking away and leaving me standing there. Brooklyn tapped me when he appeared at the door. An amused smile on his face as he examined me in his doorway. I examined him right back, mostly because I didn't remember having to look up quite so much at him.

"I brought you an ice cream," I told him in leu of saying hello. He frowned but it was amused. "Well, I've found that ice cream just make everything better, you know, and Quincy said you were sick, so I thought if you were sick you might need something to make you feel better and I thought, ice cream, because they make everything better."

"Take a breath," he whispered.

"I remembered you telling me you liked Crunchies, so I got you a Crunchie ice cream but it's fine if you want the Smarties one instead."

He shook his head as he laughed, then nodded towards the stairs so I stepped into his house. He led me upstairs and into his bedroom. I watched as he climbed onto his bed, crossing his legs then sitting down, I warily sat down opposite him.

"Are you sick?" I whispered as I passed him the ice cream. He took it happily, grinning as he mixed the ice cream.

"No," he whispered then cleared his throat.

"Why aren't you filming with us? I missed you."

"You missed me?" he said a little louder.

"Well, I mean, we had to work *extra* hard because you weren't around."

He laughed. "Sorry for the inconvenience," he mocked. Well I figured that was how he wanted it to come across, it didn't quite get there as his voice cracked mid-way. His cheeks flushed almost instantly.

"What?" I asked, tilting my head at his blush. He ate more ice cream then cleared his throat.

"Dad said I'll be back in a month or so, maybe before." He was back to whispering again.

"A whole month?"

He shrugged one shoulder at me.

"What's wrong?" I asked.

"Puberty," he smiled.

"Oh," I said, frowning. "You started your period?" then I grinned at him, he grinned right back, the laughter playing across his face as he ate more of the ice cream.

Series 10

Day 13

I quickly wiped away at my cheeks when the room filled with light.

There was a pause from both of us. A completely silent pause where we both made a decision for our next move.

Mine was pulling the duvet over my head. I thought his was leaving the room, but that was because it went dark again.

I let out the breath I was holding, tears rolling down my cheeks. I swallowed deeply, jumping when I felt a hand on my waist. The thumb stroking against me in a comforting action.

I lowered the duvet, Brooklyn sighed gently using his free hand to wipe at my cheeks.

"Come," he said. I shook my head trying to pull the duvet back over my head. "Come on, Oz," he whispered, before kissing the side of my head.

He left our bedroom.

I watched after him, pushing myself to sit up and wiping my eyes with my palms as I took in deep breaths.

"Shoes," I heard called from the hall. I frowned towards it but pushed myself out of bed regardless, picking up Brooklyn's hoodie as I passed it then stepping into my Vans.

He was leant against the front door when I finally emerged, twirling his keys around on his fingers.

He caught them when he saw me, so I walked towards him. I stopped just in front of him.

He watched me, not saying a word as I took in long drawn breaths, then I pulled on the arm of the shirt he'd tied around his waist.

He laughed as he caught it before it fell, then wrapped his arms around my head, pulling me towards him, swaying us side to side kissing the top of my head.

"Come on, Nugget," he whispered, letting me go to retie his shirt and open the front door.

It was dark out as we walked towards his car. Very dark, proper night-time kind of dark. I was surprised to read 1AM on his dash as he turned the engine on.

"Did I wake you?" I whispered. He frowned, confused, as he took a stick of gum out of his door.

"I haven't been to sleep yet," he offered me some gum. "Have you?"

"I don't remember," I admitted, taking the stick from him then pulling myself up onto the seat. Crossing my legs and putting the hood up.

He drove.

I didn't pay any attention to where he was heading, until he pulled into a drive-thru. I watched him as he pulled up to the speaker, lowering his window and taking his own breath as the lady on the other end asked to take our order.

"A Smarties McFlurry," he said. I covered my face as I smiled. "And a Crunchie one too, please."

"Course, drive around, Brooklyn," the lady replied, he rose his eyebrow.

"We're too famous for this," I murmured. His laugh

was very nasal, as he put the car back into gear and drove around to the window.

The lady was blushing brightly, as she fiddled with her headset.

"One ninety-eight, please," she practically whispered. Brooklyn smiled a winning and totally put-on-smile as he tapped his card against the machine.

"You a fan of the show?" he asked.

She nodded laughing in a dismissive way. "Been watching it since I was like seven. Never miss an episode"

He nodded, laughing, as he put the handbrake on.

"Can I get a selfie?" she asked as she reached into her pocket. "Totally get it if not and…"

"As long as you don't mind that I haven't shaved," he teased. She shook her head as she seemed to forget how her phone worked. He requested it, she handed it over practically swooning as he took a couple of selfies with it, then passing it back, nodding to her thanks before taking the handbrake back off and reaching across to squeeze my thigh.

I let out another deeper breath as he let the car roll to the next window. We were given our ice cream without further interaction.

He drove into the car park of the supermarket next door, turned off the car then sighed leaning his head back as the car settled.

He glanced at me, then held the receipt to me.

"Spit," he whispered. I did. The gum had well lost it flavour anyway. He spat his too then folded it in on itself.

I reached for the tub. Turning in the seat so my back was against the door, my knees raised. He began stroking my shins as he seemed to watch me.

"You're definitely already on her Twitter," I muttered.

"Insta story," he teased then stroked his chin. "I must look rough."

"If it's any comfort, not as rough as I do."

"You're doing indie band album cover aesthetic well."

I laughed burying my face into the seat then taking a spoonful of ice cream.

"I'm sorry," he whispered

"You don't need to be, you tried to help, you…"

"I'm sorry about how they're treating you."

"I felt so… vulnerable. So exposed." I swallowed shaking my head at him. "It sounds so stupid, but…"

"It doesn't sound stupid," he interrupted then took his own spoonful of ice cream. "At all. They were asking you to do something that'd make you uncomfortable."

"We're actors, sometimes you've got…"

"No," he shook his head. "No, no, Oz. We should never do anything that makes us uncomfortable. It doesn't matter that we're not kids any more. If a director, or writer or whatever asks something of us that we don't want to do, we don't have to do it."

I swallowed, holding the spoon in my mouth. We both looked out the front window as it began to rain.

"It sucks," I muttered. "Because I really like having sex with you."

He snorted, then gasped holding his hand in front of his mouth as he began to dribble ice cream - this was Brooklyn, international teen wet dream.

"I don't think this show displays just how good at it I am."

"Modest. That's what I like about you."

He winked at me. "I don't think this'll help," he assured me. "But it might make you laugh."

"What?" I whispered.

He winced mixing his ice cream, then he sighed.

"You remember the first sex scene I did with Dakota?"

I nodded as he shook his head.

"You guys all got kicked out because you were not helping, at all." He paused as I smiled at him, he smiled back in such a natural response. "We had to stop filming after you guys left, like we were all ready to go and..." he rose his fist. I frowned then giggled like a child when he rose his first finger. "We couldn't keep shooting, and besides I was far too embarrassed to act cool. Dakota found it hysterical, she couldn't stop laughing at me but she swore she'd keep it secret."

"She did," I gasped. "I never knew."

"It took us about thirty extra minutes to shoot, because it wouldn't go down, and when it finally did, I was too embarrassed to even look at Dakota."

"You were far cooler the evening before," I teased.

"The primary difference was that I wanted you to see my erection."

I nudged my foot against his knee.

"I love you," I told him. He nodded and didn't reply like he would normally, instead he waited for what I was about to say next. I sucked the ice cream from around a Smartie as I thought. "But I think I need to tell Eliza, and everyone, that I am not going to partake in any on-screen sex scenes."

"Hey."

I looked up at him.

"You loving me has nothing to do with your on-screen decisions." He shook his head. "Us working together and sleeping together do not go hand-in-hand and I fully support your decision."

"Thank you," I sighed. "I just... I don't want to be a part of a diversity stunt. We saw what they did to Quincy, it was..."

"Horrible," he agreed. "They've never forgiven

them." He held the side of my head, scratching his fingers lightly through my hair. "I will stand by whatever decision you make, and I will not allow you to be used in that way."

"We're a team in this," I whispered.

"Team Broz."

"Oh, I hate that and you know it."

He kissed me. It tasted like ice cream.

Series 4

Day 120

Quincy found me. *Well*, I wasn't necessarily hiding but Quincy was the first person to stumble upon me. They pulled on the thighs of their trousers, before crouching in front of me. They weren't wearing their jacket yet, nor their tie or whatever neck piece they were going for, even their shirt was still undone.

I still had time to go home, I guess.

"What is wrong, my love?"

I shook my head, burying it deeper into my arms. They sat beside me. I felt their body nudging against mine but not as if they were trying to get my attention. They didn't speak, but I'm sure they did speculate.

I eventfully looked at them.

"I can't help you if you don't tell me, you know," they whispered. "You kind of having to give a little to get a whole damn lot."

"I don't want to wear a dress," I said.

"Then don't."

"Mum said…"

"Darling, I don't give a fuck what your mother said, if you don't want to wear a dress. Do not wear a dress."

I shook my head.

"No, no, think about it. These pictures are going to be everywhere, if you don't feel comfortable with what you're wearing, you should change because you're going to be seeing them forever."

"I don't have any other clothes." I cleared my throat. "I don't have anything else to wear."

"Come with me," they offered, then they stood. I frowned up at them so they pushed their hand out to me. "Come on."

I took their hand, swallowing deeply as they pulled me up to my feet. They walked me through the corridor into the boy's dressing room.

Brooklyn was shaving over a wash basin; he also didn't have his suit fully on. His reflection grinned at me before continuing to shave.

"Why are you gracing our presence?" he asked without taking his eyes off his reflection.

"We don't want to wear a dress," Quincy said as they crossed the room.

"Do you want to wear a suit?" Brooklyn asked.

I shrugged one shoulder at him, looking down at my fingers. "I don't know. I just don't want to wear this dress."

"Do you have a second set of clothes?" Brooklyn laughed. Quincy grinned as they lifted a suit bag off the rail.

"I do," they whispered. "I have the plain black suit that my okaasan thinks I'm wearing and what I actually am."

"I love you." I laughed as Brooklyn grinned at us.

"You can wear my black suit if you want, we're about the same size." They rose the hanger to me, tilting their head as if asking me a question. I nodded biting my lip. I was increasingly thankful for running the same size as Quincy *and* I truly dreaded the day that I grew too much outwards for their clothes to fit.

"Yes, please."

"Awesome," Quincy whispered then shook the hanger at me, so I took it from them and pulled down the zip. It was simply a black suit, black blazer, black trousers, and a white shirt, no tie though.

We all turned towards the knock on the door.

"Ten minutes, kids," Eliza called through. Brooklyn squawked as if that was an appropriate response before wiping the shaving foam off his cheeks. I hesitated.

"It's okay, darling," Quincy whispered as they buttoned the top of their shirt. "You can change in the bathroom if…"

"It's not that," I said as I let my eyes trail Brooklyn watching as he tied his tie without thought. "I don't know, I'll get in trouble."

"With your mum?" Quincy asked. I swallowed nodding. "If it's only your mum you're worried about, you don't need to worry. My okaasan will be pissed I'm not wearing a simple black suit, but she isn't going to punish me for it. She'll tut and tsk, but…" they shrugged. "I'll help you, okay?" they grinned. I nodded clearing my throat before turning and moving my plait.

"Can you unzip me, please?"

"Damn," Brooklyn said from his perch on the back of the couch where he was waiting for Quincy and I to finish getting dressed. I met his eyes as he beckoned me towards him with his finger. "No tie, so…" he opened the top two buttons of the shirt. His fingers running down the buttons when he did.

"Shall we?"

I jumped, turning from Brooklyn towards Quincy as they straightened their blazer.

"Where is my damn—" Quincy gasped. Brooklyn

shrugged as he stood from the couch, his arm draping over my shoulder.

"Eh?" He tapped my chest.

"You get a *damn* for the record," I told Brooklyn. He grinned, appearing pleased.

"I scrub up well," he told me, then jumped against me at the knock on the door.

"Move it, kids," Eliza said as she opened the door, pausing when she saw me. "Wrong dressing room," she said. "You look good, though, suits you."

I grinned turning away from her.

"Move, people, move. You need to get into the limousine."

I inhaled deeply. Brooklyn squeezed my shoulder then pushed me forward, so I began to walk. I caught up with Quincy as they stepped through the door. I squeezed their elbow.

"Thank you."

"Always, my darling, always." They took my hand, kissing the back of it before climbing into the limousine

Dakota cocked her head at me as I took my seat, she appeared mostly confused.

"You've gotten changed," she said.

I pointed at her. "No one said you weren't quick, sweetheart."

"Now…" Eliza interrupted. "Remember, no matter what people ask, you cannot say *anything* about series four."

"Bold of you to assume I remember the plot of series four," Brooklyn muttered. I choked when I tried *not* to laugh.

Series 10

Day 27

Eliza didn't look all too pleased as she let herself into the room. She closed the door, leaning back on it and cocking her head at me. I held my script to her.

"I am not comfortable," I stated then threw my script onto the table. "Not with these words."

She walked towards me, frowning lightly before picking up my script.

"Page fifteen," I continued. She hummed, nodding, as she flicked through. "And I know it's the Halloween special, I know Costumes and whatever bullshit they're trying to pull, but if you want a boy in a dress, ask Brooklyn, you know because he would. He so would comply, but I know if I do this, if I willingly put myself on that set, they'll use it against me."

She looked up from the script. "I understand why you're frustrated." I could hear a *but*, a loud *but* that would probably have a guilt-tripping explanation to it. Our eyes met.

"It's not even just this, though. This a dress on Izzy doesn't fit in anyway. It's not Izzy's character, she has never worn dresses, or done stereotypically girly things. They're just doing this because I've transitioned. I know they are."

"I will talk to Jordan, but I think you know as much as I do, he doesn't really…"

"Care," I finished.

She sighed. "Have much say."

I looked away from her.

"Oz, you know I will always try to make sure you're comfortable."

"I know," I whispered. "I know, Eliza."

She sighed. When I turned back towards her she was gone, the door closing behind her.

Brooklyn, or I suppose Kevin, was in a very low-effort Vampire costume. A black t-shirt, impossibly skinny jeans, and fake fangs that actually looked remarkably real. He was currently taking grief from Dakota, Ally, who was dressed as a cactus. Yes, a cactus.

"Coming from a cactus," Kevin teased back as he pushed himself on the desk, sitting with his feet on the spinning chair.

Ally rolled her eyes. "Look, see Todd made an effort."

Quincy was dressed as a ketchup bottle. They were not all too impressed at that, even they'd have preferred to wear the dress.

"Todd had no choice," Todd commented, then I heard Freya's, laugh. Her character, India, was dressed as a Mustard bottle.

"What do you think of our couple's costume?" she chirped. Ally laughed, them both complimenting each other on every element. Todd sighed, leaning against the desk Kevin had sat on.

"I thought we could go find an actual haunted house," Ally said, and that was my cue. I walked onto set. I wasn't in the dress yet. It wasn't scripted for me to be, probably so Quincy and Brooklyn didn't raise hellfire when they received their scripts, but I knew it was in the dresser behind me.

"You didn't make an effort, either," Ally proclaimed in full on aghast with me as I walked through the door. I held up my hands.

"My hoodie has a skeleton on it."

It did. It was adorable and proclaimed happily that it was a bones day.

"Izzy," she said in the tone of voice that suggested I was her student and she the teacher who thought I should've tried harder.

"See, I thought…" I took a deep breath, turning on the spot and heading for that dresser. I paused with my hands on the knob. "…given on Halloween you can dress up as anything…" I pulled on the knob. The doors opened and there it was, worse than I could've ever imagined; big, puffy, and princess like something Izzy would never have worn and something I got dysphoria just from looking at. My face must've done something to portray this.

"Izzy," Brooklyn said. I swallowed, because kudos to him for staying in character, but I could hear his concern. I pulled the dress from the dresser, the frills brushing against me. The dress heavy, so heavy. I met Brooklyn's eyes for the slightest of seconds before turning back to Dakota.

"I thought I could dress up as me, you know, before all this. The…" I took a breath, closing my eyes for a second, "…the real me."

"Oh, hell no."

I turned as Quincy stood up straight shaking their head.

"No, no way. Cut!" they proclaimed. Jordan rolled his eyes, he looked very frustrated, but he did call cut.

"It's a joke," Jordan said. "You know, boy in a dress, ha, ha."

"What are you, six?" Quincy snapped. Jordan rolled his eyes. "Why did your so-called humour not leave Nursery? There is nothing funny about a boy in a dress, but if one of us must wear one, I will, or Brooklyn will. You do not put Oz in a dress."

"Izzy…" Jordan began.

"Izzy is a fictional character. Oz is a real person," Quincy barked. Jordan sighed. I met Brooklyn's eyes as he examined me.

"Comfortable?" he mouthed. I shook my head. "You don't want to?"

I shook my head again, he swallowed. I watched his Adams apple bob a few times and then he stood up.

"I quit," Brooklyn said.

"*What?*" Jordan and I stated at the same time.

"No way," Quincy whispered.

"I quit." Brooklyn stood and began to walk off set, Jordan went after him. Grabbing him by the arm to stop him.

"You can't quit. You have a contract."

"Whatever," Brooklyn stated, pulling his arm from Jordan's grasp. "My contract ends this year, I have plenty lined up. I don't need you anymore, you need me, and I quit."

"Let's talk about this," Jordan offered. "Don't be rash."

"I'm not being rash," he said, still eerily calm. "I don't like your values. The first strike was Quincy. You were disgusting to them."

"We sorted it out with him," Jordan attempted.

"*Them*," Brooklyn corrected. "And now all this shit with Oz. it's disgusting, and I will not work for anyone who is blatantly transphobic."

"Brooklyn."

He looked up over Jordan's head at Eliza as she approached with wariness.

"What's going on?"

"I quit," he repeated. "Good luck with the end of the series."

He turned to walk away. I watched as Jordan looked to Eliza, pleading with his eyes to get Brooklyn back. I glanced at Quincy, they rose their eyebrow at me, then shrugged.

"I'm out," they said, mostly to me, then they turned back to Jordan. "Bye." They walked off set.

"Quincy," Jordan stated.

Quincy turned to look at him. "What are my pronouns?" they asked. "What should you refer to me as when you're talking about me, to my face, behind my back, and to the press?"

Jordan stuttered. Quincy turned and walked away.

I glanced across the set to Dakota. She winced at me. I let go of the hanger. Letting the dress fall to the floor like a deflating balloon.

Jordan turned to Eliza. "Get them back," he demanded.

Eliza walked towards him. "Don't you ever use that tone of voice with me," she said, almost as calmly as Brooklyn had spoken. "I am here for the young people on our set, not to placid you."

"They can't just walk off set."

"No," she seemed to agree, as she glanced at where Quincy and Brooklyn had left, "but I assume Brooklyn will actually be driving, not walking."

I laughed.

It made Jordan look at me. I caught my breath, watching him as he examined me. I reared myself up for an attack. He didn't quite get to the point of saying words.

"Oz," Eliza said. I looked at her, deflating like the dress at the kindness in her expression. "Would you like a lift home?"

I nodded.

"You could be fired for this."

"I could be fired for a lot of things I let you kids get away with."

"I'm twenty-one, I'm not a kid."

"Yes, you are, darling." She sighed. "And I'm sorry about how shitty they're treating you."

I looked out the window as we left the studio.

"Pity Happy Meal?" she asked. I laughed, shaking my head. "I usually get the scripts in advance; I usually can forewarn with this."

"The issue is prominently that they don't see an issue," I sighed. "I didn't ask Brooklyn to do that."

"Oh, I know. I know he did that from his own free will. I know Brooklyn would've done it even if it wasn't you because you know that'll come into it. They'll try to argue that because you're having sex, you're manipulating him or whatever. I know it's bullshit. I know it is.

"Brooklyn is so hard to sway. I've known him since he was twelve years old, I know that. I had to persuade him to stay when everything happened with Quincy. It was tough, but he eventfully agreed to stay."

"I didn't know that," I whispered. "Did I break my contract?"

"No."

"I sometimes think I deserve this. That I shouldn't have come out, I should've just waited it out. Finished the series, not taken any other jobs and hidden away to transition and when I come out the other end, no-one would know I was that girl from *Adolescent Summers*. I sometimes regret coming out, and I hate that I feel like that. I hate so deeply I feel that.

"But I'm scared, I'm so scared about the response of the studio that I am terrified about this series going out. Not only that, the moment I came out, I deleted my Instagram, my Tiktok, my Twitter, because I didn't even want to give anyone the platform to feel like they could hide behind a screen and say anything."

"I want to apologise," she said. "But it's not my place to and I truly don't want to minimise your feelings with an *I'm sorry*. Have you spoken this aloud to anyone, else?"

"No," I whispered. "Brooklyn's just trying to be as supportive as possible and I know that Quincy gets it, but I don't want to be constantly dumping on them." We glanced at each other. "It's easier to just get some weed and get high on our roof."

She snorted gently. "Imagine if the studio got wind of that."

"Fired," I teased.

"Oz," she whispered. "Have you told your mum?"

I looked down at my hands.

"No?"

"Complicated."

"Oh, I know, sweetheart. She'll find out you know, she'll see…"

"And it'll be too late. Too late for her to do anything, too late for her opinion to matter." I cleared my throat. "That doesn't directly affect this, though."

She nodded. I looked at our house. The only evidence that Quincy and Brooklyn had come home was Brooklyn's car which was parked on a slight wonk in front of us. He didn't seem to still be in it.

"Would you like to come in for a coffee?" I asked.

She smiled at me, turning off her engine and nodding. "I would."

I smiled back at her, getting out of the car and climbing the steps to our front door. I pushed on the door, it opened.

"You keep your door unlocked," Eliza commented. I looked at her. "You're some of the most well-known, highest grossing actors in the UK, and you leave your door unlocked."

I shrugged one shoulder. "Lucky, really, as I didn't have my key. Brooklyn knew that so he must've left it open for me."

"Brooklyn did."

I looked up, smiling sadly at him as he stood in the doorway, his head leaning against the doorframe.

"I am so sorry I left without you."

I shook my head, turning to point at Eliza. She waved, he waved back then almost fell over as Bud crashed through his legs into the hallway. Eliza leant on the front door to shut it before crouching, offering her hand to Bud.

"I shouldn't have left without you."

"Did you leave without Quincy?"

"They just about caught up to me. I…"

"Stop apologising." I pulled on his shirt. "I'm not even a little mad at you."

Bud woofed.

"I think they would've caught up, but they took time to completely destroy their ketchup costume."

Eliza laughed gently. We turned to her together.

"Coffee," I said, then passed Brooklyn going through to the kitchen. Quincy was sat at the breakfast counter. Scrolling through their phone with one finger whilst they leant their cheek on their other hand.

They visibly jumped when they heard me step into the room. They shook themselves off. "Hey. You okay?"

"Are you?"

They smiled at me, big, wide a laugh in their expression but completely fake. "Of course, darling, of course."

"Quincy."

"No," they laughed. "AJ's working, too, so he won't be home for a while, not even picking up his phone and…"

I hugged them.

"I'm sorry, it's so selfish."

"No, no, it isn't…" I gasped sitting on the seat beside them. "No. It affects you as much as it affects me, it's been going on much longer for you, too. You can be upset."

Their smile didn't even falter as the tears started down their cheeks. "I don't even care if they treat me like shit." They swallowed wiping their cheeks with the back of their hand. "I'm just so pissed that they're treating *you* like shit."

"Hey…"

"And you're so much braver than me, doing this…"

"You walked so I could run, Quincy."

They looked straight at me, then frowned so I turned.

"I adopted her," I said. Eliza smiled as she carried Bud into the kitchen. She stood him on the floor in an effort not to drop him as he wiggled around.

Series 4

Day 121

She'd been angry. *So* angry. Unnecessarily angry. She'd kicked me out on the spot.

Get out of my house until you grow up and start acting like a girl.

I wanted to scream and shout, tell her I *wasn't* a girl, but then I didn't really know where that had come from or, in fact, how true that was. It was a rash thought, that's all, a quick, rash thought that didn't make *any* sense.

I called Quincy. They answered and told me in no uncertain terms there was no way their mother, their okaasan, was going to allow me to come stay because she was pissed at Quincy for changing their suit, but she was still making some Chawan Mushi for them because she truly loved them and was merely pissed because she was their mother, and they *were* a nightmare.

Unlike *my* mother, who I sometimes believed hated me.

I called Dakota next. She didn't even pick up. I figured she was busy, so I ultimately bucked up enough courage to call Brooklyn.

"You could come here," he told me from the other end of our video call. I blinked, shifting my focus from his necklace that was hanging over his bare chest to his face as he examined me. "But Dad will only allow it for *one* night, he'd totally expect you to go home tomorrow."

"There's nothing I can do?"

"Call Eliza," he suggested. "I promise. Call Eliza. She'll help you out." He smiled, so I took a breath. "Where are you kid?"

"The alley behind my house. I didn't know where to go. I just left."

"Are you safe?" he asked. I swallowed looking down the alley towards the road. "Hey."

I looked back at my phone. "Safe enough."

He scoffed standing and pulling on a t-shirt.

"Brooklyn, it's okay, you don't have to—"

"You're fourteen," he said. "*Not* just that you're alone and it's dark and…"

"Brooklyn."

"Call Eliza. I'm coming to you."

I sighed. "I'm almost fifteen."

He smiled, his laugh soft as he looked at me.

"I'm coming," he whispered.

I was still on the phone to Eliza when Brooklyn's dad's car pulled up outside my house. He got out leaving the headlights on. I heard him calling my name before he closed the door.

"Is that Brooklyn?" Eliza said into my ear.

"You don't have a driving licence," I said. Brooklyn shrugged one shoulder at me, taking my backpack from me flinging it over his shoulder.

"I've got my provisional," he replied. I smiled at the floor. "Is that Eliza?"

"Yeah," I sighed, as she called Brooklyn's name through the phone. He took it.

"Yes, I know, I'm not meant to drive without an

adult. This was an emergency." I shook my head. "Has the situation been explained?" he asked, looking at me. I nodded once as Eliza must've confirmed the other end. "I want to activate loco parentis."

He nodded, chewing on his lip.

"I'll drive," he said. "W1D..." he recited aloud, so I made a mental note of it. "Come on," he said to me, turning and going to the car. I followed running around it to get in the passenger side.

I shivered when I closed the door.

I hadn't realised I was so cold.

Brooklyn passed me my phone as he got back into the driver side. Shifting the car into gear, then pointing at the display.

"Type that postcode in for me, please."

I did.

We'd reach our destination in twenty minutes. Traffic depending.

Brooklyn was quiet. In a very uncharacteristic Brooklyn way so instead I asked; "What's loco parentis?"

"It means in place of a parent," he said then he looked at me. "It's a law in, I think, America, someone who takes on the role of a parent."

"What did you mean, you wanted to activate it?"

He exhaled gently. "Do you remember last year..." he looked at me. "...when my mum showed up?"

"I do."

"When everything went wrong my dad essentially gave me to Eliza." He glanced at me before looking back at the road. "She looked after me until my dad got it all sorted out."

I remembered. I didn't remember his mum showing up. I remembered the feelings associated with it, but the details were blurry. I hadn't really wanted to impose. I wanted to give Brooklyn space because who wants a thirteen-year-old hanging around you whilst you're going through stuff.

"She basically took on loco parentis because, you know, *underaged*. I said I wanted to activate it because you need someone to look after you for a little while, at least until your mum cools off and because I said that Eliza feels somewhat obligated to help out."

"I don't want to intrude on her," I whispered.

He smiled at me. "Don't worry. She's a great host." He reached across the central panel, squeezing my hand gently. "And you're going to love her partner."

"You do *not* have your licence," Eliza said from her garden path as Brooklyn walked towards her with my backpack.

"Give me a ticket. I had to save the day," he stated turning back to me and flashing his hands at me as if saying *ta-da*.

"You could totally be Superman."

"That *is* a role I could play," he said to Eliza, grinning. "Right?"

"I'm not your agent, sweetheart. I'm just your well-paid babysitter."

"I'm sorry," I whispered.

"No, no, no, no, darling." She reached her hand out to me, so I went to her. Squeezing her hand when I could reach. "You're going to go in, take the room at the top of the stairs, get a shower. Warm yourself up and I'll make you a hot chocolate and we'll chat. Okay?"

I nodded.

She squeezed my hand gently.

"We do have a rabbit that roams. If you stumble across something small and furry."

I laughed. "Thank you, Eliza." I turned, Brooklyn dropped my backpack from his shoulder to his hand holding it towards me. "Thank you," I whispered then cleared my throat. "Thank you, Brooklyn." I walked towards him wrapping my arms around him.

He laughed gently into my ear before wrapping his arms around *me* and lifting me from the floor.

"This is the first time you've initiated a hug."

"You deserve it," I replied, tipping my head back to look at him, he grinned, winking at me before shaking me gently.

"Text me *all* night. I will stay up *purposely* so you can continue texting me until you feel comfortable."

"Don't get taken into custody for driving home," I whispered back, instead of stuttering over a thank you. He laughed then gripped me a little closer as I jumped.

"I love you, kid," he laughed. "Stay safe, yeah?" He put my backpack onto my shoulder. "Trust Eliza, she's got you."

I nodded. "Thank you."

Brooklyn let me go then blew a kiss to Eliza.

"Go straight home," she said as I started towards her,

"What are you going to do? Call my dad?" he mocked, she rose her eyebrow at him.

"You bet your ass I am."

"Oop," Brooklyn laughed, waving at me before getting back into the car.

"Come on, hon."

I took a deep breath, following Eliza into her house.

"What's your rabbit called?" I asked as she led me towards the stairs.

"Nunchuck."

"What?" I said as she grinned at me.

"Chuck, but yeah, official title Nunchuck." She smiled at me, squeezing my shoulder gently.

"I'm going to need to meet Chuck."

"Agreed." She pushed me by the shoulder upstairs.

"Shower, pyjamas, hot chocolate."

Nunchuck was placed on my knee the moment I took a seat on her couch. He was a big fluffy grey bunny, who was so chilled out he made me feel calm.

The mug of hot chocolate was nearly as big when Eliza passed me it. She sat beside me.

"The suit, right?"

"The suit," I agreed. "She's so angry about gender. I don't understand it." I rubbed my forehead. "I'm unsure about too many things to comprehend what her reasoning could be."

"Do you want to talk?" she asked.

"Complicated. Far too big and complicated, and confusing."

"Hey."

"I think I fancy Brooklyn a little."

"A *little*?" she replied.

"Ouch."

"It's obvious, lovely," she said then shook her head. "Has been for a while." She stroked Nunchuck between the ears.

"Really?" I winced.

"He's a gorgeous boy, truly beautiful inside and out. His heart is so pure and honest. I understand why so many fall for him. Yourself included."

I chewed on my lip. "It's not just that, but I'm not ready for *that*."

"That's fine," she replied. I swallowed nodding as I lifted the mug and drank from it. I very obviously jumped when the door to the room opened. Eliza attempted to soothe me, as I'm sure Nunchuck grunted at me for disgruntling him.

I examined the person who came through the door.

Eliza smiled turning back at me.

"This is my partner," she said. I didn't drag my eyes away because I was so fixated on the rainbow dyed into the shaven part of their hair. "Arden," she added.

"Hello," I offered.

"You adopting again?" Arden said, their voice deep, gravelly. It almost made me shiver. Eliza laughed in a sigh.

"This is…"

"Oh, sweetheart, I know who this is."

I tapped Eliza on the shoulder.

"I'm famous," I informed her. She rolled her eyes as she stood, walking away from me, then bending to kiss Arden on the side of the head.

"Be nice," she said, then looked at me. "I'm talking to both of you."

I laughed before burying my nose into the mug, although I could still look at the multicoloured stars that were clipped onto the spokes of their wheelchair.

"Hi," Arden smiled. I figured I must've blushed.

"Hi," I whispered back, then cleared my throat. "I'm sorry that I'm intruding, I don't think I'll be here long, I don't…"

"Don't worry. We practically fostered Brooklyn," they smiled.

"Please don't think me rude." They tilted their head at me, a curious thing that I, for some reason, mimicked. "What are your pronouns?"

"That is the least rude question you could've asked, and I'd like to thank you for asking it."

I smiled like a child who'd been praised.

"Ey, em," Ey said. I repeated them back, practicing over the syllables.

"I've never heard those pronouns before."

"I'm androgynous," Ey said

"Like… Quincy?" I paused. "Although Quincy's

nonbinary. Is there a difference?"

"There can be. I personally don't identify as nonbinary, sometimes I identify as genderqueer, but the label doesn't always fit me," Ey paused. "And that's okay."

"That's okay," I repeated. Ey smiled at me, I drank more hot chocolate. Eliza came back into the room, she walked around the couch so she could retrieve Nunchuck from me. "I didn't know you were queer."

"Well, why would you, sweetheart, I didn't tell you."

"Well..." I cleared my throat, looking to Arden before back to Eliza. "I'm sorry that I assumed you were straight."

"Apology accepted," she grinned at me. I grinned right back.

Series 10

Day 28

Four hundred and ninety… one, two, three sheep had jumped over the imaginary fence in my mind as I'd tried in vain to sleep.

Brooklyn was asleep which wasn't to say he *hadn't* stayed awake with me as long as he could. I knew he was a goner when he rested his head on my stomach. He was asleep within the hour, and I only resented that he could sleep, not that he was.

My head was swimming.

My feelings were hurt.

When Brooklyn moved, his head falling from my stomach onto the bed, I got out of our bed. I paused as he frowned in his sleep, but it soon relaxed, and he didn't wake so I pulled our blanket off the end of the bed wrapping it around my shoulders and going downstairs.

The alarm was off and I was *sure* the TV was on.

Bud stopped me at the bottom of the stairs, raising on his little back legs, panting happily at me. I sat on the bottom step, scratching between his ears.

"What are you doing up Bud?" I whispered. "Who's up with you?"

He licked my hand in response.

"Come on, then," I whispered, standing and stepping around him. He ran at my side, then ahead of me into the living room. I followed him in, wrapping my blanket a little tighter then sighing as Quincy looked back at me from the couch.

"Couldn't sleep," they sighed, I looked at the TV, frowning at the credits rolling.

"What are you watching?"

"Glee."

"Glee?" I repeated, laughing lightly as I went to sit beside them. They snuggled in close the moment I was fully sat.

"I was going to watch Pose, but I think we've had to deal with enough of our own trans issues this week."

"Preach." I sighed as the next episode began. "Oh, season one."

"Course," they laughed. "Comfort show vibes."

"Necessary," I sighed. They nodded resting their head on my shoulder.

"I'm so sad, Oz," they said then watched as Bud jumped onto a cushion that had fell to the floor, then onto the couch. He trotted along until he could rest his head on Quincy's legs, rolling onto his back and looking up at Quincy with a tilted head *requesting* they immediately compile with the stroking rule.

Quincy, of course, did.

"How do you feel?"

"Like shit," I nodded. "Genuinely the worse I've ever felt. It's all my fault."

"Yep," they whispered. I gasped as they turned to me. They smiled gently. "It's not your *fault* but you are the catalyst and, well, they've had a hell of a reaction."

"Have you read our emails?" I whispered. They frowned at me. "Comic Con."

"When?" they groaned.

"Weekend after next, apparently we've already been announced, *apparently* we've already said yes. I don't want to go, I don't want people to see me."

"What do you mean?" they whispered.

"I'm… I'm not ready. I wanted to do it slowly, you know, resuscitate my Twitter account, *then* maybe Instagram. When I know they're both doing well, maybe Tiktok, by then series ten will be out, and people will have familiarised themselves with Oz."

"Honey," they sighed. "I'd never push anyone out of their closet before they're ready, but people know."

I closed my eyes.

"I *know* that. I know that people speculated after our live sessions. I *know* that it was all over Pink News, because I had Brooklyn read them and make sure it wasn't wrong, I guess.

"I'm terrified, I don't care if it's news, or reporters, paparazzi, I don't give a fuck but the moment I'm putting myself out there, that's *different*."

"Oh, I know. I know, sweet pea. I remember the first time I went out after I came out, *yeah* it was scary but you don't realise who you're inspiring until you do these things."

"They haven't helped."

"No, they're assholes." They sighed. "What are we going to do, Oz?"

I shook my head, frowning.

"What do you mean?"

"About the show. About work, what are *we* going to do?"

"I think Brooklyn's formally quit," I sighed. "I think it'd take some higher power to get him to finish filming."

"And yourself?"

"I don't want to," I whispered. "I don't want to go back unless I have a say in the script."

They rose their eyebrow at me,

"That isn't an unreasonable demand. I'm not suggesting you *write* them, but Eliza can only do so much when she receives the scripts. If you or I had a say in the content we wouldn't get to *this* position."

"But…" I paused. Bud whined so I scratched his ears.

"But?"

"I don't feel like I've been trans long enough to dictate words."

"My love, you've been trans your whole life," they held my chin. "Every time you've looked in the mirror and thought something was wrong, every time you put on clothes and they felt like someone else's.

"Every time you touched yourself and paused because something wasn't there, because something felt like it was missing.

"When you couldn't look at yourself in the mirror, when you hid under baggy clothes, when you tried to make yourself invisible so no one could see your pain.

"No one is more trans than anyone else, and *everyone* experiences being trans differently. You have as much of a voice as someone who's been stealth for forty, fifty, sixty years."

"You know…" I whispered. Quincy met my eyes. "You're the real love of my life."

They rose my hands, kissing my knuckles.

"We will get through this."

"Together," I agreed, nodding as they smiled at me.

Series 5

Day 66

I really hadn't had very many scenes opposite AJ or, I suppose, Daniel – as his character was named. He was pretty good but even better at playing the villain.

I was thoroughly enjoying the *evil Daniel* storyline that had developed – as I think was Quincy but for completely different reasons to myself. It was potentially the best storyline we'd done so far, even though it had thoroughly pissed off Eliana as it wasn't from the books.

Today was AJ's last day of filming. We all had a number of scenes left to film, a number of weeks left of this series but we were walking into AJ's last scene. We sat on the floor, in line with Jordan's chair. Brooklyn, Dakota, and I and a bag of Haribo that was getting passed back and forth.

"What do you think they're going to do to him?" Dakota whispered. I shook my head as Brooklyn sighed biting on a Haribo ring pulling on it until it broke.

"Has he been renewed for next series?"

"I don't think so," I whispered. Brooklyn glanced at me.

"Oh, shit. He's going to die."

"No, surely not. Maybe they just haven't reviewed his

contract yet," Dakota whispered. Jordan shushed us.

We turned to him, all pulling a face at him. He rolled his eyes, muttering something about working with teenagers, then he called *actors to set*.

Quincy walked on first. They looked livid. Eliza followed them on, standing behind them, her hand on their shoulder. I glanced at Brooklyn as he frowned at the set.

"I told you, he's going to die."

AJ walked on the opposite side of the set. He also looked pretty livid.

"Okay, everybody ready?" Jordan asked. Quincy rolled their eyes turning to Eliza, they exchanged some silent words before Quincy walked to their mark. AJ turned on his spot being stopped by wardrobe and donned in a cape.

"He looks hot," Dakota sighed. Brooklyn laughed as I exhaled.

"Lights," Jordan declared, "camera." He nodded to Dave, the cameraman. "Clear the set." A pointed eyebrow at Eliza, "episode twenty, scene fifteen, take one."

Quincy took a deep breath.

"Action," Jordan called. Quincy nodded another deep breath and then they crumpled.

"Stop!" they shouted as they ran onto set. "Stop, stop it Daniel, stop it."

AJ, *Daniel,* didn't but he did look in their direction.

"Please, please stop. I figured it out. No-one else knows but I do."

"You know nothing," Daniel boomed. We could feel the bass all the way through the floor, he turned fully to Quincy so they were stood looking at each other.

"I do, I do. I know you were struck by the light. I know when we open the door to look out at the universe,

I know the light hit you, and buried deep inside you." Quincy took a breath. "*And* I know the only way to get this out of you is to kill you."

"No," I whispered as Brooklyn gasped.

"Only I know. Not Kevin, not Ally, none of them. Only me. This is between me and you." They blinked hard, a tear escaping down their cheek.

There was no way that they were controlling that tear. They swallowed deeply, taking a breath as they reached behind them. They shook their head, squeezing their eyes shut, tears falling one after another rolling down their cheeks, then they pulled out a gun.

Brooklyn grabbed for my hand. Stroking his thumb over my knuckles because I was crying too.

"It's just you and me, okay. No-one else, we go out together."

"Your words are meaningless," Daniel replied, *then* caught sight of the gun. He laughed, a joyless, hollow laugh. "You think that'd work, you think you could do it?"

"You still love me, I know you do."

"I do not…"

"I know you do," they turned the gun on themself. "It'd kill you inside out," they paused, "if I pulled this trigger."

"You wouldn't," Daniel sneered. "You're not brave enough."

Quincy walked towards him, the gun still firmly aimed at them.

"I'm braver than you'd ever know, Daniel. I would walk head first into danger for the people I love. I would fight tooth and nail until my dying breath for my family." They stood directly in front of Daniel. *AJ* just a little taller than them so they had to look up at him. "Aishiteru, Daniel."

"I don't love you," he whispered. Quincy shook their head, tears still streaming down their cheeks.

"You're lying," Quincy sobbed, then cleared their throat, the gun drooping at their side as they reached to hold the back of Daniel's neck.

They knocked their heads together, closing their eyes and taking a breath.

"Aishiteru," they repeated, nodding gently so their heads moved together. "Aishiteru." They kissed him. Deep, true, and meaningful. They took a joint breath, them exhaling together, their lips still close, *and* the shot was fired.

We all jumped together.

Then, there was a moment of silence. A moment of pure silence, not even a breath.

Daniel choked. A cough so low and wet sounding before blood began to run down his chin. He staggered back away from Quincy. The gun rose between them.

"I'm sorry," Quincy whispered, as Daniel fell onto his back, his hands clasped around his stomach. Blood seeping through his fingers.

"Todd," he rasped. "Todd…" he reached for him, Quincy dropped the gun, running to AJ's side, stroking his fingers through his hair. Whispering that they were sorry, over and over.

"Cut!" Jordan called and Quincy fell into AJ's chest. Their shoulders shaking as AJ sat up and wrapped his arms around them. "Okay, reset, we're going to do that again."

"You're fucking kidding right?" Brooklyn said as he stood, he bypassed Jordan completely running to kneel behind Quincy, also hugging them.

"Clear the set," Jordan pushed, Eliza walking onto set.

"Don't you dare move them along," she stated,

Jordan, not to be out done, stood too walking towards her.

"We need to do another take," Jordan growled back.

"They're fifteen years old. They've just performed a highly emotional scene. It'll do you well to give them a minute to express that emotion."

"He's an actor. It's his job."

"They're a child," Eliza snapped back. "I am here to look after the children on set. *They* are one of the children on my set."

"Ten minutes. Reset," Jordan barked.

I turned as Quincy sat up. AJ wiping their tears, whispering something to them as Brooklyn rubbed their back.

I stood, going to approach them. Eliza stopped me.

"When you said it was a publicly stunt?" I whispered.

She sighed. "I was *wrong?*" she replied turning to look at me, a curious look on her face. "It was far worse than I thought."

"What do you mean?"

She shook her head.

"It doesn't matter sweetheart, it doesn't matter."

"Why did they kill Daniel off? What was the meaning behind that?"

"Next series, Quincy, sorry. Todd will be with a girl." She said then cleared her throat. "They'll be with this girl, who is currently not cast until the end of series ten. No negotiation.

"I don't know if AJ was a stunt, an experiment or a warning, *but* I know that I'm *not* going to make Quincy act that scene again."

"A warning?" I whispered. She looked at me then shook her head.

"It doesn't matter," she whispered. "Forget I said anything." She smiled at me, I didn't fully believe it *but* she walked away from me before I could say anything in response. Walking towards Quincy, offering her hand to them so they stood. She hugged them, wrapping her arm around them and walking them off set.

AJ followed behind, a small run in his steps as Brooklyn sighed sitting himself on the floor. I walked towards him. He offered me a Haribo fried egg.

Series 10

Day 34

Eliza dropped the staff lanyard over my head. It bounced against me, the little plastic sleeve read *staff* and had a little sticker that declared I was someone of importance.

"I don't think I want to be here," I told her. She smiled squeezing my shoulders and giving me a little shake.

"If you want to get off that stage, do so," she said. I tilted my head at her. "I mean, let's be honest, you're big enough of a name to just stand up and say 'no more' but honestly, everyone in that audience is here for you guys." She smiled as she reached to fix Brooklyn's hood over his lanyard. "All you guys. I've been out there, the buzz is indescribable."

"Really?" I whispered.

"Really." She squeezed my shoulders again, I nodded swallowing deeply.

"Just a question," Quincy said, their arm falling over my shoulder and patting me. "Innocent and pure, and all…"

"What, Quincy?" Eliza cocked her head at him,

waving her hand as if saying 'don't waste my time'.

"We can't mention walking off set, right?"

"Honestly?" she asked. Quincy knocked their head against mine. "I don't give a fuck if you do," she whispered. We both gasped dramatically. She rolled her eyes. "What they've done is wrong, and I am not going to quieten you guys if you want to speak out about it. Just be careful, be vigilant."

"Got it," Quincy said. "Like the Comic Con when I told everyone AJ and I were a thing."

"A thing," I mocked. "You're considering marrying the guy."

Eliza rose her eyebrow at Quincy.

"Are you?"

"It was a fleeting thought." They hit me, I coughed out a laugh. "You've ruined it now," they mocked, so I grinned at them. "I was going to get down on one knee during our panel, but it's not going to be a surprise now."

I crowed out a laugh. Brooklyn looked up surprised, his eyes raising as he looked between us.

"I have picked out the ring though," they said. Eliza touched her chest in an affectionate way.

"We're going for a drink after this, okay? We're going to chat." She waved her hand. "I extend the invite to you all, by the way."

"Sounds like my kind of night," Brooklyn said then stroked through my hair. "You okay, darling?"

I sighed, sending it right down my body before turning to smile at him.

"No?" I offered. He kissed me. Soft and considered

before knocking his forehead against mine. He pumped his chest three times, I exhaled and did it back.

"Freya's walking on first," Eliza said softly, as if she didn't want to interrupt the moment. "Then Quincy."

"Wow, second-lowest billing," they laughed.

"They love you and you know it," she stated. "Dakota will follow Quincy."

"Really?" I laughed. "I'm getting a higher billing than Dakota?"

"You're coming out last," she said. "As a precautionary matter, because we know the audience will go batshit crazy with you. No-one would be able to follow you."

"Ha," I pointed at Brooklyn. "I'm more famous than you."

Brooklyn gasped. "That's it, we're breaking up. I cannot be outshined within my own relationship." He held his hand up dramatically, I almost choked on my laugh.

"Can be outshined in the bedroom, though." Quincy muttered.

"I have skills," I proclaimed, raising my hands.

Eliza sighed. "Get ready to go on stage you naughty kids."

"We, Eliza honey, are legal adults," Quincy helpfully said.

"Ssh, you're kids," she said, hitting the back of their head. She clapped her hands. "Break a leg." She walked ahead of us, opening the door to the back of the stage. The sound of the audience was unmistakable. It made my stomach feel a little hollow.

I reached for Brooklyn's hand. He squeezed mine.

"I've got you, my love," he whispered. Lifting my hand and kissing my knuckles. "You come onto stage, and you can grab my hand instantly, okay?"

I nodded, swallowing deeply as Freya was announced.

"Freya McDonald."

The cheer was thunderous. Go Freya. Brooklyn laughed softly; he must've been thinking that, too.

"Quincy Ikeda."

There was a scream as Quincy stepped out onto stage. I heard them laugh, loud and genuinely joyful. The cheering had barely subsided when the announcer said, "Dakota Chidubem."

Her cheer was as loud, as full. I knew she was blowing kisses to the audience like she always did. Brooklyn started up the stairs. Not letting go of my hand until we heard.

"Brooklyn Sampson."

He gave me one more squeeze then stepped onto the stage. I moved closer, watching as the audience soaked Brooklyn up. They fucking adored him, and so they should because he was sensational. He glanced towards me in the wings, nodding to me and *not* taking his seat like we were supposed to, instead he waited, bouncing on his heels like an excited puppy.

Eliza reached for me just before my name came over the speaker. She nodded, stroking my arm. We both took a breath in together.

"And Oz Campbell."

I took a deep breath, that I felt as my lungs emptied before refilling them with staggered breaths. It wasn't quite as thunderous, there was definitely an anxiousness, so I locked onto Brooklyn. He was smiling out at the audience, something keeping his attention and I wanted to know what that was so I walked onto the stage.

It hit me like a shockwave. The sound taking a moment to catchup to the audience.

I took a few steps back, gasping as the audience cheered and shouted, trans flags rose above their heads, and signs, so many signs. I didn't have enough time to read them before my eyes filled with tears. My hand lifting to my nose so I didn't begin instantly sobbing, and so it didn't echo around the entire theatre.

Brooklyn wrapped his arms around me.

Whispering *I got you* into my ear as the audience continued to go crazy. Eliza was right, we weren't moving on anytime soon

"Oh my god," I managed through the tears that were choking me. Brooklyn laughed, kissing the side of my head and sending another wave through the audience because, even though they all totally knew Brooklyn and I had been sleeping together for years, it had just been confirmed right in front of their eyes and I was glad of it. So glad that I didn't give a second thought to turning to him, wrapping my arms around him, burying my face into his chest.

"Oz Campbell." The announcer repeated, and the audience screamed again as I let Brooklyn lead me to the couch. He let me sit first, Quincy standing quickly and scooting Dakota down the couch so they could sit beside me. She went with an overdramatic roll of the eyes that made the audience snigger as Quincy wrapped their arms around my neck, knocking our heads together.

"You good?" they whispered, so low the mics couldn't pick us up. I nodded, smiling at them as Brooklyn sat on my other side, his hand resting on the back of my neck, stroking the bottom of my hair with his thumb.

"Welcome the cast of *Adolescent Summers*," the moderator said, being cut off *instantly* by another wave of screams. "Now, we're all still in the afterglow of Series Nine but I believe you're all well into filming Series…" she paused as if there was *any* other word to follow that, than the number ten. "Ten."

Another scream.

I glanced at Brooklyn, he laughed although it sounded somewhat pained.

"Can you tell us *anything* about the next series?"

We all exchanged a look with each other, over-egging it *for* the audience. Quincy clearer their throat.

"Absolutely nothing," they said.

"Oh you're teasing us."

I'm sure she flirted, I glanced at Brooklyn, he rose his eyebrow as he obviously agreed with my assumption.

"Well if you're not going to tell me *anything*, I guess we'll open to questions. Boy in the front row?" she said, and a boy stood. He was wearing a hoodie in the colours of the trans flag and a backwards cap. He looked young. Young enough to have not been able to watch series one the first time it was aired.

He cleared his throat.

"For Brooklyn and Oz…" he started, his voice cracked, and honestly, *same*. "Do Kevin and Izzy finally end up together this series?"

I looked up at Brooklyn as he grinned.

"I couldn't possibly say," I answered before clearing my throat. "I mean…"

"We really haven't got a clue," Brooklyn teased. I knocked my head against his shoulder as the audience sniggered.

"And?" the boy asked. I glanced at him as he chewed on his lip anxiously. "Are you guys… *together*?"

Brooklyn glanced at me, he nodded gently. I returned it.

"I can honestly tell you, I love this boy with my entire heart."

The audience screamed, so I decided to enable them by reaching up and kissing him.

They went *bananas*. I laughed as I pulled away, my microphone picking it up – I heard it back, it sounded far too giddy. Brooklyn winked at me as Quincy laughed, too, squeezing my thigh. I tapped their hand.

"For Oz?"

I turned back as a girl stood, she wore a t-shirt with our clubs name and logo on it.

"Yes, darling?" I asked. she blushed bright red, I bit my lip.

"Does Izzy transition in this series?"

Quincy barked, before clapping their hand over their

mouth. I snorted gently.

"That's… *complicated*. We…" I began, then I decided to bullshit. "We get our scripts out of order, so we don't really know what's going on until we see it all edited together. Izzy might have transitioned but I haven't received that script yet, so I guess we'll both have to wait and see." My voice betrayed me towards the end, a crack as clear as if it was in glass. I sighed, as Brooklyn smirked at me. I punched his thigh gently.

"Happens to the best of us," he whispered. I scoffed as the girl who asked the question grinned at me. I smiled back looking down at my knees as I took a breath. Brooklyn's hand rubbed my back.

"Brooklyn." He turned to the voice. "Who's better to kiss? Oz or Dakota?"

Brooklyn laughed so happily,

"That's so unfair," he whined, the audience laughed with him. "I'd have to do it again. To see…"

"You're not coming anywhere near me," Dakota stated. Brooklyn pulled his tongue at her.

"Well, I have to say Oz, don't I, if I don't want to sleep on the couch tonight."

"So true," I said.

"To Quincy…"

They gasped, sounding excited to be included.

"Will Daniel return in Series Ten? Even just in a memory or something? I loved Daniel and Todd, the chemistry was *out*standing."

Quincy sighed dramatically.

"Unfortunately, my love, I can say with some

confidence that Daniel will not be returning to our screens. I'm as devastated as you are, believe me."

"Dakota? What's been your favourite outfit you've worn?"

And it went on, and on.

"Okay, okay, last question," the moderator said, then smiled pleasantly at the singular raised hand amongst the crowd. "Take the floor."

"Quincy?"

I looked up instantly because I *knew* that voice. I lived with that voice. I hit Brooklyn at the exact same time he hit me.

AJ climbed onto the chair he'd been sat on. Quincy frowned at him as the audience began to whisper because, *of course* they recognised AJ, they adored Daniel.

Brooklyn grabbed onto my hand excited, shaking our hands together – I think we'd both come to the same conclusion. The conclusion that Quincy hadn't yet.

"AJ?" they asked. He grinned as the audience cheered at the confirmation.

"Quincy Ikeda, I have a question for you."

I glanced off stage at Eliza as she stood in the wings. A massive grin on her face. I nodded to her. She put her finger on her lips.

"Will you marry me?"

Quincy gasped, shaking their head as they stood walking to the edge of the stage then pointing at AJ.

"That's not fair," they stated. AJ laughed although he was frowning. "I was going to ask you."

"Is that a yes?"

"Of course it is! I love your fucking face," Quincy stated. The entire audience cheered as AJ jumped from the chair and ran towards the side of the stage. He took the steps two at a time until he could run towards Quincy, collecting them in his arms and kissing them. When they pulled away, AJ grabbed the mouthpiece of Quincy's microphone. Holding it in his closed fist so he could speak just to them. I only caught AJ saying *I love you*.

"Now *that* was a better plot twist than Series Ten," Brooklyn said.

"Comic Con London had everything this year," Brooklyn read from where he was sat behind me against the extra poofy pillows provided by the hotel room. I turned to look at him, leaning against his raised leg as I ate a piece of pizza.

"Blah, blah, blah, Doctor Who, Supernatural, etc. Ah, Adolescent Summers." He moved his leg side to side, so I moved with him. "Series Ten leaked." He laughed. "Bullshit."

I smiled at him,

"Fans were very excited to see…" he gasped. "Rude. Deadname… for the first time since… I'm changing pronouns here… he has transitioned. He took to the stage, under new name Oz and wowed fans with how much he in fact… oh, shut up."

I sighed, as he waved his hand.

"Skip, skip, skip. Confirmation of the relationship that has been forming between Brooklyn and Oz, click here to see nine pictures that prove their relationship."

"Did you just click the link?" I asked, then passed him some pizza. He looked at me wide-eyed.

"No."

"Liar."

"They're really stretching with these pictures." He paused to eat pizza. "Actually, except that one."

"Brooklyn, back to the point."

He nodded. When he finished chewing, he continued.

"Fan favourite, AJ Lawson, made an appearance, ugh, wrong pronouns for Quincy, too. Bear with." He continued to scroll. "Pink News."

"Promising," I said. He nodded as he finished the pizza.

"Oz Campbell looks fantastic in first public appearance since he started his transition. At London Comic Con, Oz's appearance caused a storm before the confirmation of his relationship with Brooklyn Sampson, teen heartthrob who came out as bisexual three years ago. Click here to see Brooklyn's coming out."

"Don't click it."

He bit his lip. I sighed fondly.

"This was not the only queer news that came from the *Adolescents Summers* panel this afternoon. Fan favourite, Quincy, and their long-term partner, AJ Lawson, took the next step in their relationship, with AJ getting down on one knee (figuratively) and proposing marriage.

"Quincy of course said yes!

"We wish so much joy to both Quincy and Oz in

their futures, following the end of filming top series *Adolescent Summers*."

I exhaled.

"You do look good," he said. I turned to him and he winked.

"We're already going to have sex tonight; you don't need to try."

He laughed.

"Are you going to gate crash my meet-and-greet tomorrow?" he asked. I hummed resting my chin on his knee,

"I don't know. Dakota has one, too, right?"

"She does, and we have one together at three or something."

"I'm gate-crashing Quincy's. They said I should, it'd probably be good to see."

"Please come play with me. Or at least come sit on my autograph table."

"That I'll do."

Series 3

Day 12

The producers suggested during *school* scenes we should *actually* complete our school work. Our teacher, Ms Jen, was a lovely woman who truly tried her best to keep us on track but, with both Brooklyn and Quincy under her care, it was a near impossible task.

Which was how we ended up with leftover work for said school scenes.

Leftover work for varying degrees of intelligence, given Brooklyn was two years older than us so allegedly at GCSE level. His work was far more complicated – his maths had *letters* in it.

"Do either of you get this?" Brooklyn whispered across our two desks whilst a scene with Dakota and our fictional teacher, Professor Diggory, played out. I hadn't been listening to the scene; primarily because I wasn't in it, secondly because I was looking at my Chemistry homework trying to figure out the structure of the atom.

"Get what?" Quincy whispered back. I buried my head into my hands, rubbing my fingers against my temples.

"How does Lady Macbeth use language to manipulate her husband in the play?" he read off his sheet.

I turned my frown to him. "I've never read the Scottish play."

He sighed as he looked past me at Quincy. They shook their head. "What?"

"Well, how does she?" he egged.

Quincy snorted gently. "Honey, Todd is the Asian stereotype, not me."

I laughed out loud, then gasped clapping my hand over my mouth as Jordan side-eyed me.

"What are you doing?" I requested.

"Maths," they said with a sigh. "But to say I'm doing it would definitely be a lie."

"Which bit of maths?"

They passed the sheet to me and I swapped mine back. Quincy laughed softly but *did* begin to fill out my answers, so I happily did their maths.

"Okay, I'm bored," Brooklyn whispered. I glanced at him, watching as he fiddled with the pin badges on his lapel. Once Brooklyn was bored, Brooklyn was *not* present. He glanced back at me, a twinkle in his eye giving me an internally bad feeling that he was about to cause trouble.

"Don't do anything," I whispered. "Jordan will kill you."

He turned looking down the set towards Jordan. "But it'd be so much fun."

I turned too, groaning lightly because it so would but I also *really* didn't want to be the one blamed for Brooklyn, *Brooklyn-ing.*

"What are you going to do?"

"Never mind, Jordan," Quincy whispered. "Dakota will kill you."

Brooklyn swallowed, "That's true."

Quincy grinned at me then turned to one of the extras. "What?" they whispered; they were shushed. They laughed.

"Don't you know who he is," Brooklyn gasped. Quincy's laugh got a *little* bit louder.

Dakota glanced in our direction, a slight frown of confusion. I buried my face into my hands.

"Sorry," Quincy whispered loudly so I turned my head, grinning at Eliza as she shook her head at us.

Brooklyn sniggered like a child, sinking down in his seat. He gasped when Jordan yelled *cut!*

We all turned towards him together.

"You three, off set," he stated.

"Oooh," Brooklyn whispered. I punched his elbow, he grinned at me as he stood from his desk.

"Oh, now we're in trouble," Quincy whispered. "That's your fault." They pointed at the extra.

I rose my hand. "I behaved in all of this."

"Git," Jordan stated. I stepped off set.

Eliza rolled her eyes at us. "Go to Ms Jen."

"No," Brooklyn whined. "Please don't make me."

"You didn't take your Ritalin did you?" she said, smiling at him.

Brooklyn sighed. "You can't prove that."

"Brook."

"Sorry."

"You two, go to Ms Jen, she's expecting you. You come with me."

"Have you got emergency Ritalin, are you like an ADHD superhero?"

She sighed nodding towards the break room. Brooklyn did follow.

"We could *not* go to Ms Jen," Quincy whispered. I gasped a little too dramatically, so they laughed. "Don't alert the elders. Besides, I want to tell you something…" they whispered, squeezing my hand. "Let's get some cinnamon buns, ooh or Ben's Cookies, okay?"

"Yes," I whispered. "Can I put some pants on first, though?" I added, as I held the edges of the school skirt I'd been put in as if I was going to curtesy. They grinned.

"Yes, definitely." They led me to costume so we could change.

It felt far later than it actually was given it was practically pitch black when we stepped out of the studio. Quincy took my hand, theirs freezing so I squeezed a little tighter.

"It's almost Christmas," I whispered as I watched the festive lights above my head. I didn't know when they'd been turned on, I wasn't even aware they were up. "Wait, sorry you don't celebrate Christmas," I said quickly.

Quincy laughed. "You can still say the word, you know. I won't explode or anything."

"What do you do, you know?"

"It's just another day off," they shrugged gently. "I'm thankful for the two weeks off, honestly."

"But, no gifts, or anything?"

"No," they laughed. "We do that during, Oshogatsu."

We looked at each other.

"New Year's," they translated. "But on the twenty-fifth, okaasan and I order KFC and have some Christmas cake. What do you do?"

"I swap Christmases, so this year I'm spending it with Dad. I prefer spending it with Dad."

"This'll sound weird, but I didn't know you had a dad."

I smiled. "He lives in France now. Usually when I spend Christmas with Dad, we spend a few days in Disneyland Paris."

"What happened with you parents?" they whispered. "If it's... *okay?*"

"They were dating. When Mum got pregnant, just

dating. They broke up before I was born but Dad never left me. Well, *until* he moved to France." I smiled. "He got a new job, there was no question he was going, and I was happy, Christmas at Disneyland, summer in the South of France. I think I would've moved with him, honestly, I still think about it sometimes, but I was in *Mary Poppins*, and Mum got it in her head that I was going to be famous, so wouldn't let me go with him. I got *Adolescent Summers* a year later, so I guess she might have been onto something."

"Wow," they whispered. "I had no idea."

"They're civil. Or at least as civil as my mum has the ability to be with someone. It isn't at all hostile."

They nodded as we turned into the Cinnabon.

"Do you have a dad?" I asked then cleared my throat. "I mean..."

"Otosan," they said softly. "He died."

"I'm sorry."

"It's..." they sighed. "Okay, yeah, it's a bit shit. I was four. We were living in Yamakoshi and we were hit by the Chuetsu earthquake. Otosan was injured, he died a week after the earthquake. We moved over here a few months later. Okaasan considered staying in Japan but nowhere felt right, so London it was."

"I didn't know you *actually* lived in Japan."

"Born there," they smiled at me. "None of this was what I wanted to tell you, though," they laughed as they retrieved the box with the giant cinnamon bun in.

"What did you want to tell me?" I whispered.

They looked at me, their eyes scanning my entire face. "I'm gay," they said, with no qualms about themself. I practically beamed back at them.

"Yeah?" I whispered.

They laughed, covering their face. "Yeah."

I hugged them, they knocked their head against mine,

"Oh, now I've said it," they exhaled then laughed, "but there's also not even a singular doubt in my mind. I just…" they looked at me, burrowing their eyebrows in thought, "really fancy boys."

"I'm so happy for you," I whispered. "For figuring it out, for being confident in it."

"I've told my okaasan, she knows. She's fine, more than fine, couldn't care less almost. You're the only other person I've told. For now. I don't quite know how I'm planning on keeping such a thing secret. I'm *so* gay."

"I love you," I laughed. They grinned, nodding as they lifted their cinnamon bun and took a bite from it. I followed by example.

Series 10

Day 35

I'd spent most of the morning sat beside Brooklyn at his autograph table. His line never dwindled, his fans devoted and more than willing to pay the additional fee to get Brooklyn's autograph, or a selfie, and if Brooklyn was feeling it, a cuddle.

I was apparently also in demand. I didn't have my own table, and I wasn't charging for my goods like I usually did. Instead, I got to try out my new signature over and over. Some said *Oz*, some *Oz Campbell*, some a intelligible scribble, one was just a fancy *O* but I'd soon settled on how it should look, or at least what felt right for now.

I'd had a few people gasp in delight in my direction, not expecting me to be out, as such, but I hadn't been expecting it either and I told them as much. A few I'd seen had walked past and whispered behind their hand to someone – but they always came back later, with a piece of art that some incredible artist had drawn of me, or a POP figure – I still hadn't gotten over being made into a Funko – or something else *Adolescent Summers* for me to sign.

When Brooklyn had gone for his photo op, I'd walked the stalls. Incognito of course. Clark Kent was really on to something with the glasses thing. The amount of people I'd met eyes with haven't even flinched – although, saying that, maybe I just wasn't as famous as I was led to believe.

I eventfully found the amazing artist of who's work I'd seen numerous of. I approached the table after a moment's hesitation primarily because there was a huge A3 poster behind her, it was our Series One promotional poster, well kind of. She'd recreated the pose immaculately, all the way down to our shoes and then, she'd drawn us now. Stood behind our younger counterpart.

But the thing that had stopped me initially, was that she hadn't drawn me as I was when I was ten. There was no long plait, there was no girlish inclination to my costume – as apparently the wardrobe didn't want the audience to mistake me for a boy.

No, the irony is not lost.

I audibly gasped and was obviously close enough to the table to make the artist look up.

"Do you like *Adolescent Summers*?" she asked in a very pleasant customer service manner.

"You could say that," I tilted my head, laughing. "Although, I think it went a little downhill when Ally and Kevin got together."

"I definitely prefer Izzy and Kevin," she agreed then flicked through her postcards, until she showed me one. I think I suddenly understood love at first sight.

"That is gorgeous," I said as I took it. It depicted a kiss between me and Brooklyn, or I suppose Izzy and Kevin, but it wasn't the kiss from the last episode of Series Nine as it very clearly showed me, as a boy. Me as Oz. Behind it, painted in watercolour was a rainbow. "I think I'm going to need this," I told her, "but do you have others?"

"I have a few," she nodded. "Why?"

"Want them signed?" I laughed, because I was nervous. I'd been a household name for eleven years, a full eleven years but I still wasn't used to this whole 'famous' thing. She frowned, a questioning expression on her face. I took off my cap, and down my glasses, she laughed out in shock.

"Oz," then, "*shit*. Oh my god, I just straight up showed you art of you without any reservations."

"I had to come find you," I admitted. "So many people were bringing your prints for me to sign. I didn't think anyone was creating art of me now."

"I started during lockdown. When the speculations about your transition started then, you know, it was confirmed and I started posting the images. You make me a lot of money."

"I could say the same about you," I teased. She grinned then filtered through her postcards, she pulled out four. "Brooklyn's doing a photo op right now, but I can get him to come here, too," I said as I crouched at the table, "he usually does as I say." I rose an eyebrow at her, she laughed like a fangirl.

"Usually."

I tilted my head as I signed my new signature again, and again.

"He gets distracted easily," I said.

"Thank you, Oz," she whispered as I handed them back.

"Thank you for drawing… me." I sighed. "I love that, by the way." I pointed behind her. "If it's still here at the end of today, I'm buying it."

"No, no. I'll give you it, it's fine."

"No way. You probably spent hours on that and, damn girl, you're talented."

She blushed, shaking her head at me coyly.

"You think I'm making you blush. Wait until Brooklyn sees these."

"Okay, okay." she laughed, then, "can I?"

I looked up at her, as she dug into her pocket.

"Get a selfie."

"Of course."

This Con, had the photo ops in their own hall. Everyone was placed into an aisle with a white background behind them, and the vast majority of them had looping queues that I worried would never end. The people in attendance had to go into a draw for the people they wanted to meet, and every person had a different limit.

I knew Brooklyn's was at least fifty meets an hour. Which was technically one-minute-twenty per person and he did it with such ease. His bouncy puppy vibe really aided with those.

Quincy's was about thirty an hour, as requested by them, a whole two minutes per person, and they both filled that with ease, a few times over. Brooklyn's meets could go on for hours at a time, and I marvelled at that.

But it was Quincy's meet I was gate-crashing as I walked the hall. They were holding court before their greets opened, stood behind a barrier talking to the front few people, but their entire crowd was hanging on every word.

I started down their line quietly, trying not to draw too much attention to myself and it worked mostly. No one even rose an eyebrow at me skipping the queue. I finally reached the barrier, leaning on it as Quincy laughed.

"Hey," I heckled, they stopped looking up then they beamed. "Nice dungarees," I said, because they were. The pattern looked like a kaleidoscope of rainbows. I could never have pulled them off.

"Oz," they squealed, and suddenly everyone in my near vicinity was squealing, too. Quincy laughed, pushing the barrier back so I could step through it. They hugged me excitedly, before clapping. "Strip."

"Excuse me?" I laughed.

"Coat off, cap off, get comfortable. You're staying."

I scoffed as I laughed, taking my coat off then throwing my cap like a Frisbee towards the table of water bottles. Everyone screamed as if I was in the Full Monty.

"Get here, get here, get here," they stated, pulling me across the floor until we were in front of the white screen. "I wanted you to crash mine because these are your people, okay?" they said. I frowned as they walked away from me, they retrieved something from behind the set.

I laughed as they shook out a trans flag.

The crowd cheered unanimously and without prompt. Quincy grinned at me as they wrapped the flag around my shoulders. They kissed my nose then turned and rose their hand.

"Completely compliant. We live together," they stated as the audience began to whistle at us. They grinned at me then retrieved their nonbinary flag. They put it over their own shoulders, then walked towards me and wrapped their arms around me.

I laughed into it. Only noticing the camera when I opened my eyes.

"Now, come on," Quincy said to their fans. "We all know he's madly deeply in love with Brooklyn, and I am a kept woman."

They all screamed in response, as Quincy laughed and held my hand. We swung our hands between us and the photographer took picture after picture.

"Okay, okay, okay," Quincy said before turning to me, resting their forehead against mine, holding their flag between us in their hands so I rose my own, our flags touching. I pushed the flag back, grinning as I stroked my finger over the silver ring with a rose gold stripe running around it that sat, like it was always supposed to be there on their ring finger.

"Gorgeous," I whispered. They grinned, nodding as they looked at the ring themself, before looking up at me.

"You good?"

I nodded against them, taking a breath.

"Want to meet some fans? Or do you want to get out of here?"

I smiled. "I'll meet some, but I won't take too much of the spotlight from you."

"Impossible," they laughed, kissing my forehead. I smiled, as they turned. "Let's get this started," they proclaimed, everyone cheered again. "Who wants to meet Ozzy, too?"

Another scream. I'd forgotten how much I fucking love this. The fans, the cons, the community.

The first teenager ran at us, a genderqueer flag pin badge on their t-shirt. Quincy grinned at me, nodding as I hugged the fan.

"This was why," they whispered, then they squeezed the teenager before placing them between us for a photo.

I left Quincy's meet-and-greet after the first hour. The trans flag still wrapped around my neck as I walked the photo ops. I soon found Brooklyn's, his line near its end. An attendant standing watch to ensure nobody else joined the queue.

He eyed me for a few seconds, frowning confused.

"I'm Oz Campbell," I offered. He cocked his head. "Well, then…" I laughed. "I'm Brooklyn's boyfriend."

"Oh, yeah," he preened. "Boyfriend, huh?"

I rolled my eyes, reaching into my pocket and pulling

out my phone. I turned it to him, the selfie of Brooklyn and I from a few weeks ago.

"That could be from anywhere."

"For real," I cocked my head. "What do I have to do, show you his dick pic?"

He smirked at me.

"Come on."

He nodded, waving at me as if he couldn't care less. I joined the queue.

The person in front of me instantly noticed, I put my finger to my lips.

"*He* doesn't know," I said pointing towards Brooklyn. They began to giggle, whispering to each other before taking a step closer.

It only took twenty minutes or so to get to the front of the queue. I watched the two girls meet Brooklyn, although I was *actually* watching Brooklyn.

Poor, poor Brooklyn who was obviously shattered. He was still bouncing, his smile wide, his words still excited but there was a slump in his shoulders, his hand kept rubbing the back of his neck, as if there was an ache there and he was stimming, more than he usually did. More than his leg bounce, more than his taking three steps forward and two back.

He waved happily as the girls walked away from him then spun and opened his arms to me all before he fully registered who I was.

"Hello, darling," I offered. He swallowed, his arms dropping then he groaned.

"Hello, love of my life."

I walked around the barrier and wrapped my arms around him. He slumped against me. His head meeting mine as I rubbed his back.

"You did so good today," I whispered.

"So did you," he agreed then tugged on the flag.

"Look, you even got a cape."

"I did, I got a cape," I laughed. "Do you want to take some time backstage?"

"I do," he whispered. "I think I need to take another dose."

We looked at each other, I watched as he seemed to count something in his head.

"There's only about three hours left and you don't even need to be out."

He groaned against me.

"I want to walk around the stalls, but I'm so tired."

"I saw some doughnuts," I whispered. "Come on." I took his hand and spinning him on the spot. He grinned, swinging our hands as I directed him towards the backstage area.

There was a big box of Krispy Kreme's, practically untouched just sitting on the table between the multiple couches.

Luckily, the backstage area was empty, nee a few other people – sometimes backstage was as bad as being on the floor. I sat on a bright orange couch, when Brooklyn had chosen his doughnut, he sat beside me, his head on my shoulder as he began to pick from the doughnut. I stroked my fingers through his hair.

"Look at this," I whispered. "You don't need to lift your head."

I felt his smile against my shoulder as I went into my pocket and pulled out the postcard. He gasped when I held it out in front of us.

"That's gorgeous."

"I kind of told the artist you'd come sign her other copies."

"Kind of?"

"Definitely did."

He laughed.

"Okay," he whispered. "That's fine." He ate more of the doughnut. "Where did you get your cape?"

"Quincy." I whispered.

"Ah, of course." A pause. "I want a cape."

"A bi cape?" I laughed. He nodded against me as I retrieved my phone. "Well, then I'm going to get you a bi cape," I told him. His hum sounded pleased. I kissed the top of his head.

Series 4

Day 7

@**IncyQuincySpider**: hey world! I've got some news for you all. From now on, I'm only going by THEY/THEM pronouns and I'd appreciate it if you respected that.

@**IncyQuincySpider**: TL;DR I'm nonbinary bitches

I approached Brooklyn with a frown. I wanted to say, *what's up with your face* but I didn't quite muster up enough balls too before he looked up at me.

"Hey, kid.," he said.

"What's wrong?"

"Nothing," he shrugged.

"Your energy is normally…" I held my hand at my head. "But it feels like…" I lowered it to my hip.

"I was told to sit and wait."

"And you obeyed?" I teased.

He grinned at me then held a bright blue drink to me. "This looks… toxic."

He began to hum Britney, because of course he did.

"Wait, what are you waiting for?"

"Quincy's being told off."

"For?"

"Coming out," he mumbled, then drank from the

blue drink.

"What?" I whispered.

"He… shit sorry, they were called into a meeting with management the moment they walked in. Eliza is in there too, they were saying something like Quincy broke contract by making an announcement without okaying it first, but Eliza stated that was bullshit, and well… that's when they closed the door."

We both looked towards the office.

"Apparently something like coming out should be handled delicately and should definitely be pre-approved."

"Oh, yeah, cool," I murmured. "Remind me to inform them when I lose my virginity," I said without thinking.

"Don't you remember though…" he said under his breath. "I had this thing with Molly, and they were on me like a tonne of bricks."

"But you were with a girl… didn't they set up a date to get pictures?"

"Yeah, but I was still controlled. She had to sign an NDA," he frowned. "That's when she called it off with me."

"What's an NDA?"

"Non-disclosure agreement. Basically, she couldn't say a word about our relationship. Not to the press, not on any socials, nothing. If she broke it, legal action would've been taken. Which you know, was a bit much for a fuc—, fling."

I rose my eyebrow at him, giving him my best *I'm not buying your bullshit* expression. He grinned. I waved my hand.

"What's that got to do with Quincy being nonbinary, though?"

"Oh, nothing," he assured me. "They're just idiots, so

they don't know the difference between gender identity and sexuality. They've made their coming out sexual."

I crinkled my nose. "They're fourteen."

"Correct."

"I don't understand."

"Join the club, kid," he sighed, tightening the lid on his bottle, and proceeding to bottle flip – reasonably unsuccessfully.

He successfully got it upright when the door to the office opened. Quincy left, they looked angry, so much so when they reached the upright bottle, they kicked it.

Brooklyn whined sounding like a sad puppy.

"Hey," I grabbed for Quincy. "Hey, talk to me."

They looked at me, their expression softening as they shook their head and rose their hands to their face.

"They said I broke my contract," they swallowed. "Said I'd acted inappropriately."

"Hey," Brooklyn whispered, standing and wrapping his arms around Quincy.

"Eliana was in there. She was pissed. Said I had no right to manipulate a character like I had. I couldn't get it through to them that I said I was nonbinary, not that *fucking* Todd was. She said I was in a lot of trouble."

"Why?" Brooklyn asked. "Why are you in trouble?"

Quincy sighed shaking their head then walking away from us to sit on the edge of the set.

"They couldn't possibly *just* change Todd's character like that. I kept saying they didn't need to; I wasn't asking them to. I just wanted the pronouns I identify with to be used."

"I understand that," I whispered as I sat beside them. They squeezed my leg before wrapping their arm around my thigh.

"They've restricted my social media. Told me if I Tweet, or put an Instagram post up at all I will be sanctioned. If I reply to anyone, or endorse this *statement* of mine, I will also be sanctioned."

"They can't do that," Brooklyn said shaking his head. "They… they can't, right?" he asked me. I shook my head back because I had *no* idea.

"They're apparently discussing my appropriate punishment and will let me know whether I'll be kept on."

"Kept on?" I repeated.

"Everyone's replaceable."

"You need to tell your mum," Brooklyn said. "She'll be pissed."

"She will. But what can she do? If I broke contract, I'm in the wrong."

"You couldn't have broken contract by coming out as nonbinary, that's ridiculous."

They looked at me, then to Brooklyn and then began to cry, shaking their head before resting it against my chest. I wrapped my arms around them, shushing gently as Brooklyn sighed, and crawled forward to hug Quincy too.

Series 10

Day 37

I groaned. Brooklyn looked mildly alarmed before raising his hands above the quilt.

"I'm not doing anything," he said. I laughed shaking my head at him. "Are you doing it yourself?"

"Brooklyn," I barked.

He grinned then took my phone from me, "Oh."

"I could just *not*."

"You definitely could just not," he agreed. "And we could have morning sex."

I sighed as I turned to look at him, he grinned.

"Well, we don't have anywhere to be."

"Are you never going back?"

He hummed.

"I can't think of *anything* they could offer me that'd make me look past… everything."

"Really?"

"Can you?" he whispered. I reached for his shirt, stroking my fingers over the pattern.

"I don't know, I'm so scared that I'm over reacting."

"Talk to me."

"I don't know if I'm just sensitive to it all. If I'm

blowing things out of proportion because it's so new to me, and I don't quite know what's normal and what isn't."

"Oz, my darling," he sighed, stopping my hand from tracing. "None of it is *normal*. All of it is out of order, and so wrong. I'm not suggesting they should've put banners up and wore trans flag colours or whatever, I'm not suggesting any of that, but they should've at least provided the bare medium for you. For Quincy, too."

I looked away from him, sighing lightly as I let my eyes trail the trans and bisexual flags that were newly hung over the edge of our wardrobe.

"I'm not happy with the way they're treating you, and if I'm blowing it out of proportion so be it, Oz. Them asking you to take your binder off during the sex scene was disgusting, and the way they responded to you saying no was just as disgusting. The way they don't even say your name on set, they're referring to you as Izzy.

"I also hate how they've changed the plot line to make it so you want to change back to a girl, how you've been cursed or some shit. I hate that, and I hate even more that the reason for you changing back is to placid Kevin. Like, fuck no." He sat up, rubbing his forehead, the palms of his hands digging into his eyes. "I'm so annoyed with the treatment, I'm so done with the quiet bigotry. It's just getting too loud."

"If I go and see my mother, she'll tell me to get back on set."

He frowned at me.

"She'll fight their corner."

"And I'll fight yours." He cleared his throat. "In fact I'll come with you."

I sat up, shaking my head as I rested my hand on his. "You don't like my mother."

"She doesn't like me. It's nice that we have a mutually

exclusive relationship."

"Brooklyn…"

"Oz. If you choose to meet up with your mother I want to be there."

I inhaled sharply, then nodded. "Okay."

He nodded, almost as if he was saying, *I win*. I pushed his shoulder, he fell back onto the pillows. He grinned at me, his fingers threading through his hair, the quilt falling low on his hips. I groaned.

"Ha. Morning sex," he whispered. I rolled my eyes over dramatically.

"T is making me so horny," I stated whilst covering my eyes.

"I'm not complaining," he said, stroking his fingers down my back. I shivered with every touch. "In fact, I remember it well." He sighed so I actually turned to look at him. "I remember itching to get off set just so I could touch myself."

I rose my eyebrow at him. "Excuse me?"

"Puberty is hard," he laughed. "At very least you're going through at an age that's acceptable to have sex."

"Did you really?"

He exhaled, nodding before putting his hand flat on his head. "You have no idea how many secret wanks I've had in that bathroom."

"And you never got caught?"

He rose a finger to me. "Quincy. The little asshole. They didn't tell anyone, though, so there's that."

"What on earth did you have to sacrifice for that?"

He shook his head, placing his finger on his lips. "I'd never tell."

I tutted. "I'm not committed enough to this story. I'll text my mum back after we've had sex."

"Result," he laughed punching up then slipping his fingers into my hair, pulling me over so I could kneel above him.

I gasped. He tilted his head at me as I sat up, resting my hands flat on his chest.

"You remember when you were younger and all I had to do was touch your dick and you'd basically come," I whispered. He blushed as he nodded. "T is also giving me some *sensitive* bottom growth…" I moved against him, I felt it all the way to my fingertips. "One touch, and I may blow."

He smirked at me, a slightly dark turn to it. I laughed as I took in a deep breath.

She had suggested we meet in her house. *I* suggested coffee. A no-man's land. A public place. A place with an obvious escape route.

We sat huddled in a corner, facing away from the crowds of people, my mum on the couch opposite.

We all had a coffee. Although she had commented on how I shouldn't drink coffee, given how it stunts growth. Brooklyn had giggled immaturely and I'd tried my damned hardest to not let it be infectious.

She'd been examining me since we met. When I'd taken my mask off to drink from my mug, her inspection had become far more intense. After a few, long sips she broke the silence.

"You don't look a thing like yourself."

"On the contrary," I began, rubbing my thumb over the mermaid on the mug. "I look the most like myself, I think I ever have."

Brooklyn preened next to me, I almost felt like I had to tell him to heel.

"This whole act is causing a lot of trouble…" I flinched at my deadname, sighing deeply as I looked into my mug.

"It isn't an act," I said. "*And* it isn't me who's causing

the trouble."

Brooklyn's hand found its way to my back, stroking gently, it sent shivers down my spine but not at all in the same way his hand on my back had done this morning.

"I saw you at Comic Con, it came up in a news bulletin. It was very unprofessional of you."

"Which?" I asked. "Being present?"

"Kissing *him*."

Brooklyn scoffed.

"Announcing your relationship like love-sick teenagers."

"Quincy got whole ass proposed to, and we're in the wrong," Brooklyn muttered. I squeezed his thigh.

"I've been with Brooklyn for four years. It isn't like I just rolled out of bed with him and announced a relationship, *and* he isn't even the point here. I'm allowed to have a relationship; I'm allowed to have sex and be a…"

"You're twenty-one, you're not a teenager anymore," she snapped. "You need to start owing up to your own mistakes."

"Which mistakes?" I stressed. "What mistakes have I made?"

"You shouldn't have told everyone about this… nonsense. Now you've caused controversy and plastered your face all over the internet. What is this, a publicly stunt?"

"A publicly stunt?" I repeated. "Yeah, I thought it'd be a great idea to do the hardest thing I've ever done, just to promote *Adolescent Summers*."

"Well, I don't know," she bristled. "Maybe production thought it was a good idea or something…" she paused. I looked away, focusing on the lipstick stain on her mug. "And besides, if it's so hard, why did you feel it so necessary to do it? Huh? Why bother if it's so difficult."

I swallowed.

"With all due respect, Ms Campbell," Brooklyn interjected, "and I mean that with the least amount of respect I can muster. Have you ever had to come out?"

"No," she snapped.

"Well, then, you'll never know the euphoria that comes with such a declaration. I, myself, came out as bi, what? Five years ago now, and I've never felt freer, I've never felt more honest, or understood.

"It might just be a word to you, a label, or I don't know, a slur, but it's who we are. Inside and out. I'm Brooklyn Sampson, I'm twenty-three years old, I'm bisexual, I have ADHD, and I'm in love with your son. All those facts are as relevant as each other because they make up *me*. He…"

She scoffed.

"*He*," Brooklyn stated with a little more force, "is Oz Campbell, your *son*. He is transgender, and gay. He is twenty-one years old, and he does not have to put up with your bullshit, because the *one* thing you're right about is that he isn't a teenager. He is an adult, and being an adult means he can tell you…"

"Brooklyn," I stopped him.

He turned to me, not saying anything else, simply because I'd requested he did. I smiled at him, swallowing then turning back.

"I can tell you to go fuck yourself," I stated, looking her in the eye. Brooklyn squeezed my arm. "I'm a man. Simple as. No two ways about it, and until you can understand or even acknowledge that, I don't want anything to do with you."

"Have you told your father? He'll be devastated," she murmured.

I actually laughed. "I told dad when I was sixteen. He

actually listened to me. He supported me, *supports* me, and I fully believe always will." I stood. "Come on," I said to Brooklyn who also stood.

She called my deadname after me. I *hated* myself for stopping for it. I didn't turn to her though.

"Will you still pay for the house?"

I laughed. "For real?" I whispered, turning to look at her. "No."

"You can't do that, I'm your mother."

"And I am your son."

"No, you're not."

"Well, then, I guess I don't need to pay for shit."

Series 6

Day 147

"I'll see you guys in the morning, okay?" Eliza said as she lent on my hotel door. Dakota nodded to her from her bed as I laughed. "Behave. Don't go wandering, not too far and do not cause trouble."

"So many don'ts," I teased.

"Behave," Eliza teased.

I snorted. "Can I go play with Quincy?" I clapped my hands together, sticking out my bottom lip and begging with her, she nodded although she also examined me.

"You sleep in this room, okay?"

"Not in Brooklyn's bed," Dakota mocked.

I pulled my tongue at her. "I won't end up in Brooklyn's bed. Brooklyn would never look at me that way."

"I don't need to hear this, but if I come to wake you guys up tomorrow and you're not in this room, know there'll be trouble."

"There'll be trouble," I repeated, deepening my voice.

"I'm going to go tell the boys the same thing," she pointed across the room. "Goodnight."

"Goodnight," Dakota and I replied together, we both ensured our smiles were sweet as Eliza left. We could hear her knock on the opposite door.

I glanced at Dakota, trying work out if her *not talking* to me was still an active decision she was making.

"Do you really believe that?" she asked. I frowned, startled that she'd even spoke, then confused. "That Brooklyn doesn't like you back?"

"He doesn't," I whispered. "It doesn't even matter, though." I shook my head dramatically before flopping back onto the bed.

"We should go out," she whispered. I turned my head to her. "Find someone to kiss."

I snorted shaking my head. "No, no way. That can only end in disaster." I glanced at her, she frowned back at me, it was brief, momentary before she rolled her eyes at me, a huge gesture that was far too over egged. We both jumped when there was a knock on our door.

"Open up."

"Quincy," Dakota and I said at the same time as I stood from my bed, walking slowly to open the door. I stopped in front of it, resting my hand on the door handle. They knocked again.

"You guys know I'm still stood out here, right?" they stated. I snorted gently opening the door and raising my eyebrow at them. "Grab your shoes, we're going out."

"Where?" I asked as I heard Dakota cheer behind me.

"I don't know, but Brooklyn's practically scratching the door like he needs a walk, so we're going out."

"You never know," Dakota teased as she approached me. I narrowed my eyes at her. "You might end the night kissing Brooklyn."

"Don't tease," I moaned as I grabbed my shoes.

"Ah, we're still riding the Brooklyn train," Quincy sighed like a lovesick Disney Princess. I turned as they collapsed dramatically against the door frame, their hand covering their heart. A whimsical look on their face.

"You two are," I stated pushing them back out into the corridor. "I'm fully aware he'll never like me like that." I pushed him again, they giggled as their bedroom door opened. Brooklyn stepped through and caught Quincy as they stepped back.

"I was thinking roller skating," Brooklyn said excitedly.

"I was thinking of not going to A&E, to be honest," Dakota said.

Brooklyn pouted although he soon shook it off. "The disco place, they're having a UV foam night, or something."

"They really threw everything at that, didn't they?" Quincy mused.

"We're fifteen," I reminded him. He frowned, his arms draping over Quincy's shoulders before he shrugged.

"So?" he looked at Quincy, they glanced back. "Are you planning on drinking?"

"You really asked Quincy that?" Dakota snorted. "It doesn't matter, we're famous. We can get in anywhere, do anything we want, no one will question us."

"I think fame is going to his head," Quincy whispered dramatically, raising their hand to cover their mouth for maximum whisper impact.

"I have our key card," Brooklyn announced then spun Quincy around, before dragging them by the hand down the hallway. Quincy looked back at us, their face alarmed so I ran after them. Dakota shouting something to me as she disappeared back into the room before closing the door behind her.

It didn't take her too long to catch up to me given we'd come to a domino effect stop at the door to the lobby. Brooklyn peeking through the window, probably trying to figure out if we had a clear route.

"Ready?" he whispered. "We're going to have to bolt."

I turned back to Dakota as she scoffed at the word bolt.

"Three." He lifted three fingers. "Two…" he dropped one, his hand on the door ready to push. "One." He pushed the door and he ran.

I'm surprised I got any momentum behind me with the giggles that overtook my body but I did, getting all the way to the automatic doors before they closed on me. Which broke Quincy, them creasing in the foyer, sinking to their knees as they laughed. I got through the doors, catching Quincy as I ran past them, towards an also laughing Brooklyn.

We, as a group, barely got out the carpark before we were stopped and asked for a selfie.

"Fame, huh?" Brooklyn lamented as he hugged my shoulders, walking us towards the town centre, his hip bumping against my elbow – I really needed to get on with getting taller.

"It's a hard life we lead," I mocked. He grinned down at me, knocking his forehead against the side of my head.

"I love it when you're sarcastic," he whispered, his breath against my cheek making me shiver. Then he let go. Just let go and began to skip – which was very Brooklyn of him. I turned on the spot, walking backwards and lifting my arms in a shrug to Quincy. They shrugged right back.

"Let the night lead the way, darling," they exclaimed.

"You know, I might take up drinking." I exclaimed.

"I support this."

"You're a bad influence," Dakota called to them, as they rose a peace sign to the sky.

I'd definitely lost Brooklyn amongst the foam. We all had

Dayglo stripes on our cheeks, neon pink, green, and yellow. The foam had made our hair droop but had also somehow made the glowsticks around our necks and wrists glow brighter.

I left Quincy to find the bathroom. Weaving myself around the club like I was in a labyrinth. No wonder we'd misplaced Brooklyn. He was like a toddler; if we were not holding his hand, we were guaranteed to misplace him.

I don't know which one of us had let go of his hand, but it didn't matter. I had found the bathroom and successfully achieved that task, so I refocused my aim to Brooklyn.

He couldn't have gone that far. Surely. There'd have been a screaming mob if he was in plain view though so he must've been hidden away.

I turned out of the backdoor towards the alley. That was where I found him with someone. Their lips stuck together in a what looked like a sloppy embrace. I swallowed, as he backed away from the person he was kissing. Smiling at them, whispering something.

I got a look at the… not-girl he was kissing. Wait, *not* a girl.

The boy was pretty, so damn pretty. He also had neon colours on his cheeks, except his hair was still immaculate. No wonder Brooklyn wanted to kiss him. He was laughing at whatever Brooklyn was saying — which made sense, given Brooklyn was hysterical. His head resting back on the brick wall as Brooklyn's hand rested above it, his hand flat against the wall. Keeping his balance I guess as he leant down to kiss the boy who was shorter than him.

I left them be.

"I didn't know he was gay," I whispered to Quincy as they sat beside me in my hotel room bed. Dakota asleep on her bed next to us.

"He's not gay," Quincy whispered back, we looked at each other.

"He was doing some pretty gay things."

"We all do some pretty gay things," they said. I sighed shaking my head and rubbing my eyes. When I took my hand away, it glowed.

"I'm literally fooling myself, I thought. Well, I don't know. In some fantasy world I could've ended up with him, could've had him love me but it's hopeless. He likes boys," I swallowed, as Quincy wrapped their arm around my shoulders. Knocking our heads together as they cuddled me a little closer.

We both jumped when their phone vibrated. They pulled it out to read it, laughing lowly.

"Brooklyn. I guess I can go back to my room now, he's returned with our key." They stood from my bed. "I think you should talk to Brooklyn," they suggested as they crossed the room.

"What do you know?"

"What I know isn't for me to share," they wiggled their fingers at me. "Come, speak to Brooklyn."

They opened the door.

Brooklyn was stood in the hallway. On his phone, the key card in his hand.

"Why didn't you let yourself in?" Quincy queried, passing Brooklyn and taking the key from his hand. Brooklyn shrugged.

"Got a text," he whispered, then he smirked as if it was a secret.

"From a boy?" Quincy asked. Brooklyn looked up at them, a smirk on their lips until Quincy nodded towards me. He turned to look at me, frowning confused until he seemed to get it.

"What?"

He didn't get it.

Quincy sighed, leaning on the door as it opened.

"You were spotted," Quincy smirked. I watched as Brooklyn processed the information he was receiving. "Up against an alley wall, your tongue in…"

"Oh," Brooklyn laughed. "He was gorgeous though, no?"

"Not by me," Quincy whispered. "Although I'm sure he was a ten." They stepped into the room. Brooklyn examined me.

"I feel like Quincy's hinting at something, but I can't figure it out."

"I didn't know you were gay," I whispered. He laughed shaking his head and following Quincy into their room.

"I'm not," he said before tossing his phone onto his bed.

"You're not…" I swallowed, "you're not just playing them, right?"

"No," he gasped. "Sweetheart, I'm bi. There's so much more than gay and straight, kid," he shrugged. "He *was* gorgeous, though, right…?"

"He was pretty," I agreed, then swallowed roughly. "You like girls and boys?"

"I like girls *and* boys," he agreed then took his top off. I glanced at Quincy. They shrugged gently. "I was going to apologise for not telling you but, you know… it's kind of my thing to tell people and I shouldn't apologise for not sharing that fact about myself." He pointed at Quincy. "Quincy's been teaching me how to be a proud queer."

Quincy snorted. I sighed.

"Wait…" Brooklyn lay back on his bed, frowning at me, "is it a problem?"

"Is what a problem?" I asked.

He waved his hand. "Me liking boys. Me being bi? Is that a problem? It feels like it's a problem."

"It isn't a problem, just a surprise," I whispered.

"That's rude," he frowned. "Did you just assume I couldn't be queer, or was it something else?"

"It wasn't…" I stuttered. "I didn't…"

"I just don't get why it's a surprise. I don't think that's right, you know? If you came out to me tomorrow, I wouldn't be like 'that's surprised me', I'd be like thank you for telling me, I wouldn't be making assumptions about—"

"It's because I like you," I stated. Brooklyn paused, Quincy gasped as I took a step back. The wall however was far too close so I bumped into it. "I… I mean…"

"Hey…" he got up from his bed.

I shook my head. "It doesn't matter, Brooklyn." I turned to leave the room. I knew he followed so I didn't resist too much when he grabbed for my arm, stopping me from going back into our room.

"Talk to me."

"I just, when I saw you kissing that boy, I thought I had no chance." I glanced behind him as Quincy lingered in the doorway. "I thought you were gay and, like, that's awesome, I would've wished you a world of happiness but it also made me sad. It was just a shock that you're… that you like girls *and* boys."

"Why didn't you tell me?"

I laughed. Right at him.

He winced, then turned. "Go away," he said to Quincy. Quincy sighed throwing Brooklyn's t-shirt back at him.

"Put some clothes on."

Brooklyn did, then grabbed my hands a little tighter, pulling me down the corridor, leaving Quincy behind. I looked back at them, they blew a kiss then crossed their fingers. Oh boy was I also crossing my fingers.

Brooklyn walked me out the hotel then back towards the club we'd come from. I went to question his route, when he diverted, turning a few corners before coming to a billboard. I frowned up at it, then laughed when I saw the Series Four promotional poster on it. It was a simple one; the four of us stood, side on, looking out as if something dramatic was coming. Electric sparks exploded behind us, *Adolescent Summers* written in a straight font with dark tree silhouettes.

I knew what series four was about, and even I was confused by the poster.

Brooklyn sighed, looking up at it then he started climbing it. I followed him when he stepped onto the platform in front of the poster. He sat down in front of it, his legs stretched out. His converse were both untied. I decided to focus on that as I sat beside him. Not close, not yet.

"Why didn't you?" he whispered.

"You'd have laughed in my face," I said.

He frowned at me, almost looking panicked. "I never would've. Never, never ever."

"I was always just that kid to you. You call me *kid*."

He frowned.

"Always. You're seventeen. Like what would you want with me?"

"How long?"

"How long?" I repeated.

"Me, how long?"

I exhaled. "You remember when your voice broke," I said.

He laughed but I think it was more out of shock. "And you bought me a McFlurry?"

I nodded. "Yeah, I was pretty fucking invested in you by then."

"You were…" he whispered. "Twelve." He shook his head. "How is that even possible?"

"You're gorgeous," I sighed. "It was a crush, back then, I'm certain it was simply a crush but things just snowballed, I guess. I like you, I really do but I had started to believe it was never going to happen so I just… let it rest."

"I don't understand why you keep saying it was never going to happen?"

I met his eyes.

"I like you, too. I mean, granted, I didn't fall for you when you were twelve. That'd have been weird," he laughed.

"When?" I whispered.

"The suit," he moaned, sinking down until his head butted the board. "Oh god, you looked…" he sighed. "And then I was like, shit, maybe I kind of like you, too."

"Is that why you took me to Eliza's?"

"No, that's because I'm a good person."

"If you like me, why did you go around kissing boys?"

"For fun," he squinted at me. "Kissing is fun. I didn't know you liked me back. I don't know, I just want to have fun, is that too much to ask?"

"Not at all," I whispered. "I still don't fully…" I swallowed. "I don't fully know who I am."

"You're fifteen, I'd be shocked if you did kid." He swallowed deeply, his Adams apple bobbing precariously. "Sorry, not kid, you don't like kid."

"I don't mind kid," I shook my head. "I just… when did you figure out the bi thing?"

"Approximately three months ago."

I rose my eyebrow at him, he mirrored me.

"Genuinely. I didn't, like, I didn't think about that kind of thing. I just acted with Dakota, and if girls came into the picture, I took it as far as I wished to. I've always liked boys, though; it was just always a little more complicated.

"I literally told Quincy last night. I know they're queer and they're proud so when we were lying in bed just talking. I told them I thought I was bi, and they got out of bed and gave me a hug."

"That you were so confident, you were so…"

"I'm an actor, my darling," he stood, quickly, almost toppling over from his laces. He spun around, raising his arms like a ballerina before opening them and bowing to me. I grinned up at him letting my eyes track him, taking him all in because I hadn't really looked at him, not for a while at least.

He was taller, so much taller than when we'd met. His chin squarer, his shoulders boarder. He'd soon start looking like a man.

When had we gotten so much older? I stroked my chin, tilting my head back and stroking down my throat. Swallowing against my fingers. It felt like something was missing, something wasn't quite there. I wonder when the point is that I'll start looking like a woman. I wonder how long I could put it off.

He smiled, it was almost nervous like he was trying to figure out what I was looking at.

He definitely wasn't wearing enough clothes for the night air. Just a t-shirt, simple and bright purple, high-waisted jeans that were turned up at the ankles – jeez he really was bi.

He was still beautiful. That hadn't changed, I truly believed that wouldn't change, ever. Not to me at least.

He pointed at me. "I want to take you on a date."

"A date?" I repeated. He nodded, his thumbs running under the waistband of his jeans until they slipped through his belt loops. "Why? We could just…"

"No," he whispered, crouching and remaining impressively solid as he balanced on the balls of his feet. "I… I haven't been treating you much like a partner."

"Partner?" I repeated. "Not…"

"I don't see why I should gender it," he tilted his head. "It's stupid, I know, but I figured I'd rather have partners than boyfriends and girlfriends, and what if I fall for someone nonbinary, I…"

"Partner is fine," I said. "Partner, is good."

"I've been treating you like a mate, like a friend. I want to take you on a date, then you can decide if you actually want this."

I knelt up. "I think you're projecting."

He cocked his head. "You'll be the one deciding if you actually want me."

Series 10

Day 40

Brooklyn always, without fail, winced when I injected my testosterone into my thigh. I frequently reminded him; he didn't *have* to be in the bathroom when I did it, but he always found his way back.

He usually ended up shaving, an easy cover-up because he had a five o'clock shadow by midday, and yet, even though he was holding a blade to his throat, my use of a needle was what made him squirm.

"You're never going to get used to it, are you?" I laughed as I dropped the needle into the box.

"How did you?"

"When you do something every week, you kind of get over it," I said as I sat on the lip of the bath. He waved his razor at me. "Yeah, I'm still a little afraid of that," I whispered, stroking the back of my hand down my neck. It had *surpassed* stubble now, if I pulled, I'd probably have a significant handful of beard which was kind of awesome – even though I didn't particularly *want* a beard.

"Would you let me do it?"

I tilted my head at him as he held the razor between his first two fingers, tittering it side to side.

I nodded. Swallowing deeply as he bit his bottom lip.

"Really?" he whispered. I nodded again. He turned

picking up his lather. He inspected it, I assume trying to figure out if there was enough left in it.

He seemed to decide there was and covered the brush in the soap before painting a beard onto my face with it.

He was gentle as he moved my head side to side, using my chin to tilt it back and forth. I could barely feel the blades as they ran over my cheeks.

Brooklyn's smirk was playful, his tongue poking out between his teeth but his eyes were focused, *so* very focused, almost Ritalin-focused, even though I knew he hadn't taken any today.

If it wasn't necessary, it wasn't taken.

"What?" he whispered.

"You're so… here," I said, because I knew he'd understand what I meant.

"I'm concentrating," he laughed. "Can you imagine the shit I'd get if I decapitated you."

I swallowed, my hand clasping around his wrist for a pause. He actively laughed.

"How very Sweeney Todd of you," I said, my voice wobbling which had nothing to do with the testosterone.

"I won't decapitate you," he assured me as I released his wrist. "I'm almost done," he added as I hummed softly. "I can't wait until I'm doing voice work for a while and I can grow a beard."

"You want a beard?" I asked.

"Not, like, full on Santa but just, Ryan Reynolds."

I grinned at him as he took a step back and retrieved a towel to wipe my face.

"I think you've just given me an erection," I teased. Well, I thought I was teasing but there was the possibility.

I didn't get much time to think on it as the bathroom door opened. Quincy appeared surprised that the bathroom was occupied. They shook it off quite quickly though, unzipping their jeans.

Brooklyn laughed, presumably at what I said as he turned back to the sink.

"Have you two looked at your emails?" Quincy asked. I glanced at them as they glanced back at me. "No? Do you guys *ever* check your emails?"

"Not unless you tell us to," Brooklyn said as Quincy rezipped their jeans. They rolled their eyes dancing around Brooklyn to occupy the sink.

"What does our email state, great Quincy?" I asked, clapping my hands together in fake prayer. They looked at me, smirking as they dried their hands.

"We are required to be in attendance at an interview."

"Shit," I sighed.

"Because of rumours regarding some cast members walking off set."

"Double shit," Brooklyn whined.

"Have you shaved?" Quincy asked.

I rubbed my chin. "Brooklyn did it for me."

It was a radio interview. Which I thought was weird because we hardly did radio interviews. It was a husband-and-wife duo.

They had both been in rather successful bands which apparently qualified them to be radio DJs – which made this interview a little bit stranger because we had nothing to do with music.

Not unless Quincy was about to go solo, that was.

They came across as fake to me.

They fawned over Brooklyn because, of course they did. It was Brooklyn Sampson. International Teen Icon. They probably thought they'd be sacked if they didn't kiss the ground he walked on.

They casted wary glances at me, their smiles still plastered on their faces, their true feelings hidden by their eyes. They gave Quincy some love, though, the wife complimenting their dangling star earring, the husband scrambling for something masculine to compliment them on. *Bless.*

"Just the boys today?" the wife laughed too loudly when we followed her to the studio.

"Dakota's still on set," Quincy replied as way of explanation. I wasn't sure whether they were telling the truth or not. I hoped it was a lie. I hoped Dakota hadn't gone back to set.

"And Freya?" the husband asked. Quincy looked at me wide-eyed. It perfectly said, *shit, I forgot Freya.*

"Freya is also on set," Brooklyn said. "They're just doing a few filler scenes." He smiled pleasantly as we took our seats. I could hear the last show finishing in my headphones. A song I knew by Ed Sheeran playing them out.

I looked at Brooklyn as he put the headphones on himself. He smiled at me, squeezing my thigh gently.

"Got you," he whispered. I nodded taking a deep breath as the hourly news began in my ears.

My deep breaths continued until the husband began to speak.

"Today we're joined by the boys of *Adolescent Summers.* We've got Brooklyn…"

"Hello." Brooklyn held up a peace sign. I laughed quietly, resisting reminding him that we were on the radio.

"Quincy…"

I turned to look at Quincy.

"Hey, darling," they purred.

"And new kid on the block…" the wife *joked,* I guess. I scowled her almost instantly, "Oz."

"Hi," I mumbled, then I swallowed deeply. Brooklyn continued to rub my thigh.

"The boys will be with us for the next hour, so Tweet us your questions," the husband requested.

"We'll get right to your questions after this song…" she took over as the music started.

Quincy lowered their headphones.

"Are we able to vet the questions before you ask them?" they asked. The wife frowned at them, laughing gently.

"We won't ask you anything, inappropriate."

"No, no…" Quincy sighed. "I'm sure, but there's some subjects you *should* just avoid."

"It'll be fine," the wife pushed. Quincy turned to me.

"Do you want to do this?" they asked, *quite* obviously, they didn't sugar coat it at all.

I looked back at them. "Yes," I took a breath. "Yes. I'll see what happens."

"You want out…" Brooklyn said, so I turned to him, "just say no debate okay?"

"Okay," I whispered. I saw as the husband and wife exchanged wide eyes. The dicks.

The song ended.

The wife started laughing with no context, at all.

"You boys are so funny," she gasped. "Oh, we're back."

I looked at Brooklyn. He bit down on his lip so he wouldn't laugh at me – come to think of it, he wouldn't even look at me. "We've already gotten so many questions from you guys, so let's get right to it."

They were mostly meaningless questions. Ones we answered at Comic Cons all the time. We were used to the *what's your favourite colour? Who's your favourite member of BTS? If we were an animal, what animal would we be? If you could dye your hair, what colour would you go?*

We let Quincy answer that one for as long as they wished until they were stopped in favour of an Elton

John song.

"Okay, so there is a reason you're joining us today," the husband said. "And it's to address the rumours that have started spiralling around."

Just let Brooklyn speak, I was telling myself, but I was also trying to ESP to Quincy, to tell them to keep themselves quiet. Preferably.

"So, let us in on the gossip," the wife said. I looked to Brooklyn. "What's happening on the *Adolescent Summers* set?"

Brooklyn cleared his throat. "There's been some… disagreements," he said warily. He'd called Eliza, in the car on the way over here. Granted, he had put her on through the radio, so we could all hear the conversation but I hadn't really taken in anything she'd said and Quincy wasn't going to follow anyone's instructions.

Eliza had told him what he could say, and how much and I had no doubt Brooklyn would follow them rules to the letter.

"We haven't spoken with the studio yet, so we can't actually *gossip*, that'd be wrong anyway, but some things just need to be discussed and confirmed before filming can commence."

"Right." The wife was hugely disappointed by that answer, I could definitely tell that. "Would you address the rumours that it's due to your transition?" she asked. I finally met her eyes. *Oh*, apparently she wanted to start some shit.

"Excuse me?"

"Well, see. The rumour mill began to spill, if you will." She smiled, that bitch was rhyming to make herself sound harmless. She wanted to make me smile, to drop my guard.

She was a shark out for blood, and I always knew it.

"The whispers on Twitter were that they'd stopped

production due to yourself."

"Well, they haven't stopped production," I said. "Dakota and Freya are filming."

"Ah, so they don't share your values?" she asked.

Brooklyn frowned. "That is not the case."

"Oz?" she asked.

I frowned at her. "Are you asking if we walked off set because of *me*?"

"No," she drew out. "No, no, of course not. I'm just asking you about the rumours."

I didn't reply.

"See," she continued. "Your… change…"

"*Transition*," Quincy commented as I exhaled gently.

"… Came as quite a shock to your fanbase, no? It happened really quickly, then to hear rumours of a disruption on set, in regard to *you*, well, questions begin to get asked."

"*Quickly*," I repeated, because apparently that was the only word I heard. "You think this was a quick, and easy decision?"

"She doesn't mean that…" the husband injected. I glanced at him briefly as he waved his hand. "We all lost so much time in lockdown, it just feels like it was quick."

Damage control. I wonder how often he needed to do that. I glanced at Quincy; they didn't look all too impressed.

"I understand I am in a privileged position," I said. Quincy reached for me but I ignored them. "I understand that if I didn't have the money I do which, yes, has come from *Adolescent Summers*, that I wouldn't have been able to transition so, as you assume, quickly.

"I am lucky, so lucky that I can afford testosterone, and can afford a private doctor, can afford to have top surgery. I know there are *lots* of trans people who can't, who that amount of privilege is unimaginable.

"Quincy and I very actively donate to top surgery funds, bottom surgery funds, hormone funds. Anonymously because we're not out for credit, we *both* understand how hard it is, and if we can make it a little bit easier for *just* one person we'll feel a little bit better about our privilege.

"My transition started *way* before it visually started. Just because now you can *see* the change doesn't mean during lockdown I thought, hey I'm a boy. There has been *years* of pain, of confusion, of anger and deep, rooted sadness that you didn't get to see, and I'm *not* going to apologise that I don't share every single part of my life.

"I owe a lot to *Adolescent Summers*, I am fully aware of that. I know what the show has done for me, but there have been issues on set. Too many to just cast a blind eye over, and until I feel I am in a safe environment, I personally will not be returning to set." I quickly turned to Brooklyn, who was watching me with wide eyes. "I know I shouldn't have said that, I *know*."

"It's okay," he whispered. I looked to Quincy who was wiping a tear from their cheek.

"You're so brave," they whispered, reaching for my hand and squeezing gently. I smiled back at them.

"Let's go to a song," the husband said, feverishly, pressing multiple buttons until a Dua Lipa song started.

I took my headphones off the moment it did. Placing them on the table in front of me and standing to leave.

I didn't know if I'd be followed and I was okay with that, but I knew I wouldn't be stopped. I trusted that neither Brooklyn nor Quincy would try to talk me back.

I sat myself in the green room. Pressing the palm of my hand against my forehead and taking deep breaths.

My phone vibrated. I looked at the lock screen, reading the message without opening it.

Eliza: *I'm not mad.*
Eliza: *You did good kid.*

Lockdown 1

Day 100

Brooklyn's laptop screen filled with faces. Four boxes, perfectly in the corners of the screen, we were the top corner. Quincy, in their bedroom in the box next to us. We hadn't thought it wise for all three of us to come from the same room. We figured the fans would speculate *anything* from a polyad situation to us breaking lockdown rules

They'd grab onto anything, especially now with no content – and we frankly couldn't be bothered debunking those rumours.

Dakota was in the box below Quincy, sipping on a cup of tea. The teabag still in it, her background looked mature, very grown up. Maybe we *shouldn't* have set up the camera in front of our Andrew Garfield as Spiderman poster.

But, then again.

His face was far more palatable than the white walls and singular aloe vera plant that was behind Dakota.

Freya was in the other box. Also in her bedroom, her walls were painted a light shade of purple. She needed to turn her bedroom light on.

"Nice of you to join us," Dakota teased; Brooklyn held up a peace sign. I hid a little further into his shoulder, which was a little stupid, I'd grown up with these people.

"We beat Eliza," Brooklyn pointed out. "That means that we're on time."

"Early even," I teased.

"Why were you so late, you went into your room like, forty-five minutes ago?" Quincy mocked. I laughed as Dakota scoffed, waving her hands at us.

"Stop that," she moaned. "No, stop, behave."

I laughed, then looked up when Dakota said my name. Well, my old name, my birth name, my deadname.

"Is that you?" she asked. I waved. "You cut your hair."

"All I'm going to say is, don't let Brooklyn near scissors," I mocked. Brooklyn looked genuinely put out for a second before nuzzling his head against mine. The screen rang like a doorbell.

"Oh, good, you're all here," Eliza said. We were now three boxes on the top and two on the bottom. It was nowhere near as pleasing to look at. "Before I send the join request, do we have any questions?" she requested, we all shook our heads, well, except Brooklyn who rose his hand. "Brooklyn?" she said with an exhausted fondness.

"Yeah, what are we *actually* doing here?"

I sighed. "Really?"

"Virtual meet and greet, Mr Sampson."

"Oh," he frowned. "Oh, I thought this was a Zoom Quiz." He turned to me. "We'll keep team Super Awesome for next time."

"We'd have a better name than that," I interrupted him. "Far better."

"Hey, I want to be in team Super Awesome," Quincy gasped.

"Well, come in here, then," Brooklyn said. Quincy

laughed as Eliza sighed.

"I have a genuine question," Quincy said. "If AJ gets in shot, is that a bad thing?"

"I will leave the room," AJ's voice said off camera. "I'm okay with that."

"Is AJ clothed?" Eliza asked.

Quincy smirked. "Mostly."

AJ laughed as Quincy did.

"It won't be the end of the world."

Quincy grinned, tapping something off screen and given how their laptop moved, I assume changed position with AJ.

"Ay-up I can see AJ reflected in your glasses," Brooklyn teased. "What theory should I start?

"AJ performs or—"

"Stop," Eliza interrupted me as Quincy crowed.

"Oh my god…" they paused, their eyes wide, they must've had the intention to say my name. I smiled at them, they winked then looked at themselves on the screen.

"He isn't reflected in your glasses," Dakota said, her voice monotone like she was over our childish games. Quincy grinned.

"That's good, I really didn't want to put my contacts in."

"Where is he?" Brooklyn asked. Quincy laughed lifting the laptop and lowering their camera. AJ's head was lying on Quincy's thigh, playing on his Switch console.

"He's playing Animal Crossing," they said. "He won't even look up."

Eliza smiled, it was soft. She wasn't mad.

"Brooklyn…" Eliza said. I knocked my head against Brooklyn's arm when she followed with my name. "Are you two sure you want to come from the same room?"

"There's no need to power up three laptops," Brooklyn replied.

She held her hand up. "Okay, it's okay. I just wanted to confirm. You know they make mountains out of molehills and with your relationship…"

"I'm not going to start licking him," I stated.

Eliza rose her eyebrow at me. "I'm sure."

"I… we're sat next to each other. Most of them know we live together, they know we live with Quincy too, so it's not going to be *that* much of a shock."

"Just. don't fall into any traps."

Brooklyn saluted. I sighed.

"Eliza…" I asked. "Can we stay on after this is over? I want to talk to you."

I felt Brooklyn squeeze my arm as she nodded.

"Of course," she smiled. "Get ready kids. I'm going to let them in."

And she did. Box after box appearing, then screens multiplying, three, four, five, ten. How many people were *actually* on this call?

I looked at Brooklyn as his eyebrows rose, he swallowed deeply.

"This is a *little* more intense that your average Q and A," he whispered. I nodded reaching past the screen, I passed him the Poppit he'd thrown behind the laptop when the call had started.

"We could just put ourselves on mute," I said. He smiled lightly, leaning back against the wall. It made him look smaller than me in our frame.

"Welcome to the *Adolescent Summers* virtual Q and A," Eliza announced. She was obviously our moderator for this… farce. "Today, we are lucky enough to have all of the cast with us. It's almost like we're in a situation where no one can go outside."

I'm sure the laughter would be raucous if everyone

wasn't on mute.

"Today we're joined by… Freya McDonald."

Freya waved coyly; she still hadn't turned her bedroom light on.

I was announced next. I was always second to last in the pecking order of fame. I waved whilst smiling and trying to ignore the muted gasps at my haircut.

"Quincy Ikeda."

Quincy laughed, bowing their head in greeting. I heard Brooklyn whisper *Moshi Moshi* behind me. I turned to look at him, he laughed softly.

"I'm getting better at Japanese. I aim to come out of this fluent."

"Fluent," I laughed. He nodded then glanced up as Eliza introduced Dakota.

"And Brooklyn Sampson."

He smiled, an award-winning smile whilst raising a peace sign. Multiple of the people in the boxes returned the peace sign. The vast majority of them had bisexual flags hung within their frame.

In fact, the more I looked at the little boxes of people the more flags I saw bisexual, pansexual, trans, nonbinary, genderqueer, rainbow flags, progressive flags, ally flags.

I'd never *quite* realised how queer the *Adolescent Summers* fanbase was. I sent this in a text to Quincy. I saw as they received it. Their phone screen *actually* reflecting in their glasses. I saw them smile. It made me smile right back as Brooklyn started to answer a question.

Quincy: *Their gaydars must have been on high alert. They all must've sensed the queerness of the show from episode one.*

I almost laughed out loud then remembered we were *not* on mute.

"Hey, this is a question for everyone." A square lit

up, a teenager speaking from it. "What's your favourite dinosaur?"

Brooklyn's laugh sounded excited as he sat up better.

"Diplodocus," he said before it was requested of him. "It's so much fun to say."

"Stegosaurus," I replied to Brooklyn. "They just look so polite."

"Polite," he repeated.

"I don't know the name of *any* dinosaurs," Dakota said.

Quincy scoffed. "Gawd, Dakota," they mocked. "Velociraptor," they added as they made their arms wings.

"Triceratops," AJ said off screen.

Quincy covered his mouth. "No one asked you," they said, a titter fell through the videos we could see.

"I'm quite happy with the contribution," the teenager who asked the question said. Quincy grinned at them.

"Brook, I raise you, Dilophosaurus," Freya said.

"I will give it to you, as long as you recreate the noise they make when they attack," Brooklyn replied.

Freya laughed then gave it a valiant attempt. Brooklyn fell backwards against the wall as he laughed.

"Gold star, Freya," he said. She bowed dramatically in response.

"My question is for Brooklyn, Quincy…" and me, "from your TikTok's and Instagram posts, we were led to believe you all lived together, so why aren't you all on screen together?"

"No one can share the screen with Quincy," Brooklyn laughed. The question asker didn't look all to convinced.

"Don't you believe we live together?" I asked. They shrugged gently, "okay…" I stood, leaving our bedroom and walking the hall to Quincy's. They were obviously expecting me as they moved AJ so I could kneel on their bed and hug them.

"Brooklyn," I said. Brooklyn frowned at the screen. "I'm staying here."

"Aw," he replied, as AJ did. I looked past the laptop at AJ as he lay on his back, the Switch in the air.

"It's like an episode of Wife Swap," Freya commented.

"Freya," I laughed.

"Question for Brooklyn," a new square lit up. "Can we see Bud?"

"Yes, you definitely can," he answered. "One minute." He stood, we heard him whistle in stereo, from the hall and through Quincy's screen. Then the cooing began, he sat back down in front of his laptop, Bud happily in his arms. He seemed to be wearing a turtle neck.

"That dog's got more clothes than me," Quincy commented.

"And me, combined," AJ uttered. I laughed as Brooklyn made Bud wave. Everyone cooed appropriately.

The next question was about the next series. We let Dakota take the lead.

It was two hours, the whole Q and A, followed by everyone being carted into the waiting room, then brought back for a screenshot photo op with us all. That took a further two hours but I swapped screens halfway, when I saw Brooklyn flagging and figured he probably needed to be propped up.

AJ popped up for some, if Quincy felt they were a Daniel stan at least and then, Eliza finally said,

"And that's the last one."

We all exhaled.

"Be free, young people. Be free. I'll be in contact, I'll let you know our plans moving forward. Stay safe, okay."

We all nodded back, waving, and saying our goodbyes.

Brooklyn's head landed on my shoulder.

"I need a nap," he told me.

"Have one, gorgeous," I whispered. "I'm going to talk to Eliza first."

"I'm staying awake for that," he stated.

"I can stay too, if you want me too."

"Thank you, honestly but, it's okay."

Quincy nodded. "You know where I am, for after."

I blew them a kiss.

Now there was only two boxes. Me, and a somewhat deflated Brooklyn and Eliza.

"Are you okay, lovely? You look like when Inflatable Tube Guy's power is turned off."

I laughed, as Brooklyn did, turning his head to look at Eliza.

"I'm fine, just a bit spent, I guess."

I kissed his cheek because I could. It was *just* Eliza.

"What did you want to talk to me about?"

"I…" I exhaled. Brooklyn rubbed my back, squeezing my shoulder occasionally. I nodded. "Eliza, during lockdown, I started my transition."

Eliza smiled. "Oh."

"Oh," I agreed. "I… I use he/him pronouns and I've changed, not legally, yet, but I've changed my name to Oz."

"Oz," she repeated. "That suits you."

I exhaled. Brooklyn knocked his head against mine.

"I plan to start hormones. I've consulted with a doctor, and I just need to get my bloods done and I can start. It's been weighing on me a long time, but filming so much kind of distracted my mind away from it.

"Being alone with my thoughts has opened a few doors that are pretty tricky to close again."

"Thank you for telling me, Oz," she said. I swallowed. "If you wish to, I can ask Arden to talk to you."

"I'd like that," I told her.

"I'll talk to the studio. Don't worry. I'll sort all that out. We don't need another…"

"Quincy," Brooklyn said. Eliza nodded looking a little glum.

"I'll keep you safe, Oz, okay? I am making you a promise, right here right now, that I will keep you safe."

"Thank you," I whispered. "I'm… I'm not coming out publicly, yet. I'm not even on any socials so, if we do any more of these, you can use my birth name until I figure things out. I don't want to cause a news scandal."

She nodded. "Okay, we'll move forward like that, until you tell me otherwise."

"Thank you."

"You are most welcome."

Series 10

Day 40

Brooklyn was on the floor. His nose almost touching Nunchuck's as they munched through some lettuce.

I sat on the couch drinking a cup of tea with Arden as ey scrolled through twitter. We had already been trending before our interview, the rumours had seen to that. Now, *I* was trending. *Oz Campbell*, *#OZCAMPBELL*, *#OZSWALKOUT*, the variety of misspellings as well as my deadname. *Awesome*.

So much for resurrecting my Twitter account. I was never doing that, it seemed.

"Most are in your favour," Arden said. "Honestly. Those that listened live and know the full context fully support you, are in fact calling for the DJs to be cancelled."

I sighed, sipping at my tea. "That's not… necessary."

"Nor is reading Twitter," Eliza stated. "In fact, I very actively suggest *against* doing such a thing, and wish you didn't encourage it."

"I wasn't," ey gasped. "He asked."

"He did," Brooklyn cooed. I turned to look at him as he sat back against the couch. Nunchuck settled on his thighs still munching on lettuce.

"I like to know what people are saying about me."

"It's not always good."

I mumbled.

"He wants to know who's on his list to kill," Brooklyn cooed. I laughed, so he looked up towards me. "I agree with both sides of this. Eliza is right, don't fill your head with online nonsense, *but* Oz also has a point. We've been reading online stuff ever since we were old enough to be online.

"My twitter boomed during the first series and every single person had an opinion on me. I was *thirteen* and grown ass adults were telling me I was gorgeous whilst others were coming after me for being a shit actor, for being the *worse* male protagonist to ever grace their screen.

"Do I wish I hadn't read half of it? Of course, but it made my skin thick as fuck. I read things now, I read personal attacks that go *way* past Kevin and just go to my physique, or my personality..." he sighed looking straight at me. "My fucking teeth. Somehow these people find our deepest insecurities and pray on them like cockroaches."

"I think you may've forgotten your point," Eliza said.

"I haven't," he pouted. "My point is still valid. Our whole lives are online. Our faces are *everywhere*, it's better we're on top of what people are saying, so we're not caught off guard."

"And I never read it first-hand, it's always abridged," I said as I stoked my fingers through Brooklyn's hair. "And you're gorgeous. I thought that before you had braces, *when* you had braces, and now you don't."

He tilted his head at me, an amused look in his expression but he still didn't smile with his teeth. *God* I hated the internet, sometimes.

"Besides..." Brooklyn said, shaking the conversation off him like a dog did when they got wet. "It's always fun promoting Quincy's *Only Fans* as a response."

I snickered because when I had a Twitter, I always did that. Any slandering direct messages, any Tweet that was less than complimentary, any article that said something rude about me, *or* Brooklyn, or Quincy I. When I was called upon to respond I always said; *Thanks for the tag! I recommend you check out @IncyQuincySpider's Only Fans! Great content, for great prices!* <Link>

It amused Quincy to no-end. It amused the studio less, but it didn't stop me from doing it, nor Brooklyn when he discovered I was. *Nor* Freya actually.

"You shouldn't reply to them, at all," Eliza said. I sipped from the tea until it was taken from my hands and finished by Brooklyn.

"Then we're bad celebrities. We're not down to earth, don't interact with the *little* people. We can't do anything right."

"Maybe we should take Quincy's approach," Brooklyn muttered. "And just say, *fuck* it."

"The studio made them say fuck it," I whispered. I turned to Eliza, pinching my fingers together. "I'm about this close to doing it myself."

"I wouldn't blame you," Eliza said, with a sigh. "But I'd much rather you fix this with the studio, and you finish series ten."

"Why?" I snapped. "Why should I finish the series?"

"Because of all the trans kids who need it," she snapped back. "I know they've been treating you like shit, and we *shouldn't* stand for it but, Oz, when this series comes out and there's a bisexual male protagonist, in a relationship with a trans boy. Clear as day, no hiding."

"But that script is bad," I stated. "The script is *shit*. They're writing it so I turn back into Izzy by the end, so I'm a girl, that's not representation.

"Just like them killing off Daniel. No, sorry, them

getting Quincy to kill off Daniel, because *queer happy ever afters don't fucking exist.*"

"Then we fight."

"What?" Brooklyn whispered. Nunchuck jumped from his knee, hopping away so Brooklyn sat on the couch beside me.

"We fight for you guys. We fight for the change to the script, the change of the characters. We fucking fight, Oz."

"We tried," I whispered.

"When you were fifteen. You were kids. Of course, they walked all over you, but you're adults now. You're adults who sign their own paperwork, who can give their own consent. You've got voices." She looked between us. "You've got *loud*, influential voices. Use them."

"Are you encouraging us to cause anarchy?" Brooklyn whispered. Eliza rose her eyebrow back at him, *neither* confirming nor denying her influence.

Arden passed my phone back to me.

"You can read this one yourself," ey said. I frowned then looked back at my phone, and there I was. The picture on the article showing Quincy and I. Their arm around my shoulders, their other outstretched holding the nonbinary flag like wings.

I had the trans flag wrapped around my front and a big smile on my face. I hadn't seen a picture of me smiling in such a long time.

I stood just shorter than Quincy, my black hair sticking up oddly as it insisted on growing out from the buzzcut. I couldn't work out fully if I actually liked it yet.

My brown eyes actually looked brown in that picture, not black like normal. The flash reflecting in both our eyes. I clicked the link; it *wasn't* an article. It was a blog post. I searched out the author first.

Fifteen-year-old, trans girl, she/her pronouns,

Scorpio. The post was called, WHY THE STARS OF *ADOLESCENT SUMMERS* GIVE ME HOPE.

I've been watching Adolescent Summers for five years now. After episode one of the first series, you can bet I binged so hard. I watched, and rewatched. I stayed up to midnight for the new series, I bought merch, I watched fan videos, I wrote fanfics.

I stated my loyalty to the TODANIEL fandom. I grieved when Daniel died. I cheered when Brooklyn and Izzy finally kissed.

Adolescent Summers has been such a big part of my life. Fictional and real, as when I came out as trans two years ago, I was able to use the resources and interviews Quincy had done to help my parents through. I can't thank Adolescent Summers enough for how much it's impacted my life.

I had no clue about Oz. People ask me all the time, my friends, my family, 'did you know he was trans?' Like I have some trans bat signal that makes every other trans person a beacon - I do not, by the way, but I'm so, so excited for Oz, and I understand the relief he must be feeling.

I saw these pictures following Comic Con

Picture of Oz and Quincy with their flags (header photo). Picture of Brooklyn with bisexual flag wrapped around his shoulders.

And they filled me with so much joy, with so much hope. I was seeing people, actors, like me. Queer actors, who are so outwardly proud to be queer, who have found their own family, who have found love and genuinely seem happy. I mean, hello, AJ proposed to Quincy, if you haven't seen it yet, click {here}. I have a lot of feelings on the lead up to Series Ten. Are they going to acknowledge Oz's transition? Are they going to allow the relationship between Kevin and Izzy's character to progress? Are we going to see a completely queer rewrite into the last series? JUSTICE FOR QUINCY BTW.

Following Oz's interview this morning, I'm feeling a bit more fear than I was excitement. I'm scared that they'll erase us, they'll find a way to, I guess, avoid the subject, have you seen when actresses get pregnant, and their clothes get baggier? Yeah, that kind of thing.

This morning's interview was horrible to listen to. She genuinely goaded Oz into saying something that'd make him uncomfortable, she actively attempted to get Brooklyn or Quincy to say something incriminating. Listening to it first hand was painful for me; I can only imagine how it felt for Oz.

They'll always be my idols, the entire cast of Adolescent Summers. *Regardless of how the tenth series progresses, I know it won't be the actor's fault if there's minimal LGBTQ representation. It's not really their decision if that happens, but there is always that teeny tiny bit of hope that maybe, maybe the biggest TV show of all time will have a queer couple in their main storyline. Just maybe.*

I looked up at Brooklyn, as he read over my shoulder. When he got to the bottom of the page, he scrolled back up, saving the picture of himself onto my phone. I caught his hand *just* before he clicked the link to Quincy's proposal. He met my eyes.

"We're going to *fucking* fight."

Series 7

Day 14

"Sex, drugs, and *Adolescent Summers*. Get the scoop on the troublemaker on set of the popular TV show," Quincy read; the laugh evident in their voice as they turned their phone to us. "Dare I click it," they teased. "I hope it's me," they added as Brooklyn walked towards us, zipping up his coat. He frowned, confused.

"What do you hope is you?"

"The troublemaker on set," they said, then sat beside me. They clicked on the article as I took the offered beanie from Brooklyn.

"Teenage stars strike again. Are the young stars of *Adolescent Summers* going off the rails?" Quincy read aloud, then laughed. "Brooklyn Sampson, nineteen, Quincy Ikeda, seventeen… oh, you get the gist." They scrolled. "We've spoken to a few extras of the popular show and they all said the same thing, the high-maintenance, troublemaker on set, is none other than front man Brooklyn Sampson."

"What?" he squeaked, leaning over me to try and read Quincy's phone.

"Multiple extras stated that Brooklyn was disruptive on set, unpredictable, and hyperactive," Quincy gasped. "Dicks. This isn't even light-hearted jest." They continued to scroll. "Being the eldest of the cast comes with its downfalls, for teen-star Brooklyn Sampson, pictured here with an unknown girl…"

"Molly," Brooklyn rolled his eyes. "Poor Molly. She'll never get rid of me, huh?"

"Brooklyn was seen slinking around dark corners with her, and numerous other girls over the years. Even a few boys, too."

"Shit," he laughed, taking Quincy's phone from them. Three pictures sat underneath the paragraph. The first was with a girl, outside a club. They weren't doing anything, Brooklyn was just stood very close, talking to her, a flirtatious smile on his face. The second was a boy.

"Are your hands down his jeans?" I laughed.

Brooklyn bit his bottom lip. "*That* was last year," he whispered. I nudged against him, smirking gently as he shook his head. The last picture, he was very obviously kissing the other person, but he covered most of the other person. Well, except for the phone case.

"That's you," Quincy laughed. I smirked at Brooklyn as he also laughed, nodding back to Quincy.

"That's by your house. When we snuck down the alley to kiss so your mum couldn't see us on your doorbell."

"So, your mum sold the picture to the press?" Quincy teased. I laughed as Brooklyn scrolled through the rest of the article.

"I wouldn't even be surprised," I muttered, then leant my chin on Brooklyn's shoulder.

"Brooklyn Sampson has hit the trifactor, being seen doing drugs on set," he squawked, shaking his head as he skipped the article obviously looking for the photo evidence. He *did* find it.

"That could literally be chewies," Quincy said as they took their phone back, Brooklyn shook his head.

"It's my Ritalin," he laughed. "You know, they want me to reply to this, they want a statement from me, and if it doesn't expose my ADHD, they won't take it seriously." He frowned. "Although my ADHD doesn't affect my love life."

"No, but you're not out as bi, are you?" I whispered.

He looked at me, then laughed. "I am *not* writing a statement, or speaking one or, anything that outs me as both bisexual and having ADHD, fuck that."

"Let's tone down the language," Eliza said as she approached us, zipping up her coat with one hand whilst scrolling through her phone with the other. "We're going to turn on Christmas lights remember, big smiles, family friendly."

"Brooklyn is the resident bad boy," Quincy told her. She examined Brooklyn as if that statement was so far-fetched that Quincy couldn't have been talking about *our* Brooklyn. She took their phone, then she laughed.

"Ignore it. It's a stupid tabloid newspaper. It hasn't got a shred of reliability. Just ignore it, okay?"

"I don't want to tell everyone about my ADHD," Brooklyn said quietly. "Which I *know* makes me a terrible advocate blah, blah, blah but…"

"You don't need to tell anyone anything that you're uncomfortable with, sunshine," she said as Brooklyn stood. Eliza fixed his coat. "You're allowed some privacy," she added, smiling as she knocked his chin. He smiled back at her.

"They have pictures of me taking Ritalin."

Eliza waved her hand as if she was just brushing it away.

"I'm just pleased they don't have any pictures of me buying weed," Quincy whispered. I laughed covering my mouth with a clap, so Eliza looked at us.

"The girls are already in the car, come on," she

pushed. "Is AJ meeting us there?"

"I believe so," Quincy said, changing the app on their phone. "Yes, AJ will be meeting us there."

"Then into the car with all of you. *No* Googling yourselves on the way."

I smirked at Brooklyn as he laughed, then turned so he was stood in front of me, he pulled on his beanie that I was wearing, turning the bottom up then flattening it against my head. When he was satisfied with how it sat, he kissed me.

"I have *no* reservations about coming out as being in a relationship with you," he whispered. "Just so you're aware."

Brooklyn walked on an angle. Bumping against me every now and again as we walked the tunnel that'd lead us towards our train.

Quincy walked a few steps in front of us, turning back to watch, their expression amused as they shook their head at him.

"You're drunk."

"I'm not…" Brooklyn turned to look at me, a somewhat sincere expression on his face. "I'm not drunk."

Quincy laughed as I examined him. I didn't believe he was drunk, he'd had like two pints of beer which were probably not even real pints as they came in plastic cups. He wasn't drunk.

"I'm not drunk. Look," he repeated, then touched his finger to his nose and walked in a straight line.

"I really don't know what that proves," I said to Quincy. They laughed shaking their head as they jumped down the steps and walked ahead to the platform as I took the steps one at a time, turning back with every step to watch Brooklyn's descent, mostly because his shoelaces were untied.

He wrapped his arms around me when he got to the bottom.

"You know, markets are all romantic and I don't feel like we could be all romantic."

"No?" I teased.

"It's sad."

"So sad," I repeated.

"You're teasing me," he whispered, grinning at me. I bit my lip. "Ooh, I love it." He kissed me. It took me by surprise, but then again, who was around to see it, besides Quincy?

They sighed from the platform, we turned towards them together.

"Fifteen minutes," they read then disappeared from view, presumably to sit down.

Brooklyn whined, I turned back to him as he took a deep breath.

"I need to pee," he whispered. "But it was like low urgency when I thought the Tube would be here."

I tried to resist laughing at all costs. It didn't work.

"You're so mean," he sounded outraged.

"You'll be fine," I almost sang at him before walking onto the platform. "It's how long? The Tube to yours?" I asked Quincy.

"Twenty minutes."

I heard Brooklyn swear.

"But you live right by the station, right?"

"That I do," Quincy confirmed then looked behind me, smirking. "You okay? You look stressed?"

Brooklyn rose his middle finger at them. They returned it.

He went to sit beside Quincy. His legs bouncing at a far quicker rate than they'd normally be. Quincy smirked before reading their phone.

"AJ's home," they told us.

"Lucky AJ," Brooklyn muttered, as I scanned the platform.

"Why couldn't AJ stay with us tonight?"

"He could've," Quincy said to me, as they took presumably a Snapchat picture to reply to AJ. "I mean, my okaasan wouldn't have been all too bothered."

"But does she know he's your boyfriend?"

"Yes," they laughed. "She's well aware. She's met him and it'd have been fine because there's other people." They waved their hand. "But AJ has work tomorrow."

"Oh," I whispered, as I turned towards the time board. "Oh," I repeated a bit louder, "delayed."

"Shut up," Brooklyn moaned. "You're kidding me?"

"Extra five minutes."

He groaned, shaking his head before bolting to a standing position.

"I can't do this."

"You can probably run back up before the train gets here."

"No way," he sighed, taking my arm then he rose Quincy from their seat by taking their hand. "Come." He walked us down the platform until we reached the furthest end. "Cover me," he said. Quincy moved as if they'd done this before. I frowned back at Brooklyn. "Stay. There," he whispered as he unzipped his coat. I glanced at Quincy as they laughed, leaning sideways on the wall.

"This is how Brooklyn's night outs normally end," they teased.

"It is not," he gasped. "I'm a very well-behaved, law-abiding citizen."

"Excuse me, you're our resident bad boy," Quincy said. I laughed turning to look at Brooklyn as he shook his head, although he did seem amused. "Always out, causing… mischief."

"You're thinking of AJ," Brooklyn replied, then he sighed.

"Oh, I've had to cover AJ numerous times," Quincy tutted. "No fear has AJ. Although he did get banned from his first *Only Fans* account for a pee video."

I squawked then Brooklyn laughed - I think at my squawk.

"Geez, that's loud," Quincy continued. "How did you expect to get away with this, this whole place is literally tile?"

Brooklyn shushed them. "You were meant to cover me, keep talking. I don't want to be in another newspaper tomorrow."

"Teenage star, pisses his career down the drain." Quincy moved their hand across the air as if they could see it. I laughed.

"Gone off the rails, Brooklyn wasn't relieved for long."

"Christmas Market aftershock as Teen star is taken in for indecent exposure."

"Quincy!" Brooklyn gasped. I giggled like a child.

"People get turned on by this?" I rounded back to AJ; Quincy impressively kept up.

"Some do," they nodded. "Each to their own, I guess. AJ didn't go out with the intention to make a pee video, he just needed to go whilst the camera was rolling and he thought, why not?"

I shook my head. "Why not?"

"He was already touching himself; he didn't intend to post it just decided to and, well, he was banned within the hour."

I sniggered. "You could make content, too," I said to Brooklyn.

He snorted as he turned back to me. "I'm okay. But

thanks for the offer. Collab?"

"Not until I'm eighteen," I cooed. He smirked at me as he rezipped his coat.

"Look at the mess you've made," Quincy tutted, waving their hand so Brooklyn looked down. He stepped over the little stream laughing as he did.

"Does anyone else need to use the platform?"

"I would take up that offer but, regretfully, I don't have a penis," I sighed, overly dramatically even though there was a genuine pang of something deep in my chest. Brooklyn wrapped his arms around me, swinging us side to side. Quincy reached for me.

"I'm sure Brooklyn will lend you his," they said, tilting their head. I glanced up at Brooklyn as he nodded against me. I bit my tongue before I *accidentally* stated that we'd never done that before, but maybe I wanted to.

Maybe.

I thoroughly enjoyed the whole making out part of the relationship with Brooklyn. If I had to tier the things that came in a relationship, that ranked very highly.

Quincy was asleep. We were pretty certain of that, they'd been asleep a while and I'd been texting updates to Brooklyn on Quincy's sleeping status, until he suggested I join him.

He was on the couch that sat within the window of Quincy's bedroom. His mother, their okaasan, was strangely okay with me sharing a bed with Quincy, but not Brooklyn. It was strange, and when I'd questioned it, Quincy had laughed and shrugged telling me she had her own reasons that were not to be questioned too deeply.

When I slinked into Brooklyn's makeshift bed, and our lips were locked almost instantly, I maybe understood their okasaan's rules. He turned me so I wasn't hanging over the edge, pushing me against the window. I gasped. The cold of the glass against my back. He laughed quietly.

"That good, huh?"

I frowned at him.

"That was a sex joke, my darling," he whispered. I bit my lip as he moved me, so he could throw the quilt he had over me, protecting me from the cold of the window. He stroked his fingers through my hair, smiling almost to himself before kissing me. It was gentle, I wanted to sink into it.

I gave it a go. Moving closer to him. I'd never really been this close to him. Even when we'd kissed, our bodies didn't really touch further than our arms looping around each other in varying ways. We'd always been standing or sitting. Lying down gave us a whole different way to approach this.

Our chests had never touched like this. So close we could keep a thin magazine up if we were standing.

I wanted to attempt further.

I kissed him. My hands naturally going into his hair, holding the back of his head, as I brought my knees up. Until I think they were knocking against his thighs.

He laughed into my mouth.

"You're daring tonight," he whispered.

"Should I stop?"

"Definitely not. Keep going, experiment, enjoy." He smiled at me, I grinned back. It felt childish. "Want some help?" he whispered. I nodded because I didn't quite know how to make the move to get our middles touching. The part between our chests and his thighs at least. He nodded back, his hands running down my back, until he was holding my thighs.

He stroked his fingers down them, it tickled and made me shiver but that stopped cold when he pulled me towards him.

I took a moment to adjust, my breath caught in my throat and he watched me, a light smile on his face as he chewed on his bottom lip.

"Yeah?" he whispered.

"I support this," I assured him. He laughed softly. "Like, I'm upvoting the shit out of this."

"Good," he whispered, then he kissed me. I deepened it. Deeper, and deeper.

"Oh," I whispered. "That's new."

"What?" I moved against him. He laughed; it sounded a bit like a surprised chicken then he nudged against me. "Oh, yeah, that happens sometimes," he whispered. "Especially when the hottest person I know is grinding against me with their tongue in my mouth."

I sniggered, resting my head against his, looking down between us. Although I couldn't quite see what I could feel.

"You want to see?"

"I…"

"You can," he nodded. "I mean, I'm happy to show you." He laughed. "That came out really professionally, and I didn't mean…"

"Brooklyn," I laughed. He grinned kissing me again before reaching between us.

"Come here," he whispered, lifting the quilt over our heads. He rose his finger to his lips. I grinned, a weird sense of excitement bubbling within me.

He knocked against me gently, before pulling on his bed shorts.

I very actively, and obviously choked.

"Damn, and it isn't even in your mouth."

I hit his chest.

"Oh, you got that one."

I shook my head at him, laughing until it just stopped.

"Can I touch you?"

"Oh, yes. Yes, you can," he said quickly. "Yes. Do so."

"How?"

"Oh." He took my hand, lacing our fingers together before tugging on my hand so I let him move it. "Open your hand." he laughed, gently. "You're not getting anywhere with a fist."

I did so, he stroked my hand down, well down his *penis*.

"That is your penis," I told him, in case he wasn't fully aware of that.

He gasped, and I seriously questioned his acting accolades.

"Is it?"

"Brook," I laughed. He kissed me, letting go of my hand, letting me stroke him, and touch him. Until he gasped, and I wanted to make him make that noise again.

"Oh, god, we're not doing this dry," he said lifting my hand from him up closer to us. "Spit."

"What?" I said

"Spit. If you don't, I will."

So I did. Frowning at him curiously until he moved my hand back down his body, before clasping my hand around him. He nodded to me, I nodded back, taking a breath then whining lightly as he began to move my hand.

It turned out Brooklyn had an issue with staying quiet which in turn created the issue of me giggling. Us both shushing each other breathlessly just in case we woke Quincy up.

When we settled, I knocked my head against his, a gentle thing that didn't have much of anything behind it.

"Brooklyn?" I whispered. He nodded biting his lip

gently so I kissed his cheek, then rested my lips next to his ear. "Can you make me feel like that?"

He swallowed.

"I would love to," he gasped then kissed me. Rolling us until I was lying flat on the couch, the cover falling down his shoulders.

I whimpered, as the street light caught him. The light streaming in and streaking across his chest. I let my eyes soak him in. He grinned at me before pulling up his shorts. I tutted.

"I was enjoying the view."

He smirked. "You can play with my dick to your hearts content and I can assure it will get hard again whilst I do this, but this is for you, okay?"

I nodded, swallowing, as he stroked over my thighs.

Series 10

Day 45

Eliza called a meeting. A meeting with myself, with Quincy, *herself*, Jordan, Eliana, and two producers who's names completely escaped me. I didn't even catch them on introductions because everyone just assumed that everyone already knew who the others around the table were.

The office we were in was completely surrounded by windows. We'd called it the Fish Bowl since we'd first stepped onto set because we could see it from where we filmed, and *occasionally* the producers and Eliana watched us from there. Like *we* were fish in a bowl.

We, as the actors, hardly ever got called into the Fish Bowl, it wasn't ever really necessary. Given we had our own break room and if we had to be told anything it was down to Eliza. Nine times out of ten because we'd give her more consideration than anyone else in the team.

Which was fair, because I was barely listening to them as they read through our contract looking or, I guess, trying to show us loopholes that didn't exist. We'd had five days to prepare.

I'd sent my contract to my dad. Quincy had their okasaan read over it, and AJ's cousin who was studying law. Arden had read it. Not one of them had found anything in there so instead of listening to their bullshit, I was watching what I think was Bargain Hunt on the TV in the hallway.

"So, as I'm sure you'll understand. There's not much we can do."

"No," Quincy sighed, sounding oddly calm. "There's nothing you're *willing* to do." They glanced at me. "You all freaked out when I, at fourteen, came out as nonbinary even though it had *no* impact on you, on the show, or my character. In case you haven't noticed, I still play Todd as male. I haven't made any changes because I never intended to."

"So Oz can continue to play Izzy as female," Jordan said.

"I hadn't finished. I'd appreciate it if you didn't interrupt me."

I swallowed as Eliza smirked gently. Jordan sunk back into his seat.

"*My* coming out didn't affect the character of Todd because, even now, I'm happy to present male. It does not cause dysphoria, it does not affect my mental health to do that. I am nonbinary, and you handled that *terribly*.

"Oz is trans, and although nonbinary comes under the trans umbrella, his transition is different to my coming out. Oz has transitioned from female to male. This means presenting female will affect his mental health, it will induce dysphoric feelings.

"Some of the things that have already taken place on set are simply transphobia."

"Could you please point out an instance?" one of the producers asked.

"The dress in the Halloween special was straight up a disregard for Oz's feelings and like you were trying to, I don't know, make a point that you believe he's a girl."

"You asked me to remove my binder during the sex scene with Brooklyn," I said. Quincy turned to look at me.

"What?" they hissed. "What the fuck?"

"You only stopped harassing me when Brooklyn told you to. You didn't listen to me at all when we were filming."

"Ah yes, Brooklyn is a good point. We will have to have a separate meeting with him, *but* you influencing him is not…"

"I did no such thing," I stated. "He quit with his own free will. He cannot be swayed in any way."

"It was very clear you influenced his decision on set that day, we have footage of a conversation between the two of you before he made his statement."

I shook my head. "He asked me if I was comfortable, and I said *no*. I didn't influence him in any way."

"I fully believe this," Eliza added. "Brooklyn is not easily influenced, if *he* chooses to do something, he will."

"You are in a sexual relationship with him," one of the producers said.

"So. I'm sucking his dick, not controlling his mind."

Eliza choked as Quincy gasped then applauded. I looked at them.

"It is inappropriate in the workplace. This is why we had to remove the character of Daniel from the show."

"Bullshit." Quincy laughed, although it sounded dark. "You did not remove Daniel because AJ and I started dating. I *know* you didn't. I was fifteen, I wasn't an idiot, you couldn't get away with talking about me and thinking I couldn't understand."

"Not everything has to be gay," Jordan snapped, hitting the table and making his water bottle topple over. "I'm so sick of this. It doesn't matter that you're *whatever* you are, primarily you are actors and that means you act, you play a part, that is different to yourself."

"We're not disputing that," Quincy replied. "No, I didn't ask for AJ to come in, the writers wrote in a queer romance for Todd. That wasn't any of my doing.

"Oz didn't request Kevin and Izzy finally get together. Eliana wrote that into the books."

"I also wrote Izzy as a girl," Eliana commented.

"A bad girl," I muttered. She rose an eyebrow at me. "Oh, she was. You didn't even want to write a romance plot for her because you didn't think she was a worthy girl. You only wrote her and Kevin into the last book because of the response of the series." I took a breath. "And *on* that, yes, Brooklyn and I are in a queer relationship but not once have we forced you to include that in the show. However, Kevin and Izzy's relationship is now queer whether you like it or not, simply because I am a boy. That is fact.

"We filmed a sex scene with me presenting male. It wasn't in any way a heterosexual scene. You're creating all these problems when you could've simply put me in male costume, acknowledged my transition in one conversation in episode one, then just moved on with the same plot."

"That would not work with the show."

Quincy laughed. "It's literally a show about magic." They turned to me. "But then again, I couldn't even have purple hair."

"Brooklyn couldn't have a nose ring," I shrugged dramatically.

"You can both be recast," the producer said, almost so softly that we missed it. Quincy rose their eyebrow

"Really? Series ten, the final series, and you're threatening recast *now*? You tried that once, remember? Back when I first came out, you said to me if I did not compile I'd be fired and recast. It still hasn't happened and, sweetheart, I stopped complying a long time ago."

"Then consider yourself fired," the producer said. Quincy genuinely looked surprised before turning to me with a shrug.

"Well, then, I guess I'm fired." They rose their wrist, reading their watch. "Only took six years. Good luck Oz." They stood, kissing my cheek before leaving the room. I followed them with my eyes as they did. The news had started on the TV.

Quincy stopped, looking at the TV so I didn't look away. I stood when a picture of Brooklyn came up on the screen.

"Eliza," I said. She stood with me, turning to look where I was.

Quincy opened the door. "There's been an accident."

I abandoned the table instantly walking towards them, reading the words on the TV.

STAR OF *ADOLESCENT SUMMERS* IN CAR ACCIDENT.

Series 3

Day 75

Brooklyn was crying. No, not crying, sobbing. Full on sobs, the tears not visible as they streamed down his cheeks as he struggled to catch his breath.

Eliza was knelt in front of him, her hands on his knees, speaking to him as he shook.

I probably shouldn't have been in the room, but I'd been sent off set so I went to the break room. I wasn't allowed out the building, not until I was sixteen, so, I just stood, awkwardly trying to figure out what I should do.

I very obviously jumped when Eliza said my name.

"Can you do me a favour?" she asked. I nodded because I assumed it'd be *leave the room*. "Can you go and get something smothered in chocolate for Brooklyn?"

Brooklyn laughed through his sobs. The sound breathy as he wiped the back of his hand across his nose. Eliza smiled at me, so I nodded and left.

I walked straight up to the dessert end of the lunch selection, examining all the things we were only allowed to have in moderation. I picked up a plate, then a cream filled, chocolate covered doughnut that was bigger than my face.

I took it back up to the breakroom. Brooklyn seemed to have calmed down considerably, his breathing far more controlled, his cheeks tear-stained but no more fell.

Eliza was sat next to him, her arm around his shoulders as he tore into a tissue. They both looked up at me together.

"Oh, that looks good," Eliza said. I approached them with the plate. She took it from me. "Just don't tell your orthodontist."

Brooklyn smiled at her, the barest slither of silver showing from his brace.

"You're a bad influence," he whispered as he took the plate and rested it on his thighs. Eliza nodded as she stroked his back.

"I've got to make some calls, okay? Don't worry," she said more to Brooklyn. "You, take a seat," she added to me. I nodded swallowing deeply as I walked so I could sit where she had been.

When she left the room, Brooklyn tore an edge from the doughnut, passing it to me with a sad smile. I took it because I didn't want him to cry again. I didn't like him crying.

I cleared my throat, he frowned at me curiously.

"I was about to ask if you're okay, but that's stupid, huh?"

"Yep," he whispered, then shrugged one shoulder. "My mum came back. A bit… sudden for me, I don't know if Dad was expecting her but she arrived last night and told us she was taking Dad to court, to gain custody of me."

"What?" I whispered. He sighed nodding then gave me more doughnut.

"Dad sent me out the room, told me he didn't want me to have to listen to it." He looked at me, I wanted to wipe his cheeks. "I sat on the stairs. She basically said she had seen how successful I was becoming and wanted a piece of it.

"Dad said he'd send her money, whatever she wanted, but he wasn't letting her have me. If she took him to court he'd fight, he'd fucking fight for me. She threatened to take me. If Dad wasn't going to give me willingly she'd…"

"She wants you that bad?" I asked in a whisper.

He shrugged a shoulder. "No, she wants my money, she wants my name and the security that comes with me."

"But… but…"

"Dad told Eliza. He dropped me off because he was scared she'd follow me and take me. He told Eliza the moment we arrived, so she came to talk to me and…" he waved his hand as if to say *this* was the result.

"I'm sorry."

"Bit shit, huh?" He shrugged. "She's never wanted me, *like* me especially."

"What do you mean?" I asked.

"I've got two older sisters," he nodded. "They're twenty-two and twenty-five. She stuck around with them, she had me then went away, just disappeared. Dad didn't know *what* the hell was going on and he had me, still a baby, and my seven-, and ten-year-old sisters.

"She eventually sent Dad an email telling him she couldn't handle it, didn't want to be a mother anymore, and just needed a new life."

"Wow," I whispered. "I… I can't even…" I shook my head because, sure, my mum and I had a rocky relationship but I truly couldn't imagine her just leaving me.

"Dad said in the car that he loves me and he doesn't care if I left this show tomorrow, he's not in this for my money, or my fame, or anything, he's in it for *me*. Always has been."

I looked back at him because I truly didn't know

what to say. What *should* you say? What shouldn't you? He exhaled nodding to me, so I nodded back.

"So your dad didn't make you go into TV then?" I said, which was supposed to sound like a joke. He did smile, barely.

"Did yours?"

"Dad? No," I shook my head. "My mum, well, I was in theatre school and they sent home a letter to audition for Mary Poppins on the West End. My mum signed me up, sent me to the audition."

"You got it?"

"Jane Banks, reporting for duty," I smirked.

"How did you get from the West End to here?"

"Mary Poppins, then I went into Matilda."

"As?"

"Matilda," I nodded.

"You can sing then, like *proper* good?"

I laughed.

"I guess. From Matilda I did some adverts; Sainsburys, Matalan, Birds Eye." I smiled gently at him. "From there I got an audition for this, and it sounds *bizarre* because I went from flame-grilled chicken to Izzy."

"Impressive."

"And what about you, then?"

"It was always my choice," he said, nodding. "My first role was a cameo on Doctor Who."

I smiled at him, he laughed softly.

"I was six, it had been a Blue Peter competition. I was the kid of just a random bystander. One episode glory. Still get screenshots sent to me all the time. After that I was in a few movies, between seven and nine, just background kids, or kid of a secondary character. I got my break when I was ten, CBBC series, I was a Wizard, it was sick." He laughed. "From that, I got this. I didn't even need to audition, one of the producers worked with me on the other show, so…" he shrugged. "Here I am, but Dad always tells me; anytime I want to quit, I can. Say the word, he won't be pissed or anything, just walk away. I guess, if she won and I quit, she'd give me back in a heartbeat. Right?"

"I…"

The door opened, Eliza came in.

"You better get back to set," she said. I nodded then stood. Brooklyn reached for me, holding my arm. I looked at him, he passed me a little more doughnut.

"Thank you," he whispered. "Thanks for distracting me."

I smiled at him.

"I hope it all works out okay."

Series 10

Day 45

I barely waited for Eliza to come to a complete stop before I was out of the car. I ran to the desk, my breath heavy as I searched for the function in my brain that let me say words.

"Brooklyn Sampson?" the man behind the desk said. I nodded. "He's on the fourth floor," he told me. I nodded again. "Private room."

"Thank you," I called back as I ran towards the lifts. They took far too long to come then get up to the fourth floor.

I broke into another run when the doors opened, following the corridors around even though I didn't really know where I was going. I soon ran into a waiting room, then straight into Brooklyn's dad's arms.

He wasn't Brooklyn, of course not, but he was as tall as him, he felt like him, he *smelt* like him and he cuddled me tight.

"What happened, Tony?" I asked, as he shushed me, his hand on the back of my head as his other rubbing my back. When I had calmed, and we both felt less chaotic, he sat me on the vinyl seats.

"I don't fully know what happened, Oz." He cleared

his throat, "I…" he sighed. "I was called because he was still awake, and he told them to call me, so he should remember what happened. He should be able to tell us. When I got here, he was already in surgery." He turned his wrist upside down to read his watch. "He's been in for two hours."

"Surgery for what?"

"His arm," he nodded. "At least, he went in for his arm. They could find other things." He took a long shallow breath then stood. I turned as he walked to Quincy and wrapped his arms around them.

"You didn't all have to come."

"Yes, we did," Quincy said nodding. "I mean initially because someone *had* to drive Oz, but it's Brooklyn, we had to come for Brooklyn. I've called AJ, too; he can't get out of work but he'll come straight here."

"Quincy…" Tony sighed, although it sounded fond. "Thank you."

Quincy bowed their head, then stepped aside so Tony could hug Eliza.

"Are you okay?" Eliza whispered. Tony shook his head, speaking so quietly to her that we couldn't hear him. Quincy sat beside me.

"He's in surgery," I whispered. "For his arm. There's something wrong with his arm, but Tony said he was awake, he… felt it all."

"Hey," Quincy whispered, wrapping their arms around me, pulling me close so our heads knocked against each other. "We don't fully know what happened yet, okay? Don't speculate."

"He'd have felt all the pain. He will have, all of it."

"Brook told me you guys were in a meeting today," Tony said as he walked back towards us.

I shook my head. "It doesn't matter, it can wait."

"No, tell me about it," he said sitting beside Quincy.

"Brook sent me regular updates on what was happening. So tell me, distract me. He won't be out of surgery for at least another hour."

"I was fired," Quincy said with a frown. "I *actually* legitimately think that I was fired," they said more to me.

"I did think you were handling it spectacularly well," Eliza commented as she sat on the row behind us, on the seat that backed onto Tony's. She rested her hand on his, stroking her thumb over his knuckles.

"Wait, they really were?" I asked. Eliza shrugged gently.

"What the producers say, goes." She sighed. "We'll figure it out, filming will be *definitely* postponed for a little while."

"I don't think Brooklyn wants to go back," Tony said with a frown. "I thought he'd quit."

"Apparently you have to do more than quit on this show," I sighed. "I think it's probably the blood oath we took in series one."

Quincy laughed softly. "You mean the one in the show?" they asked. I nodded hugely, they knocked against me. "What'd happen?"

"If you all resigned?" Eliza asked.

"Well, not me, as I obviously have now been fired. Do you think I'll get jobseekers?" they asked Tony. He laughed although it was quiet.

"I have no doubt in my mind they'd recast. They'd make up some lame excuse that gets you all out of the way, *maybe* even use the footage of Kevin getting stuck in the past, and never bring him back," she sighed. "They'd make you all redundant very quickly."

"They'd be shooting themselves in the foot, Tony said. "The show's *good*, but you kids, you make it so much more. Watching you all grow up, that's been special."

"That's very true," Eliza nodded. "You've become

fantastic adults but knowing you all since you were ten, seeing it happen before your eyes. I fully agree, Tony, they'd indeed be signing their own death warrant."

"The meeting went, well then?" Tony added. I bit my lip as Quincy sighed.

"It went as well as to be expected."

AJ arrived with two McDonalds bags, an uncertain amount of time later. Quincy exhaled gently, it sounded relieved *mostly,* a little amused probably at the inclination that AJ had knew we had definitely forgotten to eat.

He was right. Completely spot on. We were starving.

The doctor had come out to see us. He'd taken Tony back into the room with him. He hadn't returned yet. No word had been spread to us, I somehow felt even more in the dark than I had before.

AJ came to us. Giving me the bag, and Quincy a hug.

"I also brought you," he said reaching into his pocket, then showing Quincy their glasses. "Didn't think you'd want to stay in your contacts."

"I love you," Quincy sighed.

"Is there any news?" AJ asked, squeezing Quincy's shoulder. AJ nodded, reaching to open the bag, he retrieved a box from it, passing it to Quincy. "Eat," he said, then went back into the bag and held a box of chicken nuggets to me. "You guys need to eat."

I took the box.

"Oz," a man said so I turned towards his voice, the doctor. Brooklyn's doctor. "You can see him, now," he said. I swallowed, standing and walking towards him. "Are you attached to your chicken nuggets?" he asked.

I looked down at the box. "I need to eat," I whispered; his smile was sympathetic before he nodded towards the room Tony had gone into before.

"He's still drowsy, coming out of surgery. Might not

be fully responsive just yet, don't worry that's okay. It's to be expected," he said. I nodded. The doctor squeezed my shoulder as I stepped into the room.

Tony was sat beside the bed. Holding Brooklyn's hand, his fingers stroking over the back of his hand.

He turned when he heard me come.

"Do you want a chicken nugget?" I asked. My voice cracking but I didn't care. I barely registered it. He gave me a sad smile.

"Thanks," he said, taking one. I considered eating one but I still wasn't all too sure if I actually wanted to eat. Not when Brooklyn was lying there, his skin waxy, his arm in a cast, scratches on the side of his face. "He was awake," he said softly, looking back to Brooklyn as he ate the nugget. "He was here for a second, then straight back to sleep. I think he'll be okay. I need the bathroom. Would…" he swallowed. "Will you be okay?"

I nodded. He stood. Squeezing my shoulder as he passed me and left the room.

I walked towards the bed, placing the box of nuggets on the chair Tony had been sat on then taking Brooklyn's hand.

"This is all wrong," I told him. "*This* was never, ever meant to happen. It's the wrong way around. You're meant to be sat at my bedside as I wake up from the best surgery of my life, *not* me sat here, after the scariest surgery of both of ours." I stroked my fingers against his hand. "I fought today. I really tried to, I told them all I was sucking your dick," I laughed. "I went in there fighting for myself, because of you, but *fuck that*. No, I'm not fighting for me anymore, I'm going to fight every single day for you, because it looks like you're going to need a little help." I rose his hand, kissing his fingers.

"I love you, Brooklyn. I loved you yesterday, I love you today, and I will love you for all of our tomorrows."

I whispered, resting my head against his hand. "I love you so, so much and if you wake up, and you tell me you got distracted whilst driving again, I'll see to killing you myself," I teased. I lowered my head to his hand and then I began to cry.

Series 8

Day 16

Brooklyn looked tired when he finally emerged from bed. I'd left him a while ago, mostly because I had been hungry and he was fast asleep, practically dead to the world.

I'd sat with Quincy eating cereal and watching kids cartoons until they went upstairs to take a bath, and Brooklyn had come down.

"Are you okay?" I asked. He shook his head before lifting his hands and pressing his palms into his eyes.

"Headache," he said. "Mostly. I feel a bit sick, too."

I tapped the couch next to me, he came and slumped on it, like a deflating balloon.

"I feel floppy," he told me. I smiled, biting my lip so he couldn't see how much it had amused me.

"What do you want? Paracetamol?"

He sighed. "Sure."

"You're a baby," I teased. He whined at me as I stood and went into the kitchen. He willingly swallowed the pill, before grinning at me as he tugged the water bottle stopper open with his teeth.

He reached for me just before I sat down. He drank more water, then paused.

"Can…" he winced. "I want to read but words are fuzzy. A does not sit next to B in my head anymore."

"But you want a story?" I asked. He nodded. "Want me to read a book? To you?"

"Would you?" he whispered.

"Which book?" I asked, smiling at him. He pointed towards the bookshelf.

"Run your finger across it until I say stop."

"That's risky. You might get one of AJ's books."

He smirked, drinking from the bottle again.

"I'll risk it. You never know, I might have an interest in…"

"Banking and finance," I offered as I continued stroking my finger over the spines.

"You never know… Stop."

I did. Pulling the spine out and showing him the front of the book.

"Hey, it's queer," he sounded pleased. "Must be one of Quincy's. Please read me it."

I nodded taking a seat on the end of the couch. He shuffled down so he could lie his head on my thighs. I began to stroke through his hair.

He impressively stayed quiet and let me read. Barely interrupting until the paracetamol had completely kicked in.

"You know, after *Adolescent Summers*…" he started, as his finger stroked over the words on the page. The words 'I'm gay'. I don't think it was conscious, *not* really. He was definitely distracted by the question he hadn't asked yet.

"Yes?"

"What do you want to do?" he looked up at me, it looked *really* awkward for his neck. I stroked his hair out his eyes.

"What do you mean?"

"Do you want to keep acting?"

"I kind of thought this was it now. I'm an actor. No go backs."

"That's not how that works," he laughed then turned, so his head was lying flat on my thighs and he could look up at me without it looking painful.

"What do you want to do?"

"Well, I want to act," he laughed. "But I want to do voice work, I want to be a cartoon character, a Disney princess, you know…"

I grinned at him as he closed his eyes.

"But I'd also really, *really* like to do some queer films. Queer TV shows. *Fuck*, I'd love to be so explicitly queer on screen."

"Yeah?" I whispered. He nodded without opening his eyes. "Do you want to be with a boy?"

He opened his eyes, then he frowned.

"What?"

"I don't know… I just… you seem to really be…"

"Hey," he whispered. "I love you. You've just sat there and read to me, like four chapters because I feel sick, you're the best. I *am* queer, that's something that is just fact. I think that makes this a queer relationship, regardless."

"Huh," I murmured. He laughed softly although it sounded a *little* pained. "Sorry," I added, shushing him as I stroked his hair.

"Sorry?"

"For hurting your head."

He tapped my hand as if comforting me.

"I don't *want* to be with a boy, I want to be with you. If I stop wanting to be with you, I'll let you know by formal letter, with at least two working weeks' notice."

I laughed, resting my head back against the couch.

"God, I love you."

"So, what do you want to do?"

"I…" I sighed. "I don't know."

"Liar. It's like when Daniel was killed, AJ just went *fuck it*, and did his exams and is now in university studying to be a money man."

"Banker," I laughed. "It was a *big* U-turn."

"He wanted to be making the money." He rose his hand, rubbing his first finger and thumb together.

"He could've been a kept woman," I said. "I don't think I want to keep acting," I added. "I don't know, it's complicated. I don't feel like I've had *much* of a chance to explore other things."

"Then we explore," he offered, then opened his eyes. "We explore cooking, and painting, and…" he laughed, "aeroplane model making."

"You'd do that?"

"Oh yes, let's build an aeroplane."

I laughed.

"Do you feel better?"

He moaned, turning so his face was against my stomach.

"You know what might make me feel better?" he whispered, as he stroked his nose against my stomach.

"If you say chicken nuggets, I swear."

"Jam toast," he laughed, then looked up. "Chicken nuggets, though."

"No, I'll make you some toast." I tapped his back. "Never know, I might become a chef."

He grinned at me, sitting up so I could stand. He drank from his water bottle, watching me as I left the room. He called my name just before I got into the kitchen.

"Can I have a cup of tea, too, please?"

I laughed. "Yes, I suppose you can."

Series 10

Day 46

There was a hand stroking through my hair. Pulling, almost, as if trying to get my attention. I had fallen asleep. I don't know *when* I had, I didn't know when I'd stopped crying and fell asleep or whether I'd stopped crying at all.

I assumed the hand belonged to Tony.

I looked up, my eyes blurry, my head hurt. The hand stilled in my hair; their hand flat.

Brooklyn was smiling at me.

"Are those chicken nuggets?"

I leaped on him. My arm wrapping around his neck, my head burying itself in his shoulder.

He moaned lightly; I must've hurt him. Shit. I looked at him.

"It's okay, it's good pain," he said. "Okay, maybe not good, but…"

"Hi," I whispered.

"Hello, darling."

I kissed him.

"What the *fuck* happened Brooklyn?"

He looked past me; his eyes landed on the chicken nugget box again.

"Hey, come back to me."

"I'm hurt," he whispered, but did meet my eyes. "I'm sorry."

I sighed lightly reaching past him for the nurse buzzer.

A nurse came in pretty sharpish. A nice-looking man who I hadn't met yet. I glanced at Brooklyn he rose an eyebrow.

"Tell me, honestly," he said reaching for me. "Are we on set?"

"What? No? Have you got concussion?" I shook my head.

He smiled gently at me. "Nurses aren't supposed to be *that* attractive."

"Well, then," the nurse said in a laugh. "I'm your day nurse. Shift change," he shrugged as he walked towards the bed. "Good morning."

"Brooklyn wants to know if he can have a chicken nugget?" I asked.

The nurse laughed. "How do you feel?"

"My arm hurts," he said, then crinkled his nose at the cast.

"Would you like some pain killers?"

"Do you have morphine?" he gasped.

"Let's start a bit weaker? Yeah?"

"Yeah," Brooklyn muttered then watched, intrigued as the nurse, who I'd found the name tag of and discovered was called Andy, administered the pain killer.

"Yes, you can have a chicken nugget."

"Winner," Brooklyn muttered. "I need to take my Ritalin, too."

"It's okay, we'll have a bit of a drug holiday."

"But…" he frowned. "Okay."

"I'm available at your beck and call, okay?" he said. "Both of you," he added with a sympathetic smile to me. I nodded my thanks. "Do you want me to invite your friends in? The two in the waiting room?"

"Quincy," I explained to Brooklyn then I frowned. "You don't know who we are?"

Andy smirked at me. "I know *full* well who you are. My wife loves you but here, you're my patient, and I am your nurse. You're just kids, who have been involved in an accident," he sighed. "I figure you don't want to be treated like *celebrities*."

"Your wife loves us?" I repeated.

"Before we had our baby it was our show, but we watched every single episode, multiple times, because she loved *Adolescent Summers*. I'm just waiting for my baby to get a little older, then I'm sure we'll rewatch it all."

I turned back to Brooklyn, smirking lightly then scoffing and getting off the bed to retrieve the chicken nuggets.

"Thank you, Andy," I said.

"I'll send Quincy in," he said softly, leaving the room as I sat back on the bed.

"Do I need to goad you with chicken nuggets?"

"Potentially," he whispered. I got one out of the box.

"What happened Brooklyn?"

"I crashed," he said meekly.

I moved the nugget away. "I'm going to need better than that. I... I was so scared."

"So was I," he whispered. I gave him the chicken nugget. "I swerved. I was... I was going to get us some food, because I knew you'd be drained after your meeting, and I wanted to cook and get us some wine and..." he ate the chicken nugget. "I guess my car is public knowledge."

"What?" I frowned.

"A group recognised my car, I was sat at the lights, so I *saw* them recognise it, I could actually hear them but I really thought when I drove away, they'd move on."

"They didn't?" I asked.

He shook his head. "They ran out in front of me, so I swerved."

"And that's how you crashed?"

"That's how I crashed," he repeated. "It kind of shook me, because I swerved sideways, straight into a parked car. The traffic coming the other way didn't quite stop immediately."

I swallowed deeply; his forehead creased.

"The group just disappeared. When the car rammed my door."

"Your arm," I whispered.

"It hurt *so* bad I thought I was going to be sick. I just kind of went dizzy, and then began to cry."

I whimpered lightly; his forced smile looked apologetic. I hated that he felt like he had to apologise to me, but I'd address that later.

"The ambulance woman came. I got my dad's number up on my phone told her to call him, then I'm pretty sure I passed out." He seemed to think about something, his nose crinkled as if the thought process was painful. "The next thing I remember was waking up, and seeing you asleep, then being *so* hungry."

"You were in surgery for hours," I whispered.

"Hours," I heard behind me. I turned as Quincy sighed and leant against the doorframe. They took their glasses off, rubbing their eyes.

"Quincy," Brooklyn said cheerfully.

"Haven't lost your memory then?"

"No, course not. You're straight, right?"

"Sacrilege," Quincy gasped, "careful I don't break your other arm."

"Meow," Brooklyn whispered. I laughed as Quincy walked towards us. They sat behind me on the bed, wrapping their arm around my shoulders and knocking their head against mine. "Can I have another chicken nugget?" Brooklyn asked. I grinned passing him the box.

"Have them all."

"Nuh uh," Quincy said. "You haven't eaten yet, eat something."

I took a nugget.

"What happened in the meeting?" Brooklyn asked.

Quincy scoffed. "You were *literally* in a car crash; you don't need to hear about our metaphorical car crash."

"Hear, hear," I muttered.

"Where's AJ?" Brooklyn asked.

I glanced at Quincy as they laughed softly. "I'm getting conversational whiplash, Brook."

"I'm on a drug holiday," he said. He sounded somewhat pleased. Quincy sighed.

"AJ's calling work. Telling them he can't come in, then he's going to get some breakfast."

"He's a good wife," I teased. Quincy laughed nodding into my shoulder.

"He doesn't have to stay off work for me."

"He isn't," Quincy whispered. "He's staying off work because he's shattered."

I laughed.

"You're family Brooklyn. We would go to the end of fucking universe for you. But if you get into a crash again, I *swear*."

"It wasn't his fault," I whispered. "This time." I rose my eyebrow at Brooklyn, he snorted lightly, knocking his chest three times. I did it back to him.

"Last time I was an idiot, and it wasn't quite so... *hospital*."

"And that's why your car has *character*," Quincy teased. Brooklyn smirked gently although it dropped.

"I was so scared," he frowned. "Scared of so many things, in such quick concession. For a moment, I genuinely thought I was going to die."

"Hey," I whispered reaching for his hand. He squeezed my fingers.

"I think I was more afraid that I was going to hit them. That's why I swerved so much, I guess," he shook his head, so much his hair flopped back and forth. "How long will I be in here?"

I shook my head as Quincy sighed.

"A week."

We turned together, Tony smiled from the doorway.

"Looking rough, kid."

"Feeling rough," Brooklyn nodded. "Why a week? That sounds excessive for just a broken arm."

"Somewhat," Tony agreed. "But it's more so for your safety," he added. Brooklyn frowned, then paled when Tony opened the window.

Screams flooded the room, Brooklyn's name being repeated over, and over.

"My god, they should solve crime," Quincy said as they stood from the bed, looking through the window. They must've been just out of sight considering the screams didn't increase in volume. "Has there been any reports?"

"Only that he was in an accident, no information has been released," Tony said as he leant on the wall looking out of the window. "You should see Twitter." He exhaled. "Your fans *are* a little bit scary. Which is why when I spoke to Nurse Andy, he said it was wise to keep you for at least a week, because you'll get swarmed the moment you step outside."

"Oh," Brooklyn murmured.

"Can I stay with him?" I asked.

"I believe so. I think Andy can make you up a bed."

"I can't share with him?"

Tony smirked at me.

"I don't think that'd be too wise, no?"

Brooklyn smiled at me. I smiled shyly back at him. The screams intensified, I looked to Quincy as they covered their mouth.

"Oh, poor AJ." They glanced at Tony. "But I hope you know I will *not* be helping him."

"True love," Tony laughed.

"He's a big boy. He can handle it," they smirked as Tony squeezed their shoulder.

"So you're going to need to tell me what happened," Tony said. Brooklyn sighed dramatically, leaning his head back against the pillow.

"Can you wait until AJ gets up here, and I'll tell everyone in one go?"

"Where has AJ gone?"

"Breakfast. He's getting you a coffee."

"He's my favourite," Tony nodded. Brooklyn lolled his head towards me, so I kissed his fingers.

AJ appeared in the doorway, he looked a little wide eyed.

"It's like you're famous or something," he breathed, then placed the paper bag on the end of the bed. "Coffee," he offered to Tony. "Coffee," he gave to Quincy, they hummed appreciatory, the steam fogging up their glasses.

"Adrian-Jacob, you are an angel," Quincy said. AJ smirked as Brooklyn laughed.

"I *never* knew what AJ stood for."

I shook my head. "I genuinely didn't think it stood for anything."

"Adrian-Jacob Lawson was a bit of a mouthful for Equity. And I told you that in confidence."

Quincy squeaked.

"They're going to hear it at the wedding anyway," they said, their voice high. AJ gave, wrapping his arms around Quincy, a special kind of smile on his face.

"Excuse me," Brooklyn interrupted. "I have been in a serious accident, can I please be the centre of attention again?"

"I think he's going to be okay," Tony said.

Series 7

Day 127

Brooklyn looked like a child as he walked towards me with a big grin on his face. His hands behind his back, his costume on. Kevin's outfit was surprisingly low-key today; just a long white Vans t-shirt with the sleeves turned up, and light blue skinny jeans with big rips in the knees and a pair of mulberry-coloured Vans. He must've been filming present day. Fillers, I assume.

He almost looked frustrated that I didn't ask after his grin straight away.

I thought about dragging it out a little longer. I decided it wasn't quite worth it.

"What have you done?"

"I got told off," he said. I bit my lip so I wouldn't laugh.

"Why did you get told off?"

"I'm not wearing appropriate boxers," he nodded. I rose my eyebrow at him.

"Want to see?" he grinned.

I snorted. "Was this just a ploy to get me into your pants?"

"No, no…" he laughed, shaking his head at me. "No, I genuinely got told off."

I eyed him, he nodded again. "Well, now I need to

see why."

He opened his arms to me, as if saying have at it. I watched him for a second longer, then reached for his button. I pulled on it, then laughed in a moan type way when four more popped open instead of a zip fly. He lifted the bottom of his t-shirt too, I assume be helpful.

I pulled on his waistband, then I cackled.

"Brooklyn," I gasped.

"Speaking of boxers," Eliza said. We both jumped, Brooklyn turning his head to her as I hid my flustered face. "As Quincy is now eighteen, GQ has been in touch to do a shoot with you. They will be expecting an underwear picture or two."

Brooklyn grinned, a mischievous grin that I knew meant he was about to play with Eliza.

"Can I choose my own boxers?"

Eliza looked pointedly at me, and where my hand still remained against the waistband of his boxer shorts.

"Can I go to watch?"

She rolled her eyes. "Before you make any decisions, I am going to have a conversation with Quincy." She looked between us pointedly. "Behave."

"Never," Brooklyn laughed. I snorted gently as Eliza walked away.

"Why did you get into trouble? No one should be able to see your boxers, right?"

"I'm doing a change scene," he waved his hand. "Modern day to future, I think." He looked confused, I accidently let my fingers slip lower into his pants.

He gasped at me, smirking when he did.

"Can't wardrobe redress you?"

"Apparently, Jordan found them funny so, requested they didn't."

I smirked. He grabbed my wrist so quick I almost jumped because I wasn't expecting it. He lifted my hand, so it kind of just flopped in front of us.

"You're going to make me hard."

"That was the plan."

Quincy had agreed to the GQ shoot. Surprisingly quickly, given Eliza's response. She'd allowed me to go without further conversation, she probably figured it'd be easier than making me stay on set.

She let Brooklyn drive.

She was being *particularly* lenient with us, or maybe she was just tired of us, it was nearing the end of the series after all. I was the designated Satnav, holding Brooklyn's phone to ensure he actually went to the right place.

"It'd have been quicker to walk," Quincy commented as we sat in back-to-back traffic. They lent their elbow on my seat, looking out of the front window. I glanced down at Brooklyn's phone, another minute had been added to our arrival time.

"Why did you agree to this?" I asked.

Quincy shrugged gently. "I like GQ, I think they'd treat me okay. And I got an afternoon off set."

"And everyone's already seen you in your underwear, right?" Brooklyn laughed as he ran his hands around the steering wheel.

"Less," Quincy laughed. Brooklyn turned his head, his expression amused. "It blew up. Almost instantly. I made the account because of AJ's ban, I put it on my private Snapchat and an hour later we had like a *thousand* subscribers."

"Who'd have thought you be in such high demand?"

"Uh, me," Quincy laughed. I grinned at them as the traffic moved. "It's so much fun. Like if this whole *acting* thing falls through I think we could survive off it."

I grinned at them, they winked as Brooklyn's phone

proclaimed *turn right*.

"I would," Brooklyn replied. "But there is no right to turn."

"Brooklyn," I said. He looked at me. "Brooklyn stop."

We bounced off the car in front.

"Fuck," Brooklyn muttered, then groaned when the car behind us bumped into our back. The car jolted.

I dropped Brooklyn's phone. Quincy fell forward, colliding with my chair. I heard their light moan as my car moved. Brooklyn hit the steering wheel before being flung back against the seat. He punched the steering wheel lightly.

"Fuck," he repeated, then turned the keys in the ignition. He got out the car as I turned to Quincy.

"Are you-" I stopped. "Your nose is bleeding."

They rose their eyebrow at me, then wiped their hand across their nose. Their sign was almost amused when they saw the blood streak.

"I'll be fine," they shook their head. "Just headbutted your chair."

I searched around until I found a packet of tissues.

"Your boyfriend is a risk," they laughed as they took a tissue out and held it to their nose. I looked out the window as Brooklyn spoke to a man and a women, both were shaking their head, and waving their hands at him. None of them looked all too angry.

"At least we were hardly moving," I said as I searched the footwell. I soon found his phone. It was fine, no *new* cracks in the screen, or at least I didn't think so – he wouldn't be able to tell if his life depended on it.

Brooklyn got back into the car.

"Well?" Quincy asked.

Brooklyn shook his head. "All fine. The man was mildly annoyed, then the woman told him I was famous, and proved it, so he shrugged it off because his kid loves *Adolescent Whatever's* and it wasn't really that much damage anyway.

"So, of course I couldn't be pissed at the woman for whatever damage to my bumper, so I took a selfie with both of them and we just went our separate ways." He turned to Quincy. "Shit, you okay?"

"I'll live," Quincy waved their hand.

"Can we agree to *not* tell Eliza about this?" He looked between us, I waved at him because, sure. Quincy laughed.

"And when she asks what happened to your bumper?"

"Lamppost, or whatever," he sighed. "Come on, Quincy."

"I won't say anything, don't worry," they laughed. "I've got your back as much as you've got mine."

"Shit," Brooklyn laughed, then shook himself off. "Okay, are we still up for going to this shoot?"

"Sure," Quincy laughed.

"If you're not, I'll put on some boxers and pose with Brooklyn," I offered.

Brooklyn snorted as he turned the ignition back on.

"We can do that any time you wish, and you *are* already wearing my boxers." I sniggered, looking out the window as I bit the tip of my thumb so I didn't tell him how much it delighted me, *or* how giddy it made me. The car moved, I looked back at him.

"Are you okay?" I asked.

"Fine, fine. Not hurt, just a bump."

I reached across and squeezed his thigh. He rested his hand on mine. Squeezing softly, before lifting it and kissing the back of it.

Series 10

Day 48

Andy made me a bed. A surprisingly comfortable bed *but* I still ended up lying with Brooklyn. Facing him, my hand under my head, the other stroking over Brooklyn's cast, which was now green after he'd asked Andy if it could be coloured, and Andy had compiled with the request.

I could feel his knees against mine, his elbow knocking against mine whenever he breathed. We hadn't shared a single bed since we were fooling around.

We weren't fooling around now, it wasn't even a consideration. Tony had been around most of the day, Eliza too. AJ had gone back to work and Quincy had somehow managed to escape the hospital and go home.

Brooklyn had been putting a damn face on all day. The first night, in my makeshift bed, we'd slept. I slept because I was exhausted, *he* slept because he was drugged up to his eyeballs but today, Andy had lessened the pain medication and Tony had stayed until the last possible visiting minute which I know Brooklyn had appreciated. He loved his dad of course, but he still put on an *everything's okay* persona, which I saw drop when Tony left.

He excused himself to the bathroom, took some time

to himself, then returned and we got ready for bed. We watched some TV on the far-too-small television then acted as if we were going to bed.

We did try or, at least, I did but I gave up all attempts when I heard him crying. I got out of my makeshift bed and climbed into his without another word.

He'd cried a little harder, burying his head in my chest and I let him, I let him until he began to quieten and now we were just lying looking at each other.

"Sorry," he whispered.

"Don't be sorry, you're more than allowed to have feelings."

"More than allowed?" he laughed. I knocked my elbow against his. "I'm feeling a lot of things and I can't even rationalise them."

"What's the most prominent?"

"Pain," his voice wobbled. "My arm hurts so bad. I think Andy's torturing me."

I smiled because I could hear the tease in his voice, *the* Brooklyn-ism that made even the worse things in his head light-hearted.

"What do you mean you can't rationalise them?"

He sniffed. "I can't hold onto one thing long enough to think about it." He moved around a little, his knees bumping against mine. "Like, I think about how much worse it could've been than just my arm, then all of a sudden I'm thinking, I could've hit that group of kids.

"I could've gone into them and injured them, I could killed them, or I could've been killed then, would anyone have heard my side, or would I be sent to jail, or…"

"Brooklyn."

"Sorry," he whispered. "My head's so busy." He headbutted me. "And my body isn't busy enough to keep up with it."

"Let's go for a walk," I whispered. He frowned, I

could feel it more than I could see it. "Just a walk, no funny business."

"Can you put my hoodie on?"

"I think it might be a bit big on me," I said.

"Oz," he moaned, as I got off the bed.

"I'm going to turn on the light," I warned him. I heard his groan before I even found the switch. It just intensified when I successfully flicked them on.

I found his hoodie quite quickly. Draped over the visitors chair. He was sat up when I turned back. His cheeks tear-stained, his eyes red-rimmed.

I walked to the bed, climbing on and kneeling in front of him. I gathered his hoodie in my hands, making it easier to pull over his head.

I didn't even attempt to pull the sleeve over his cast, opting for pushing it in so that it didn't annoy him.

I wiped my thumb over his cheeks, sighing gently as he shook his head away from my hand. Instead, I reached for his duvet.

"What are you wearing?" I whispered. I looked back at him as I smirked at the grey joggers. "Not your normal bed attire."

He laughed weakly. "I couldn't very well sleep naked, could I?"

"I see no issue," I whispered as I got off the bed again and retrieved his chucks.

"Imagine if someone saw me dressed like *this*, though?" he sighed as he pulled his chucks on, one handed. "I'd be featured in *Hello* within the hour. *Teen star lets himself go.*"

I smiled sympathetically at him as I walked towards him. I lifted his foot, tying his lace. He moaned.

"You're ruining my aesthetic," he mocked. I laughed as I lifted his other foot.

"I'm saving you from breaking your other arm."

He pulled his tongue at me, I did it back. He stood, as I crouched to tie the laces of my Air Forces. I paused.

"What?" he whispered.

"I was just…" I stood up. "Wouldn't you like to go outside and *not* be wearing brands?"

"Sometimes, yes," he sighed. "Don't you remember when I left the house in sweats and a Crystal Palace top?"

"Oh god, yes," I almost laughed as we started down the corridor. "I saved a lot of the zoomed in pictures of your sweats."

He punched my shoulder lightly.

"I remember fans sent you Crystal Palace merch for *months.*"

"Literally," he sighed. "And Jordan thought he had something to talk to me about." He shivered dramatically. "It was frightening. I don't know. It's shit, but also, the best thing ever. I love when we get random parcels from ASOS or Boohoo, or…" he tapped his foot against mine, "Nike. It's so exciting. Like big brands just send us stuff because we're on their radar. That's *exciting.*"

"When you put it that way," I said looking up at him. He smiled back at me. "I think I might've figured out what I want to do after all this."

"Really?" he breathed. "Do you want to be a Disney Princess, too?"

"No," I laughed. "But if you ended up in a queer film, I wouldn't say no to an audition." I tilted my head towards him, he did it back.

"You want to keep acting?"

"Glutton for punishment," I nodded. "I want to go back onto the stage."

"Oh, yeah?"

"Plays, musicals, I *loved* doing musicals. Shakespeare." I took a breath. "Can you imagine, a trans Hamlet, a trans…" I waved my hand, "Romeo."

"That'd be *incredible.*"

"I'm going to have to train my voice back, since I broke it."

He laughed childishly. "Since you broke it?"

I nodded to him, biting my lip so I wouldn't laugh.

"But I also can't wait to say goodbye to *Adolescent Summers,*" I shook my head. "It's kind of sad that the best thing in my life, turned into this…"

"Hear, hear," he sighed. "But new horizons. I think a break first, though. I need some time to stop and stand still. To *exist.* I think lockdown told me that. I loved being at home, with you and Bud, just being twenty-fucking-three. I don't care if my fame goes away, or people stop following me on Twitter, or whatever.

"I'd rather do one indie film that has strong values I agree with, over a multi-million pound TV series that haven't even sent a card after their lead was in a car accident."

We stopped by a vending machine.

"I think that's what's fucking me up right now. I could've died, and they would've just recast."

I dropped a pound into the machine, he sighed leaning against it.

I looked at him, he closed his eyes.

"They fired Quincy," I said. "At our meeting. They sent me a text this afternoon, said they'd received an email confirming termination of employment."

"You're kidding?" his voice was low. I shook my head as the bar of chocolate fell to the bottom of the machine.

"They forwarded me it. There was a list of reasons. One was pornographic content."

"Shit," he sighed as I dropped another pound into the machine. I held the two chocolate bars up to him. He took one, then walked ahead.

I followed until he took a seat on a window ledge. He sighed, resting his body and his head against the window then attempted to unwrap the bar. I sat opposite him, watching, waiting to see if he'd ask for help.

He didn't, opting to use his teeth.

"I know why you didn't tell me about your meeting," he said. "But can you now?"

"You want the highlights?"

"I want what happened, why Quincy got fired, what they did to you."

"They didn't get to me," I said quickly. "You saw to that. '*Adolescent Summers* star in car accident'."

"Did I make the news?"

"Oh, yes."

"Cool," he laughed. I smiled at him although it dropped when I began to recount the meeting to him.

He didn't have a reply straight away, so I looked out the window watching as the sky turned pink. The top of the sun just visible on the horizon.

"Things are pretty dark right now, huh?" he whispered. I didn't turn.

"But the sun *is* rising," I whispered back.

Series 6

Day 10

Brooklyn's eighteenth was *never* going to be a quiet affair. It being on a Wednesday night was strange, though.

We were all on the rota to film on Thursday. Well, actually, we were all due in, in just less than eight hours. I had been checking that; Quincy couldn't care less.

They were thoroughly enjoying the range of alcohol available as Brooklyn – and it *definitely* was Brooklyn, Tony had played no part in the chaos – had spared no expense.

There was shot pyramids and multicoloured cocktails, spirits, beers, and so much champagne. By now, a lot of it was drunk. Quincy had played a part in getting rid of most of the cocktails. Dakota had too, come to think of it, but she'd disappeared.

I'd drank my fair share. Which I'm sure was why I'd completely misplaced everyone. I'd never been drunk before. I didn't quite know if I'd succeeded in the whole enough-alcohol-to-count-as-drunk thing, but I definitely felt a little unstable.

Wobbly, I felt wobbly and a little like I wanted to find someone to kiss, but I wasn't good at it. I don't know if it was because I had a pretty intense crush on Brooklyn or because I was just bad at it. Potentially the latter.

I stopped when I found Quincy, sat on a couch, cocktails around their feet, their hands hidden under AJ's jacket as they kissed. Go Quincy.

I was *famous*, it shouldn't be this hard to get someone to want to kiss me. I leant on the wall watching as he laughed and sang loudly along to One Direction's *What Makes You Beautiful*, a bottle of beer in his hand raised above his head, his other was wrapped around Molly's shoulders.

Her long brown hair fell over his arm, stopping just above the hem of her dress. I let my eyes linger down, smiling at her knee-high socks and Doc Martens. When she turned, *also* a bottle of beer in hand, also singing loudly to One Direction, I saw she was wearing an army jacket over her dress, the sleeves turned up to her elbows paths sewn all over it. I focused in on the little heart, that was striped pink, yellow, and blue.

She was cool, *undeniably* cool, I understood what Brooklyn had seen in her, I understand what he might still. She was beautiful, gorgeous inside and out, funny, her personality like a firecracker.

I didn't *think* they were still a thing, I assumed not given how the moment a NDA was waved in front of her she'd basically told him she didn't want to be restricted in what she could say, or do, or *feel* and honestly, I got that. God, I understood that so deeply.

I continued past them. Laughing and singing along for the bit of music that Brooklyn called my name and goaded me into. *Yep* I was drunk.

Which is the only explanation for what my eyes thought I could see when I passed the room where Brooklyn's washer and dryer was.

I stopped, allowing the shock to flood out of me with

a high-pitched.

"Dakota."

She visually jumped, as did Jordan who she was wrapped up in.

They both began repeating my name in quick concession. I shook my head, waving my hands as I backed off. Closing the door behind me and continuing through the house.

Quincy was thankful all of Todd's scenes were low energy. Brooklyn, and for some reason I, were nowhere near that lucky. We were running from set to set, high stakes in every single one of them.

Todd just had to sit on the computer and speak to us on speaker phone. I was envious which I informed them of, whilst lying back on the clubhouse bed. Which regretfully wasn't a bed at all. It was just a heavy padded selection of boxes with a duvet and pillows thrown on top.

So I didn't throw myself onto it, quite like how I'd wanted to, and I truly wasn't expecting Brooklyn to. My stomach jumped when he landed with a thump behind me, I genuinely thought the bed was going to collapse but somehow, it didn't, and he wrapped his arms around me, his head resting against the back of mine.

I rose my eyebrow at Quincy. They laughed.

"Do you think they'll be able to tell we're all hungover to *fuck*?"

"I will very actively Tweet that it's Brooklyn's fault."

He laughed behind me. I felt it on my neck sending a shiver right through my body.

"Where did you end up last night?" I asked Quincy.

"I *may've* had sex with AJ."

Brooklyn groaned behind me.

"Where in my house did you have sex?"

Quincy lifted their fingers to their lips, winking at me so I laughed, turning my head to look at Brooklyn. I had a *different* question on my lips, but it died in my throat, when I lowered his t-shirt neck.

"Is that a hickey?"

He laughed instantly, burying his head further into my back.

"Shh."

Quincy gasped coming and standing over me, pushing Brooklyn back by the shoulder, he groaned lightly.

"Who was sucking on your neck? Dracula?"

"*Lady* Dracula," Brooklyn snorted gently then he sighed, resigned. "Molly and I..." he waved.

"Molly?" I interrupted as Quincy laughed. "I thought you and Molly aren't together?"

"No, no we're not. Haven't been for like two years but *sometimes* we might fall into bed together or... whatever."

I rose my eyebrow at Quincy, they laughed.

"Get it where it's good," they shrugged *mostly* at me, but Brooklyn punched up in agreement.

"We were drunk, *mostly*. She suggested it. I consented," he shrugged. "Wardrobe has already given me grief for it."

I sniggered.

"Brooklyn, darling, you should get them where no-one can see," Quincy cooed. I frowned up at them as Brooklyn laughed.

"Oh yeah? You trained AJ well, have you?"

They nodded, as I let my eyes scan their body. They tapped their thigh so I looked back up at them, they winked.

I turned when Dakota said my name.

"Can I..." she waved vaguely off set. I detangled

myself from Brooklyn, regretfully, and followed her through the set until we were obviously far enough away for her.

"Look, what you saw last night…" she said quickly.

"I saw you and Jordan, kissing," I confirmed, frowning. "Well, I assume it was just kissing, you were sat on the dryer, and I couldn't see his hands."

"Just, forget about it, okay?"

"No," I said, without hesitation. "Dakota you're *fifteen*." She looked away from me. "He's… not, *and* not only that, but he's also our director, and a dick."

"You don't know him like I do."

"No, I certainly don't." I said, "maybe I'm not his type." *Wait that was mean.*

"It's not seedy, or anything like that. I like him, he likes me." She paused. "And he's only twenty-eight."

"*Only*," I repeated. "Dakota that's so wrong."

"What do you *fucking* know? You're hopelessly in love with someone who doesn't even see you."

That was mean.

"What the *fuck*, Dakota?" I said taking a few steps away from her. "At least the boy I like is well within the legal age range for me to date. What he's doing is statutory rape."

"He's not grooming me."

"He doesn't need to be!" I snapped. "I'm going to tell Eliza."

"Do *not* tell Eliza," she gasped as I met her eyes. "If you tell Eliza I'm *never* going to speak to you again."

"I'll risk it."

Series 10

Day 48

Brooklyn was tired so I suggested he sleep. Which was like suggesting a nap to a toddler, but when I also suggested I go home to pick up a few things, sleep suddenly became appealing to him.

After, of course, he gave me a novelisation of a plays' worth of things to bring back for him.

Andy had caught us in bed together when we'd finally found some way to sleep. He'd woke us up, with an amused glint in his eyes before moving me from the bed so he could medicate Brooklyn.

He'd told me to go home.

So I guess the idea wasn't completely original.

I kissed Brooklyn, deep, and still tame. Reminded him I loved him then put his hoodie on, then my cap.

Brooklyn was basically asleep as I left and I took a minute to smile at him, to just appreciate *him*, before Andy touched my shoulder.

"We'll call you a taxi. Try to reduce you getting mobbed." He gave me a sad kind of smile. I nodded.

"Thank you," I whispered, then put my mask on and followed him as he walked me through the corridors.

"It must be exhausting," Andy said, almost absently. I

glanced at him as I sighed.

"I was thirteen when I started needing protection everywhere I went," I told him. "We went to a comic con, we did a panel because production thought we were to young to do a photo op.

"We were walking the floor after the panel and it was like…" I looked at him, as his eyes searched mine. "It was like when Simba gets caught in the stampede. We lost each other really quickly, we were separated by the flow of people and everyone wanted to touch us, and talk to us, it was like they wanted a piece of us.

"It was honestly terrifying. I mean, I was just a kid and there were some grown adults involved. Eliza, you've met Eliza?" He nodded. "She's our chaperone. She eventually got to me, grabbed my hand and pulled me free. Got everyone to back off. After that we weren't allowed to walk the floor during cons or just, kind of go out alone without security, *or* a disguise."

"That must be pretty isolating," he said. "But at least you've got Brooklyn, right? And he's got you. A nice new relationship."

I laughed.

"No, yeah, you're right. We've got each other, we love each other, it's amazing but we've been together for…" I frowned lightly, "almost four years. We just…"

"Weren't allowed to tell anyone?"

I shook my head.

"Couldn't possibly have *two* queer relationships, could we?" I said, in jest – mostly. He squeezed my arm.

"You can hide in Brooklyn's hospital room as much as you wish." He paused just before the door, so I turned to him. "But he is hooked up to a heart monitor, so no…" he tilted his head, "…raising his heart rate."

I snorted so hard I almost choked.

"Noted, thanks, Nurse Andy."

He nodded, then turned. We looked together as a taxi pulled up.

"Good luck."

I crossed my fingers and left the hospital. I stopped just before I got into the taxi, looking towards the main entrance at the swarm of people who were still chanting Brooklyn's name.

"Where are we going mate?"

I got in the taxi, then relayed my address.

Bud was *very* excited to see me when I opened the front door. He ran from the living barely coming to a stop, so I picked him up.

"Missed me?" I laughed as he wiggled and barked, licking at my hands in between sniffing every inch of me. "I'm going to have a nap," I told him, putting him back on the floor. He sat back on his legs, looking up at me with big eyes. "You can come with me," I offered, he yipped then jumped up the stairs at my side.

I hesitated outside our bedroom, looking towards Quincy and AJ's door. It was closed. I figured AJ would be at work, but I didn't know if Quincy was sleeping in.

I decided not to bother them, instead, I went into our room. Sighing deeply at the mess Brooklyn had left on our bed.

I'd left him still asleep; he'd obviously pulled out the entirety of his wardrobe to find something to wear before he settled on his hoodie.

Bud jumped up onto our bed whining lightly as he sniffed at Brooklyn's clothes.

"He'll be back soon, Bud," I whispered, as he buried himself into one of Brooklyn's shirts. I cleared the rest of the bed, unceremoniously pushing them onto the floor in front of the wardrobe.

I toed off my shoes, stepped out my jeans then pulled

Brooklyn's hoodie off, putting it on the bed as I pulled on my t-shirt then my binder.

I took a *deep*, full breath feeling the pinch of wearing my binder for just a little too long then put Brooklyn's hoodie back on. I let the sleeves fall over my hands as I climbed into bed. My sleeved hands stroking down Bud's back.

Soon I fell asleep.

Although, I wasn't asleep long. Or at least it didn't feel like it. Bud fully woke me up by running around the bed then jumping off and leaving my room. I smiled after him before turning to reach for my phone.

I gave serious consideration to reinstalling Twitter. I got as far as redownloading the app before my door opened, far too much for it to be Bud.

I looked towards it as Quincy stepped around it. They smiled sympathetically at me, sighing and knocking their head against the door. I focused in on their oversized t-shirt until they came and got into my bed with me.

"How is he?" they whispered as they took off their glasses, folding the arms and putting them between us.

"Emotional," I sighed. "In pain. He's sleeping, or he was when I left him. We were up quite late last night. This morning."

"Bud was asleep in your bed when I got back. AJ said he was sat outside your door when he got home from work, so he let him in. He's barely left."

"I had to tell Brooklyn I couldn't bring Bud back with me," I said, Quincy grinned. "Although he wants me to take his nose ring." I rolled my eyes, Quincy laughed gently. "How are you?" I asked.

"Oh, devastated," they frowned. "Which is *weird* because I haven't enjoyed that show for years, but yeah, it hurt." They shrugged. "Spoke to Eliza, though, she said to not worry too much, and to keep my phone on me, *so…*"

"I reinstalled Twitter," I said. "Neither Brooklyn or I know where his phone is. I figured I could post an update. *Something* just to say he's okay, and maybe, you know, leave the hospital."

Quincy nodded as I unlocked my phone.

"I can change my username, right?"

"Oh, yes," they gasped, turning my phone to them and going into my settings. "Password," they whispered, I typed it in. We both looked at my *current* username. I sighed as I erased my deadname.

"Do I make my name a pun, or just *Oz Campbell*."

"Just *Oz Campbell*," they repeated. "Oz Campbell is one of the most important names in history."

I smirked typing my name in and pressing okay. I took a breath as my phone flooded with notifications.

"Sure you want to do this?"

"I'm not sure I want to do anything," I admitted.

"There's *one* thing I want to do," they whispered, "that I think we should do together."

"I love you, but…"

"Shut up," they laughed. "I think we need to do an exclusive interview, with *someone* to explain what's going on. Now I've been fired I'm not under any obligation to maintain appearances. Of course, I wouldn't make you break contract, but…"

"Who are you thinking of giving the interview to?"

"I don't know," they frowned. "I can't fully work out who *our* Oprah is. You're up for it?"

"I held Brooklyn as he sobbed last night, I *am* up for it."

They stroked my cheek. I turned to kiss their palm before typing a *Brooklyn update* out.

I had one hundred likes before I even exited the app.

I sighed.

"Sobbed?" they repeated.

"It was a rough night," I nodded. We looked down between us as Bud retook his spot on the bed then at my phone as it vibrated.

New Message from **@Mol_98**

I frowned at it, opening the message.

@Mol_98: Hi Oz! Sorry for messaging but I couldn't get through to Brooklyn. I wanted to check in on him, make sure he's okay? Maybe visit? I tried to but your swarm of superfans made it near impossible. I understand completely if I can't, but please pass my thoughts onto Brooklyn.

Series 4

Day 10

I was starting to think Brooklyn was going to fly backwards off his chair if he kept swinging on two legs. Well, that, or his script was about to rip in two.

Whatever happened first.

"Hello."

I jumped, turning and making eye contact with Eliza.

"Izzy says," she hinted. I bit my lip before trawling the script in front of me to figure out where I was.

"Hasn't got a clue," Quincy laughed. I smirked at them biting my lip.

"Page six," Brooklyn whispered dramatically,

"Fourth line down," Dakota laughed.

"Let's go guys," I said with *zero* conviction. Brooklyn cackled, swinging with more gusto as Quincy shook their head at me.

Eliza smirked at me, I shrugged one shoulder. We all turned over the page simultaneously.

"Oh, I get it," Quincy read, shaking their head as they sat, their hands on the back of their neck, a slight frown on their face. "The quantum leap was active by the momentum of the atoms that passed through Kevin." They laughed. "*He* is the catalyst. Every time he sneezes we…"

Brooklyn fake sneezed. Quincy sighed.

"Leap." They actively turned to look at him. "Will you stop that?"

"It's hay fever season," he grumbled. "Can you fix it?"

"Yeah," Quincy said. "Easy, you just need to *stop* sneezing."

"Easy," I mocked. "Oh, yeah, the easiest." Then I reached for Brooklyn and squeezed his nose. "There."

He knocked my hand away after a few more pages, a laugh in his expression as he kept my hand in his, it swinging between us as he continued swinging on two legs.

"Oh," Quincy read.

"Oh? What oh?" Dakota pushed. "Todd, we don't like *oh*?"

"It's fine, doesn't matter," they waved. "Let's just keep…"

"Ahhh-chew."

Quincy *actually* rolled their eyes.

"Let's keep working," they almost growled. "Izzy, I thought you were stopping the sneezing."

"He's very tall," I said

Brooklyn laughed. "You're very small," he told me. I pulled my tongue at him, he did it back.

"If you two could *stop* flirting, please," Dakota requested. Brooklyn laughed shaking his head as I swallowed deeply, burying my head into my script.

Page after page of banter.

I read ahead as we gained on the end of the episode. *What the…*

"Todd, stop it, press the button."

Quincy took a breath. I watched as Brooklyn read the script. He frowned, his chair banging to the floor. He placed his script on the table as Quincy's breath staggered.

"You have to understand, if I press this, it'll stop."

"Yeah…" Brooklyn's voice was monotone. "So, *press* it."

"It'll stop, but…"

"Todd?" I asked. Quincy looked at me, shrugging.

"But I'll die."

"You'll…" Brooklyn began. "What the fuck?"

Eliza frowned at her script.

"No, that's a question. What the fuck, Eliza? Why are they killing Todd?"

Eliza sighed, looking towards Quincy as they rubbed their forehead.

"Because I came out, right? Because I'm nonbinary, because I *stated* it. If I'd kept quiet, Todd would just disappear into the geeky background, huh?"

"I wouldn't like to comment," Eliza whispered.

"Because it's true?" Quincy shrugged. "This is *shit* and transphobia."

"What exactly do they think he's going to do?" Dakota asked.

"They," Quincy and Brooklyn said in perfect unison.

"I'm fifteen, I'm not starting a war," they muttered. "Do I have to die? Can't the script be appealed or something."

"It's fantasy, can't you *just* come back next week?" I asked. Eliza hummed. "I'll take that as a no?"

"They're pretty set on… *this* storyline."

"Bastards," Brooklyn muttered. "Well, *I'm* not going to let it happen, I'll fix this."

"You're not *actually* Kevin, you know?" Quincy teased. Brooklyn smirked back at them.

"Oh, yes I am." He stood and left the room. I frowned after his as Quincy did.

"What's he going to do?" I whispered.
Eliza sighed. "Who knows."

Series 10

Day 48

It was like a mission to get Molly into the hospital. She drove to our house, picked me and Brooklyn's hordes up and drove me there. She had to park out front so we had to walk through the most dedicated of fans who seemed to be camping out.

They didn't even pretend not to notice me. They didn't even pretend not to gasp and take pictures of me walking with Molly.

They didn't stop to think before crowding the two of us, asking about Brooklyn, about Series Ten, and the rumours, and loads of other bullshit that didn't matter because Brooklyn was in the hospital we were *trying* to get into, and he was far more important than anything they may request of us.

"Oz."

I looked up. Tony smiled at me as he stepped on the cigarette, he was pretending he hadn't been smoking. He pushed through the crowds, pulling me through. I dragged Molly through after me.

"Oh, hello," Tony said pleased as we stepped through the doors. "I haven't seen you in a while, Miss Molly."

"I have missed you, Tony," she stressed. "A lot.

Screw Brooklyn, we need to meet up for a drink."

I laughed as Tony did, a quiet smile on his face that wasn't there two days ago. Three days ago? Time was a blur.

We walked the corridors like they were familiar, like we felt at home.

"He's only really just woke up," Tony said as he held the door for us. "The night nurse was bringing him something to eat but he was still a little groggy."

"Was he asleep when you arrived?"

"Dead to the world," he hummed. "I've been here a few hours. Didn't want to wake him, I figured he needed it." He pushed open the door. Brooklyn appeared to be eating chocolate mousse.

"You're back." He sounded happy, his smile glowing when he saw me, so I grinned back then stepped aside.

"Brought someone for you to play with," I said.

"Molly," he gasped happily. She laughed behind me so I turned, smiling at her as he crossed the room, wrapping her arms around him and cuddling him tight.

"You idiot," she gasped. "I told you that going around bouncing off bumpers wasn't good."

I glanced at Tony as he sighed rubbing his forehead.

"How many times did he do this?" he asked.

I bit my lip. "Sorry I signed a NDA."

He punched me in the shoulder.

"I'm going to have to get a new car," Brooklyn sighed.

"And by the sound of it, a new phone," Molly teased as she sat opposite him on the bed. He laughed resting his head back against the pillow. His expression relaxed. It always looked so easy with Molly.

"I could completely start again," he whispered. "New *everything*... But I wouldn't replace you, Oz."

"I love you, too," I teased.

"You're so… different," she said to me. I shook my head asking her *what* as I did. "Happier, brighter, so much *sassier*. You wouldn't say a word to me a handful of years ago. Never mind sass Brooklyn."

"He sasses me all the time," Brooklyn put on a cry. "All the time."

"Once I saw him naked he lost all his creditability," I said.

"No, but I love him," she told Brooklyn. "Seriously. He's my favourite."

"I'll sell you him for a very reasonable price," Brooklyn muttered. I scoffed, placing his backpack on the end of his bed.

"I brought your nose ring," I said. "Multiple, actually, but I can take them."

He reached out to me, his hands open and closing as if saying *want, want, want*. I rolled my eyes at Molly as I passed over the little box he had full of them.

"I also…" I said going into my pocket for my phone, I turned it when I found the picture I'd taken of Bud fast asleep wrapped up in one of his checked shirts.

"My baby," he gasped, then showed Molly who cooed instantly.

"He's missing you," I said, as my phone buzzed in his hand. "A lot."

He smiled.

"I'll be home soon, Bud," he told my phone, then, "what are you doing back on Twitter?"

"Regretting it, mostly," I replied as I took my phone. "I Tweeted that you were okay… *mostly*."

"Mostly okay, or you mostly Tweeted?" Brooklyn mocked as he chose his iridescent nose ring. I watched him put it in. I rose my eyebrow at him, he smirked. "Let's take a selfie to prove it," he said excitedly.

"Excuse me, I brought Molly for you to play with."

"*Yeah*, and I am, she's more than welcome to be in the selfie."

Molly shook her head. "Please, as you were." She laughed. "I'll even be the first to like and retweet." Brooklyn laughed, the sound light and happy *so* I got my camera up.

I switched it to selfie. *God* I looked so tired. I was twenty-one, I shouldn't have looked like I'd been working a dead-end job for the last fifty years.

Brooklyn looked tired too, but in a I've-just-woke-up-and-I'm-insanely-visually-attractive kind of way. He held his cast up, a big smile on his face.

It made me think of him at thirteen, *fourteen*, when he smiled without preservation regardless of his braces. Every picture I have of him at that time his smile is wide, until someone commented on a picture on Twitter shaming him for having braces and after that, his smile became closed mouthed and fake.

I wanted to kiss him, I wanted to turn around and kiss his no-reservations smile. So I did, and with as little reservations as his smile, I posted it.

"You trying to get fired?" Molly laughed, as I saw the little heart come up on my notification bar.

"Maybe," I said softly. "I want as long of a list as Quincy got."

Molly frowned.

"They've been fired," Brooklyn explained.

"Pornographic content."

"Disregard of contract."

"Changing appearance without consultation."

"Workplace relationship."

"Inappropriate language."

"Inappropriate use of social media."

"My favourite; disregard for authority." I smirked at Molly, as she exhaled in one long breath. "We're going to make it public," I told Brooklyn. "We're going to talk."

"You're going to talk?" Brooklyn repeated. I nodded swallowing deeply. "Have you spoken to Dakota and Freya at all?" he asked. I frowned. "Find out what they're doing, where they stand, what's going on there?"

"Dakota wouldn't answer me," I muttered.

"What?" Molly laughed. "Is she bitter you got Brooklyn?" she smiled although it dropped when she met my eyes. "What happened?"

"She'd answer me," Brooklyn said. "She always replies to me."

"Maybe we need a meeting," I suggested. "Quincy, Freya, Dakota, me and you. I have a feeling once one secret comes out, the rest will follow."

"Jenga," Brooklyn agreed. "I think we need to agree what we're going to protect, what we need to."

"I'll protect you," I said.

"And you, always."

Series 6

Day 1

"We want to introduce you to new cast member, Freya," Eliza said, backing it with some enthusiasm. We all examined the poor, poor girl who had no idea what she'd just walked into.

She was younger than us, younger than Quincy and I. She must've only been fourteen, fifteen at a push. She was pale, her hair so long and a soft mousey brown.

"New cast member, like, cameo right?" Quincy asked as they examined the girl, their eyes taking in every single details of her.

"Main cast," Eliza stated. Quincy *didn't* hide their anger all too well.

"What's your name, sweetheart?" Brooklyn asked, wrapping his arm around Quincy and pulling them back into them. Quincy barely relaxed.

"Freya," she said warily, frowning at Quincy then smiling, confused at Brooklyn.

"That's so unfair," they muttered.

"Who are you playing?" I asked. I'd actually read the book that ran alongside Series Six. I had some vague knowledge on this series. *Vague.*

"India," she confirmed.

"India," I repeated, then, "oh."

"What?" Quincy asked, their eyes narrowing at me as I bit my lip.

"Todd's love interest," I said then recoiled because their anger just *grew*.

"You're fucking kidding me, Eliza," they stated. "I end the *fucking* series pulling a gun on the *love of my life* and start the next with a girlfriend?"

"The fans won't buy that," Brooklyn muttered. Quincy pushed themselves out of Brooklyn's arms.

"I don't care about the *fans*, you know…" they turned to Eliza, "*you* know how much it affected me having to film that scene, having to do that. *You* know."

"I didn't hire Freya," she stated. "And this isn't the best way to introduce her, no?"

"She shouldn't even be here," they sighed. "*Sorry*, I'm sure you're lovely, you're gorgeous, and I'm sure it goes skin deep. This has nothing to do with *you*."

"Maybe just wait until you've read the script," Eliza offered. "It might not be as dismissive as you're predicting."

"Bullshit." Quincy shook their head. "I *get it*, they threatened to kill me over a fucking sneeze, then they actually give me a boyfriend, and have me kill him. *Now*, they're giving me a girlfriend in hope that I fall into the hetero background, never to have story development again. I absolutely *hate* it here," they stated, *then* left the room. Eliza looked after them, sighing and shaking her head as I looked at Brooklyn. He winced then put on his *everything's okay* persona.

"Don't you worry, darling," he said, a big smile on his face. "Quincy's just upset, it has *nothing* to do with you." He wrapped his arm around her. I smiled vaguely at the fact she just about stood to his chest.

She looked a *little* starstruck, looking up at him as he

spoke. I glanced at Dakota. She rolled her eyes and turned away from me.

Awesome.

I followed Brooklyn as he led Freya to our table. She took a seat, as he sat on the tabletop.

"I've been watching it since the beginning," she told Brooklyn. "My dad used to read me the books before bed. This is like a dream come true."

"Really?" Brooklyn's voice was soft, like when he spoke to kids.

"Really," Freya agreed, smiling pleasantly at him before looking at me. I watched as she took me in, every bit of me. "Do you guys have any advice on how to survive?" she joked. I swallowed as Brooklyn laughed.

"Be yourself, and don't let Quincy's feelings upset you. They're such a nice person, they're just having a bad day."

She nodded, she even looked like he believed him. She said my name, I startled, looking up at her, then shrugging one shoulder.

"Never be alone in the room with Jordan," I said. she frowned at me as the door opened. Quincy stepped through, they looked as if they'd been arguing with Eliza.

"I'm going for a cofee. Have your scripts out, ready for episode one read through by the time I get back." She paused, looking around the room. "Be nice to each other," she added. I looked at Brooklyn as he sighed, crossing his legs on the tabletop.

"I swear, we like each other," I said to Freya. "That almost made it sound like you were about to get a major scoop that we *hated* each other."

She laughed shaking her head at me

"Don't worry. I'm not a spy," she smirked. "So you can totally trust me, and tell me all your secrets."

I smirked at her, she winked at me.

"I kind of like her," Brooklyn whispered loudly to me. I laughed nodding before clapping my hand over my mouth and looking towards Quincy as they sighed.

"Where are your scripts?" Eliza asked, as she backed through the door. She hadn't even looked at us to know we hadn't done as she requested. Brooklyn pulled a face at Freya, she laughed happily as he jumped from the table and walked across the room. He wrapped his arms around Quincy. Swinging them side to side, his nose buried in their hair as he spoke softly.

I turned when Freya said my name, she looked almost confused.

"Who's Jordan?"

"Our director," I said, as Dakota passed behind her to get to her own seat. "He's an asshole. Just, take everything he says with a pinch of salt."

"I swear this is a fun place to work," Eliza stressed. "Jheeze, guys, less of the melancholy. Have some caffeine."

"My kind of woman," Brooklyn teased.

Eliza scoffed. "I'm in a relationship." She tsked, Brooklyn winked at her.

Series 10

Day 55

The lights in an interview were somehow *completely* different to the lights in the studio. It made no sense because they were obviously the same lights but these ones created so much more pressure.

I image this would be the feeling of being on *The Weakest Link*, the immense pressure that makes you forget the colours of the French flag.

Quincy was talking, talking about Series Six, about the trauma *Adolescent Summers* had put them through, but they spoke with a softness, no anger. They spoke of AJ how through all the hell they found the man they wished to spend the rest of their life with.

I really hoped the world was done fucking with Quincy Ikeda.

I took them in, in all their glory. There was no this is what the studio thinks I should wear. There was no *hetero-coding*.

They were wearing a shirt, or maybe it was officially a blouse. Baby pink, patterned with strawberries and a white dungaree dress that criss-crossed over their back. They wore bright ruby red Doc Martens and white socks like Molly's up to their knee. I almost envied them in a strange kind of way. I envied how they embraced their queerness, how *fantastic* they looked in everything they wore.

Their earrings. I envied their earrings. Their left ear was a strawberry, their right a cuff of white pearls.

I felt underdressed, and I was wearing a Gucci polo shirt which I was sure you could see the lines of my binder through. I was a little hypo fixated on that.

We all paused to watch AJ proposing. Quincy laughed through it, covering their mouth.

"Through all that, you found each other," our interviewer said. Quincy smiling at the screen as they kissed.

"Yeah, something a lot of people forget was that we were teenagers. We were *kids*. Series one, we were ten, right?" they said. I nodded.

"We were ten, yeah. Brooklyn, twelve. I hadn't even started secondary school."

Quincy laughed softly.

"We had to figure ourselves out with a whole studio of cameras aimed at us. We were going to mess up. We were going to have parties, snog each other, get together, break up." They shook their head. "It was like that surprised them."

"And that isn't *just* queer relationships. They came down hard on hetero relationships, too."

"AJ was brought in as my love interest from the off. There was a whole day on set that we just had to be together, when we were developing their relationship. I was fifteen, *just* about, he was seventeen and we just clicked instantly.

"At the end of that day, we kissed. Quincy and AJ, not Todd and Daniel, and our producers were like *that's* great but wait until the cameras are rolling." They waved their hand as if waving it off. "We started texting, and Snapchatting, non-stop. I think it's fair to say we were together *unofficially* by the mid-point of filming.

"The producers weren't too pleased by that. They were constantly separating us, making sure we weren't left alone, or out in public together, *stupid* things that just were not necessary. AJ had to sign an NDA almost instantly, promising to not *out* me…" they paused to laugh. "I was so far out even the White Witch had forgotten who I was. Promising he wouldn't put our relationship on social media or make any reference to us being romantic *anywhere*. It was shit, but being fifteen, I was fully encased in my own personal bubble. Me and AJ.

"It ripped me inside out to have to kill his character. Which I know sounds dramatic, but I was fifteen years old, and he had just become my *first* boyfriend, so…"

"Understandable," the interviewer said nodding solemnly. "And yourself, and Brooklyn? How is he by the way?"

"He's far better. He was allowed home a few days back, he's basically been asleep wrapped up with his dog since he got home. I don't know which of them was more excited to see the other."

The interviewer smiled at me, and it felt genuine. I didn't think I was walking into a shark tank.

"How did you two get started?"

"Tale as old as time," I teased. "I and, of course, he now knows this; I've liked Brooklyn for a long time. I was twelve, at least when I started crushing on him, but I didn't tell him until I was sixteen.

"We went on a few dates. Mostly to figure out if we could go from what we were to dating. It turns out we could."

"You've been a couple for five years?" the interviewer asked, whilst struggling to keep the shock from his voice. I laughed as I nodded.

"We weren't allowed to say a word. No physical

affection at events, no touching, no long glances, no *nothing*. We couldn't allow the papers even a sniff we were in a relationship."

"Why not?"

"One queer relationship is bad enough, *imagine* two," Quincy said softly. The interviewer looked between us, a light frown on his face, I knew what he was about to say.

"But, five years ago, Oz, you…"

"Identified as a girl?" I helped. He nodded. "Yeah, I did. I guess initially it was a *workplace* relationship, and we were teenagers so I think they secretly hoped we'd break up and they wouldn't have to deal with it.

"Then the fans started demanding Izzy and Kevin, and they were, all things considered, pissed. They decided that they couldn't write it into the show, if it was public knowledge we were dating, so they made us keep it secret.

"Of course, during lockdown I started my transition, and well, *that* was like trying to throw water onto a fire and discovering it was vodka."

"Oh, good metaphor," Quincy said. I laughed smiling at them as they took my hand, squeezing it gently.

"Let's talk about your transition," the interviewer said. I nodded. "I know there was a lot of whispers, speculation, after your virtual meet-and-greet."

"Loads," I almost laughed. "I was getting hounded, so I started my transition quite early into lockdown, we'd been in for a few weeks, and I'd had more time to think than ever before. I got so in my head that I ended up, I guess, knocking on that door.

"I went and spoke to Quincy about it, because I knew I'd be heard, then I told Brooklyn. Before our meet-and-greet, only really Brooklyn, Quincy, and AJ were aware. I'd shaved all my hair off and was wearing a binder, I was like starter-trans." I smiled to myself, as

Quincy laughed.

"I told Eliza, our chaperone, but I requested it be need-to-know, however, of course, the fans were onto me instantly. I was getting countless Tweets, Instagram messages. People were commenting on Brooklyn's TikTok's about me. Starting full on arguments when they stated I was transitioning and people disagreed.

"It was frightening, on so many different levels. I was terrified of the response if I actually ended up coming out. I was scared of the hate, scared of the love, even." I swallowed. "Quite frankly, I was scared of the fans." I shook my head.

"I got a trans flag through my PO Box, and I just broke down. I opened the parcel and I just began to sob because, yes it was me, but I wanted this to be done on my own terms. I wanted to be given time that I deserved.

"*That's* when I deleted everything. I uninstalled every social media app I was on. I went dark, essentially because I didn't want to know. Brooklyn started opening my PO Box, only passing on the things that didn't relate to my gender to me.

"I have since read them, I have since gone through all the letters, the flags, the drawings and they're gorgeous but, I wasn't in the right headspace for them at the time." I swallowed. "We were obviously forewarned that we were going back to set and, by then, I'd started hormones and I'd started planning for top surgery, my transition was *real* and I was about to walk into a warzone."

"Their initial argument for it all was they didn't want to make Brooklyn uncomfortable by making him act queer," Quincy said.

"Apparently, we were so good at hiding our relationship that they forgot we were even in it."

The interviewer smiled at me, so I smiled at my hands.

"So, series ten, what's happened there?"

"Right now, nothing," I answered.

"We were filming, and they were making some *poor* choices," Quincy explained. "Now…" they looked at me, "the most recent update, is that the studio have decided to terminate my contract."

"They've fired you?" they asked. Quincy nodded. "Is that because of your *Only Fans*?"

"Amongst many other reasons," Quincy smiled gently; the interviewer nodded.

Lockdown 1

Day 64

Quincy and AJ were having a date night. Which meant Brooklyn and I were ordering a pizza and staying in our bedroom all night to give them *space*.

This was okay. We were not against that arrangement. We'd come up with it about three weeks into lockdown. We'd ordered pizza and binge watched Good Omens together. It was a good night, highly enjoyable. Quincy and AJ's date night had apparently also become ours.

Brooklyn was planning on binge watching Love, Victor tonight, and as much as I wished to do that, I wanted to tell him. I wanted to come out to him.

I needed to.

He returned with multiple pizza boxes and two bottles between his fingers.

"I got us pizza, duh."

"Duh," I agreed.

"Garlic bread, some wedges, just because, and…" he grinned, "…cookies."

"Cookies," I gasped.

"But for after pizza," he added closing the box back over. "I'm going to change into my pyjamas, and we'll get started, yeah?" He stood on the bed, going to step off but

I reached for him. I got the spare material in his joggers, pulling on them and pulling them down just slightly.

He reached for my hand, stopping them from going any further before sitting down as he obviously received my message.

"What's up, lovely?"

"I need to tell you something. I need to talk to you."

"Okay," he nodded. "Take your time."

I swallowed, shaking my head because, nope I could not take my time with this. I needed to blurt this out. Otherwise, I feared the words would never leave my mouth.

"Brooklyn," I closed my eyes. "Brooklyn I'm…" I opened my eyes when he took my hand. He stroked my hand with his fingers, his expression was blank. There wasn't a smirk underlying his features, not at all.

I wonder if he knew, if he had an inkling. If he'd worked it out.

"I'm trans," I said. "Transgender. I…"

His finger stopped stroking my hand, but he didn't let go.

"I'm a boy," I whispered, before clearing my throat. "I'm a boy." When I looked up, he was smiling at me. I hadn't been expecting that.

"Okay," he whispered. "Okay. Can you tell me a few things?" he asked. I nodded warily. "Your name?"

"Oz."

"Like, the great and powerful?" he asked, not quite teasing, but I smiled at him.

"The very same."

"Your pronouns are he/him?"

I nodded.

"And you still want to be in a relationship, with me?" he asked.

"What? Yes, I… I thought you'd want to break up

with me," I gasped. He tutted, shaking his head at me. "I thought you'd leave me… because… because of… this."

He knelt up. Moving closer to me, his hands on my face.

"No, no, my darling Oz, no." He touched his forehead to mine. "I loved you yesterday, I love you today, and I will love you for all of our tomorrows. I want you to be happy, to be comfortable in your body. I'm happy you've found your truth." He sighed. "So much makes sense now," he added as if an afterthought. I rose my eyebrow at him.

"What?" I whispered. He shrugged dramatically before waving his hands at me as if ensuring I knew he didn't mean offence.

"Like, you've never wanted me to touch your chest. You hate wearing feminine coded things, you get really upset when…" he swallowed. "You remember when we first started fooling around? Not the first time, I think you were a little too shellshocked that I was touching you, but you always kind of seemed like you were looking at me and…" he shook his head.

"It was never you," I said weakly, he shook his head then nodded, his expression confused. "I just sometimes envied your…"

"Body?" he offered.

"Sorry." I sighed. "For ruining sex."

"No, no, never," he gasped. "God, never. I fucking love you, and love having sex with you. If you're comfortable with that, damn, let's not stop that. I just worried sometimes that I was doing something wrong, then I usually just realised you were… taking me in."

"I want a penis," I sighed. "It's easier to ignore sometimes. Then I see you and I'm like, fuck I want that." I nodded my head. "In both ways, granted."

He smirked gently.

"I'm willing to help you," he frowned. "Well, you can't have my penis. *Well*, you can touch it, and play with it, but I can't give it to you."

"That's okay, Brooklyn. One day I aim to get one of my own."

"I love you," he told me. "And if that's what you want, I'm *more* than happy to help, to be there for you, to help you."

"You're really okay with this?"

"Yes, god yes, Oz," he grinned then knocked his forehead against mine. "Even still, if I wasn't okay with it, it's not really up to me is it. This is your life."

"And your relationship," I whispered.

"And I've told you before, if I want out, I will tell you. I will communicate it with you, I won't just suffer."

I kissed him then I lowered my head, and I began to cry.

"Oh, my love," he sighed, wrapping his arms around me, and pushing me back onto our pillows. "How can you cry when there's pizza in close proximity?"

I laughed.

"I was so scared," I swallowed. "I *am* so scared."

"Of what?"

"Everyone leaving me. Everyone hating me. Losing everything."

"Oz, if you lost everything, your job, your fame, your fans. I'd still be there with you, every step of the way because *you* are who matters to me, not your money, not your credentials, not this stupid show. You."

"And Bud?" I teased.

"Okay, yeah *and* Bud." He tapped my chest three times. "I. Love. You," he said with each beat. "Yeah?" he bumped my chest again, before doing his own. "I love you."

"I love you," I whispered back.

"If ever you doubt that or feel scared."

I bumped my chest, he nodded doing it back then flipped open the box and pulled out a slice of pizza passing it to me.

"Eat. You'll feel better, yeah? I know it must have been terrifying telling me," he whispered. I knocked my head against his shoulder. "I'm quite proud of you," he purred lightly. I glanced at him. "Sorry," he laughed, "the feeling of your hair makes my spine tingle."

"Sensory overload?"

"No," he whispered. "No. Good sensory. Like brrrr in my spine, like good" He exhaled. "This isn't about me."

"But I still want to learn." I looked up as I took a bite of the pizza. "Like, I have no doubt you will ask me questions, and want to learn about... being trans."

"Oh," he said softly. "Okay." He reached for some pizza himself. "I feel mildly bad."

"Why?" I whispered, my stomach feeling *somewhat* hollow.

"I was going to definitely make this night led to sex."

I laughed.

"But you've just exposed your heart to me. So that's not *great*."

"Let's eat pizza, watch Love, Victor, and then I'm sure my hand may find its way onto your thigh."

"Saucy," he teased. I pulled my tongue at him. "You..." he began, then he sighed. "You know if there's something we do *during* sex, you can tell me if you don't like that."

"I know," I whispered. "I know. I always will. We're a team, yeah?"

"Yeah."

Series 10

Day 57

Brooklyn took my phone off me. Throwing it down our bed. Bud sniffed at it, almost disgruntled at my phone flying towards him, but he didn't seem too bothered by the disruption.

"Stop reading the headlines."

"I was reading the articles as well," I muttered, then sighed burying myself into his side, my chin resting on his shoulder. My body as far back as I could so I didn't bump his cast. Although I doubted he'd care, he'd become quite used to his cast.

We'd even all signed it. Us and anyone who we'd stumbled across over the last few days, they'd asked for his or my autograph, and he'd requested theirs in return.

I was starting to think he might miss it when it's gone.

"There's no point reading them," he whispered. "They'll just make you sad."

"I'm weirdly sad already," I whispered.

"Saudade," he said. I frowned. "The word for feeling sad, whilst also feeling happy."

"Brooklyn," I gasped.

"I read," he laughed. Our phones buzzed together. Bud whined lightly, nosing at my phone as Brooklyn reached for his. "Oh, shit."

"What?" I moaned. "What has happened *now?*"

He turned his phone to me.

"Oh, shit."

Our bedroom door opened.

"Shit," Quincy stated, then they sighed. "I'm so glad you're wearing clothes. Oh, my god."

I almost smirked at Brooklyn. He certainly wasn't wearing clothes. It had taken us an embarrassingly long time to figure out just because he couldn't use his dominant hand didn't mean I couldn't.

"You've read?" I asked. Quincy nodded coming to sit on the end of our bed, they began to scratch between Bud's ears.

"Did you know she was going to?"

"No," Brooklyn whispered. "No. In fact, I truly thought the opposite." He sighed. "I'm proud of her, though. I'm going to call her." He went to stand. "I'm *not* wearing pants," he told Quincy; they rolled their eyes.

"Figured out hand jobs did you," they rose their eyebrow at me. I did it back as Brooklyn got out our bed and miraculously got his joggers on and left the room.

"I know they're already in deep shit, I know I'm already fired, and you're…"

"On my final warning," I quirked an eyebrow at them.

"But Dakota coming out about Jordan," they swallowed. "That's going to stop production dead."

I nodded

"Jordan should at least be trialled. Eight years in prison," I whispered. Quincy tilted their head at me. "I read up on it because I was so angry. I didn't know what to do. I didn't even end up telling Eliza I threatened to. Dakota thought I had.

"Dakota hasn't spoken to me, not properly for four years or so. She just…"

"You didn't tell anyone?"

"Besides Dakota? No. I was too scared."

"Scared of?"

"Dakota." I tilted my head. "Jordan."

"Oz," they whispered. I shook my head. "How did *you* know?" they asked, as they obviously diverted. I sighed.

"I saw them, at Brooklyn's eighteenth. I walked past you licking AJ's tonsils."

They laughed gently.

"I'm not apologising for that. We had sex in Brooklyn's bed." They lifted their finger to their lips. I squawked.

"I passed you guys, then saw Brooklyn with Molly, *then* saw Jordan and Dakota. They were both well aware that I saw them."

"I'm so sorry, Oz," they sighed.

"How did you find out?"

"Freya," Quincy whispered. "I found her crying. It was one of those days when it was just me and her filming all day. She disappeared and Eliza sent me to find her, it was her first series. For all I was pissed at her, she was *just* a baby. I found her crying.

"She saw me and instantly stopped. Told me to go away, which I don't really blame her for, I was being a dick, but I finally got it out of her." They paused. "Gently, I mean I didn't force it. She told me that Jordan had tried to touch her. That he'd bumped into her on the way to the break room and tried to… she didn't let him.

"When I went to cause hellfire, she stopped me, begged me not to. Instead of talking to Eliza, I spoke to Dakota. She shrugged it off, told me it was just how he was."

"And you knew?"

They nodded softly.

"I feel dirty. Still feel disgusting that I didn't say anything but I was more careful with Freya after that. Nicer to her, but when they were forcing a sex scene on us, I made sure she was happy, that it was fully consensual. She was so afraid." They smiled. "I told her I was gay. I've never seen someone look so relieved to find out my sexuality."

"He tried it with me," I whispered. Quincy met my eyes instantly. "After I saw him and Dakota, he must've thought that if he gave me the same treatment, I'd shrug it off."

"Oz, I never…"

I shook my head.

"I pushed him away. I walked away from him. He followed me, tried to crowd me against a wall." I swallowed. "I almost *just* let him, almost just closed my eyes and waited for it to be over. Then Brooklyn came down the corridor." I looked past Quincy as Brooklyn came back into our room. Quincy turned to look at him.

"You remember when Jordan had a split lip for a while?" Brooklyn whispered. Quincy nodded. "He didn't get off fast enough."

"And he didn't come back on you?" Quincy asked. Brooklyn frowned as he shook his head.

"He told someone I punched him. I tell everyone he was caught touching underage cast members."

"Is Dakota okay?" I whispered. Brooklyn nodded softly.

"She's with Eliza. She went to visit her yesterday. Told her everything. Eliza helped her release a statement. She invited us all around, for a drink, primarily. A chat. A debrief."

"Did she say anything else?"

Brooklyn shook his head slowly.

"This is it," he shrugged. "This is the end."

415 days after

I licked the spoon as the Bolognese sauce continued to bubble away way in the pan in front of me. My music was on the verge of too loud, but I'd had no complaints from upstairs, so I let *The Waitress* soundtrack blast through the kitchen and I sang along. I turned when the male part of the song was sang at me then I began to laugh, turning and singing the next line back.

Quincy smiled as we walked towards each other, they wrapped their arms around my waist as the song reached the part of the instrumental that involved a lot of awkward touching.

I leant towards them, our lips near enough to kiss, before we both dramatically gasped and turned away from eacother finishing off the song. They laughed happily when the song drew to its end, the next in the playlist starting but almost completely ignored. I put the wooden spoon down hoping I hadn't gotten Bolognese sauce on the floor, or on myself, or definitely not on Quincy. This was completely disregarded when they hugged me.

"Hello, darling," they said. "Home in time for tea, I see." They looked over the pans on the stove. I nodded, lifting the spoon to the ceiling.

"Brooklyn's recording. I don't know how much he has left but…" I shrugged dramatically. Quincy returned it before twirling away out of the kitchen.

I turned my speaker down, pulled out the plates and started to lay the table. Bud ran into the kitchen, stopping by the oven, looking up towards the pan with big puppy dog eyes.

So I gave him a meatball.

"That smells good."

I laughed as I watched Bud rolling the meatball over the tile. The trail of Bolognese sauce growing as he did.

Brooklyn lifted my chin, grinning at me so I smiled back at him.

Reaching up, and stroking my finger down his beard, then I kissed him.

"Last meal you'll be getting off me for a while," I teased. He nodded, his cheek rubbing against mine.

"We'll just waste away, huh, Bud?" he said before sighing dramatically. "And when they write about us, it'll be tragic."

"So very tragic," I mocked. "Such a tragedy." I rested the back of my hand against my forehead, before stepping around him to the stove.

He sang woefully, taking a seat at the dining table.

"O, Romeo, Romeo wherefore art thou, Romeo," he recited dramatically, as he pulled his knees to his chest, his chin resting on them. Bud ran to his chair, standing on his hindlegs until Brooklyn picked him up and let him sit between his thighs.

"Shall I hear more, or shall I speak at this?" I replied.

"You know your lines."

"I better had, its opening night tomorrow," I pulled a face at him.

"Mood check?"

I paused.

"The content smile, that looks so at ease," I turned my head to him; he was smiling back at me.

"Good," he whispered.

"And yourself?"

He rose his hand into an 'okay'. "Lots of fun today, getting into the action," he laughed. "And I got the concept art emailed to me today, it's honestly the best thing ever."

"Does it look like you?" I asked, as I placed a plate in front of him. I sat in the seat beside him.

"Kind of. There's definitely parts of me, but I'm also bright blue."

"So yes, then," I teased. He smirked as he twirled spaghetti around his fork.

"Best thing we ever did with the attic," Quincy laughed. I turned as they scooped their own tea out.

"Soundproof it?" I asked, their smirk taking a slightly evil turn,

"No, Ozzy," they laughed. "Putting all the recording stuff up there. Tsk, I'd never use the soundproofing of Brooklyn's new office to my advantage."

I rose my eyebrow at Brooklyn as he moaned.

"Stop teasing him," AJ laughed, taking the plate from Quincy and coming to join us at the table.

When Quincy sat, they rose their glass.

"To Oz's last supper for…" they exhaled, as I lifted my fork, and Brooklyn lifted Bud. "A really long time."

"To a six-month run," I replied as my spaghetti fell from my fork. We raised the toast together.

"I actually got an interesting phone call today," Quincy continued when they lowered their fork. "Approached to play a lead. In an adaptation of a queer book. It's one I read, love in fact. They thought that I'd play the part perfectly, and if I was happy to, if I wanted to, the role was mine."

"For real?" I whispered. They laughed as they nodded.

"Did you say yes?" AJ asked.

"Of course, I said yes. I still want to act; I don't want *Adolescent Summers* to define me."

We all made a different noise at them, they laughed shaking their head.

"Sorry, sorry. I don't want *redacted* to define me. In fact, for most of it I was a whole ass different gender."

AJ choked on his drink as I lifted my own.

"Cheers to that."

"Besides celebrating a movie lead," they grinned between us. "They also asked if *maybe* I knew someone who'd play opposite me."

"Love interest?" I asked.

"Well, yes *and* no. There's a few other roles. It's an entirely queer cast. They're still in the early stages of casting." They looked at Brooklyn. "And I know you want to be in a queer film. I *know* you've got like, fifty-thousand voice jobs, you have to finish your movie, and then you've got the series, but if you were at all interested..."

"Would I have to kiss you?" he whispered.

Quincy rolled their eyes. "How about *you*, Oz?"

"I'll take Brooklyn's role, *yes*."

Brooklyn gasped, his voice high, *so* high that Bud sat up, whining gently at him.

"No, no, I want to be queer," he said. I laughed as Quincy nodded reaching into their pocket for their phone. They sent a text.

"Done," they laughed. "Done. Expect a call at some point. *God* you're going to miss me when we go aren't you?"

"I will," I cooed, reaching across Brooklyn to take Quincy's hand. They raised my hand, kissing the back of it. Brooklyn sighed *dramatically*.

"I don't know what I'll do without you..." he glanced

at AJ. "Both of you." He seemed just that bit more genuine about AJ.

"Are you going to leave after filming?"

"I think so, it's only a six month or so project, and AJ needs to accumulate his holidays."

"One year sabbatical in Japan," he smiled. "Work have said they'll pay six months or so, and I've accumulated three months holiday."

"You're *actually* going, aren't you?" I asked.

"I should've gone back far sooner. I should've made a point to visit my Otosan before now. I never had the time, our schedule was so demanding and I didn't want to fly to Japan for a *weekend* or what? Ten days? I needed to spend time there. I needed time to breathe," they exhaled gently. "But don't worry, I *will* be back. We will be back, if primarily to get married."

"I'd have thought you'd want to get married in Japan?" Brooklyn said.

"I do. I'd *love* to get married in Yamakoshi. It'd mean the world to me to get married where my parents did."

Brooklyn frowned, looking confused.

"Gay marriage isn't legal in Japan," AJ aided.

"Oh," Brooklyn whispered. "I'm sorry. I didn't know."

Quincy squeezed his hand, shaking their head.

"It's okay. It might change, there's a chance. Tokyo is pushing it, if it *does* become legal whilst we're there…" they glanced at AJ.

"Oh yeah, I'll be marrying you within the 24-hours of it becoming legal."

Brooklyn leant a little closer to me.

"I feel that way about you, by the way," he whispered.

"I didn't doubt that for a second."

"And your spaghetti," he continued as he fed Bud

another meatball. "This is immaculate, darling."

I smiled at him.

"Well, when I've finished my run, I'll make it again. Until then..."

"I'll just starve," he gasped. Bud howled - it turned out Brooklyn's dog was as dramatic as Brooklyn.

Series 10

Day 57

Eliza placed five beers on the table between her couches. This was, I think, the first time we, the whole cast of *Adolescent Summers*, had been together, outside, in a social capacity for years.

Brooklyn and I were sat on the floor. His back against the couch, me between his legs, my back resting against his chest. His cast was wrapped around me, resting on my thighs. I was stroking my fingers over it, somewhat enjoying the feel of it under my fingers.

I reached forward, getting us both a beer.

Freya was sat on the couch behind us, her legs drawn in to her body, but she didn't look uncomfortable. Quincy was sat beside her. They looked more tired than anything else.

Dakota was on the couch opposite, beside Arden. Looking at her, it felt like the first time we'd met. When she was smiling widely with space buns in her hair. I felt like I hadn't known her for years.

We'd just finished telling each of our sides of the story. I felt raw and I could only imagine how Freya and Dakota felt.

God, there had been so much I hadn't known.

There had been so much Brooklyn and Quincy

hadn't even been aware of.

There had been so much fighting from all of us, that now we just felt weak. We were done fighting, or at least I was and as Brooklyn was out of commission having just one arm, I think he was waving a white flag, too.

"I just wish you kids had spoken to me," Eliza said. "About Jordan…" she looked angry for a second before turning to Dakota. "I wouldn't have needed details, I'd have helped you."

"I thought Oz had told you," Dakota whispered.

"And you thought I wasn't doing anything about it?"

"I don't know," she said. "I didn't think. I was fifteen."

Eliza looked at me.

"I was *also* fifteen, and I was scared."

"And Brooklyn?" she asked. He sighed against me. "You *saw* and you didn't say anything?"

"I was scared, too," he said., I turned my head to look at him, frowning as he shrugged. "Oz and I had just gotten together. He was sixteen, and I'd just turned eighteen. I was scared that if I told someone about *him* that it'd come back on me, and I'd be painted in the same light."

"I didn't know that," I whispered. Brooklyn shook his head.

"I didn't tell you. I loved you, I *love* you and so many stories were coming out, and then I saw Jordan and I punched him without thinking, I just got scared."

"And the homophobia?" Eliza said to Quincy. They rolled their eyes.

"I thought everyone knew about that. Soon, I just began brushing it off. Water off a ducks back. For a long time, I figured it just went without saying that if I'm going to be queer on a major TV show, I'm going to get flack for it."

"Quincy, that isn't right."

"I know that now," they stressed. "I know it was wrong that they threatened to fire me, I know it was wrong they literally brought in AJ's character for me to kill him onscreen. I know it was wrong that after all that they brought in a girl just so *I* could be with a girl." They looked at Freya. "I'm *sorry* for treating you like shit for it, too, there was no valid reason for that. I was just, so angry."

Freya reached for Quincy. Squeezing their hand.

"It's okay, I forgive you," she smiled at them, they smiled right back. "I'd have been pissed, too. In fact, I *am* a little pissed on your behalf. I didn't know the half of it. I assume I still don't but I was just a fan. I was someone who loved watching *Adolescent Summers*. I actually shipped Dan and Todd; I was devastated when he died." She paused. "No, that's wrong. When he was killed. I didn't realise that was what I was coming in for."

"I was still an asshole."

"Oh, yeah you were," Freya smiled at them, they smiled back.

"You and *me*, we're going to be fucking best friends."

"Hey!" I gasped.

"Freya is going to be my girlfriend, move on, Oz."

I turned my shock to Brooklyn. He grinned at me

"I'm sorry I failed you kids," Eliza said. "I'm so sorry. I thought I was doing what was best for you all. I really did. I always."

"Eliza, I wouldn't have gotten through this last year without you. In fact, I wouldn't have survived my mother without you."

"You *literally* fostered me to keep me safe," Brooklyn added. "You took me into your home, if you hadn't done that…"

"I should've been better."

"It's okay," Dakota whispered. Eliza shook her head, Dakota cut her off. "Most first-time mums have no idea what they're doing, and you had to do it five times over." She smiled at Brooklyn. "And had to deal with *him*."

"She's my ADHD superhero," Brooklyn laughed. "Quincy was far higher maintenance."

"I am," Quincy agreed then drank from their beer.

Our phones pinged at the same time. Eliza frowned around the room.

"What have you done now?" she asked as she reached for her phone. I smirked at Dakota, she laughed softly, twisting the ring on her forefinger around as she looked at her own phone.

Email Received: admin@adolescentsummers.co.uk

"Well, that can't be good," I said. Brooklyn hummed as he looked at my phone over my shoulder. He reached over me to open the email.

Subject: Contract Termination.

Dear Oz Campbell,

We are sending you this email to confirm the termination of your *Adolescent Summers* contract. This is due to the cancellation of production; this will take effect immediately. As per the terms and conditions in your contract you will continue to be paid royalties and for any publicly events you attend. You will stop receiving your salary.

Please find this outlined in your contract that is attached. If you have any concerns or queries, please contact HR on hr@adolescentsummers.co.uk.

I stopped reading, looking up at Brooklyn as he frowned and reached for his own phone. I *guess* confirming he'd also received the email.

"What did you get?" I asked Quincy who frowned at their phone.

"*Adolescent Summers* has been cancelled; this means you will no longer receive your reduced salary," they sighed.

"Reduced salary?" Freya asked. Quincy waved their hand.

"They fired me, paid me off by dropping what I was earning to thirty percent, said I'd get that until the contract end date." They paused. "Which of us is going to work the streets then?" they added.

"I think with the four incomes we currently have; we'll be okay," Brooklyn said. "I can't believe they cancelled it."

"I can't believe they didn't cancel it sooner," Dakota muttered. "Well, I guess this'll be the last time we'll all be together, then?" Dakota said. I turned to her, my face must've done something. "I mean, there's no reason we'd meet up, is there? That became abundantly clear over the last few years."

"You stopped speaking to me," I said, "because of something I didn't even do."

"You never told me you hadn't."

"Because you weren't talking to me."

"Okay, okay, okay," Eliza interrupted, *probably* so we didn't end up throttling each other in her living room. "Let's be honest, it was a shitty situation all round, but now it's out, now Jordan will be trialled and I have no doubt will serve time.

"Now you can all do whatever the hell you want with your lives. Without restrictions."

"Voice acting," Brooklyn said. He sighed contently, leaning his head back against the couch. "I'm going to buy a microphone. And I can start *immediately,* you don't need both arms to speak."

Quincy laughed.

"I want to go to Japan," they sighed. "I just want to

go back home, for a little while at least."

"Movies," Dakota nodded. "I want to do movies."

"Soaps," Freya smiled. "I really want to be in soaps." She shook her head at Quincy as they smiled back at her.

"Primarily, I want top surgery," I said. "And I can get it *sooner* because now I don't have to wait for filming to end." I exhaled. "Then, I want to go back onto the stage."

Eliza looked at Arden. She smiled.

"Adoption?" she asked.

"Adoption."

Two years later

Brooklyn laughed, his breath tickling my neck as his beard scratched against my shoulder. I lowered my head as he glanced up at me.

"It's like, trying to unlearn something," he whispered. I frowned because I was pretty sure I didn't want him to unlearn the bits before we had sex. In fact, I'd be really quite upset if he did. "It's been years of not touching…" He opened his hand on my chest. I exhaled gently, feeling the warm handprint he left behind as he stroked down my stomach. "I kind of hesitate. Even though I know you've told me it's okay."

"Well, let's fix that," I whispered. He rose his eyebrow at me. I weaved my fingers through his hair, moving his head so he could kiss my chest.

He did. I felt him smile against my skin, his breath hot a stark contrast to how cold his nose ring was.

"Good?" he whispered. The noise I made in response wasn't quite words. He continued, stroking his fingers over my scars, before his lips followed.

Because apparently, I really, really liked my chest being touched and kissed.

"Tell me…" he whispered, his nose stroking against my nipple. "Is Romeo topless on stage at all?"

"Once," I whispered. "Twice potentially."

He tutted, before biting down on my nipple. I

choked.

"You sound disappointed?"

"Well, that means I can't suck on your chest," he sighed dramatically. "I can't make sure everyone knows your mine."

I smirked at him.

"If Quincy taught me anything when we were teenagers," I whispered, lifting Brooklyn's chin with my finger, "if its hidden well enough, you can suck as hard as you wish."

Brooklyn's throat clicked. His Adams apple bobbing precariously before he was searching up my chest, quick kisses until he focused in on my nipple, biting lightly, before sucking.

I swore. He laughed before backing away to admire his handy work.

He knelt up, the quilt falling around his hips, as he rose his fingers to his mouth and kissed as if saying 'fantastic'.

I stroked the very tip of my finger over his tattoo.

He shivered quite obviously before leaning back to give me more space. Smiling down at my fingers as I traced them over the heart rate line with three huge spikes.

I.

Love.

You.

I exhaled, meeting his eyes as my fingers drifted across his stomach then down to his dick. He laughed, the sound breathless and almost shocked although he soon relaxed into it. Leaning back on his hands, as he watched me.

The curses falling from his mouth. I gasped, *loudly*.

"How dare you? You're a children's cartoon character," I tsked. He snorted shaking his head as he threaded his fingers through my hair.

"Let's call these the bloopers," he whispered, then he laughed. "I have a lot of bloopers with swears."

I smirked at him, kissing his shoulder, then his chest as I moved down his body, he moved back, lower and lower until he was lying on the bed.

"You know…" I whispered as I kissed his stomach. "I'm so glad you've started interpreting non-verbal cues. You have no idea, Brooklyn."

He laughed, covering his eyes.

"I assume you're going to…"

I looked at him, I fully expected him to say, *suck my dick*, but of course he said, "Deliver fellatio."

"Correct," I laughed quietly, as I crossed my arms on his thighs, leaning my chin on my hands.

"Non-verbal cues are so hard," he murmured. "Use your words, you know."

"Okay…" I whispered. "Brooklyn, I'd like to suck your dick."

"That sounds like a good way to move this forward," he teased. I smirked at him *before* getting on with it.

His hand clasped over his mouth, when there was a knock on the door. I laughed, *almost* choking on him but I kept going - it was only polite.

Brooklyn took a breath.

"What?" he said.

"Get up, we have an interview in an hour," Quincy said through the door. I laughed, as I stopped moving, Brooklyn whined lightly.

"Okay," he replied.

"I'm coming in, in ten minutes. If you're not decent that's your problem," they said. I rose my eye line to look at Brooklyn. He sighed, so I began to move my hand. Keeping my mouth firmly around his tip.

He came quickly, it appearing to be as much of a

surprise to him as it was to me. I pulled off when I began to cough, laughing as I wiped my hand across my mouth, then grinning at him. He looked delighted as he deflated onto the bed.

"I'm going to get a shower," I laughed as I got off our bed, stopping to kiss him as he closed his eyes. "Take your time."

"I will move when the euphoria has passed," he told me. I shook my head leaving our room. Quincy purred at me from the stairs. I jumped.

"Look at you showing off your perfect chest."

I touched my chest, a grin on my face before turning towards the bathroom.

"But do make sure you brush your teeth, huh…" they smirked as they continued down the stairs. I rolled my eyes, laughing as I closed the door behind me.

I genuinely hadn't seen Dakota since the day our contracts had been terminated and we'd gotten ridiculously drunk in Eliza's front room.

She looked immaculate. In fact, I lost my breath when I actually saw her. I knew she'd been making movies. Brooklyn and I had, in fact, watched her first film since the series ended. It was good.

Freya looked *as* immaculate, actually. I think this had to be the first time I'd seen her as a woman. That was a shock to the senses, but she definitely wasn't a girl anymore. I shared this with Brooklyn as he sat on the makeup chair getting his beard trimmed. With some very strict instructions to the makeup artist for them not to remove the beard.

I had backed up the request, that beard was to stay.

"She does," Brooklyn whispered. "My god, when did she grow up?"

"You should invite her to your twenty-sixth

birthday."

"Shut up," he laughed. "I *know* I'm old." He turned to Quincy as they sat on the second makeup chair. "How are you? Nervous yet?" he asked, Quincy nodded exhaling.

"All checked-in, AJ is weighing our suitcases and finalising the little details. But we're ready to go." They looked at us. "I'm going to miss you guys."

"You'll be back," I said. "You *have* to come back for the premiere of your film."

Quincy laughed. "Of course. I need to outshine Brooklyn on the red carpet." They blew a kiss to him, Brooklyn caught it.

"*And* we're flying to Tokyo to meet you guys in, what? One hundred and something days?"

"One hundred and thirteen days," I told him.

"For, hopefully, our wedding." Quincy rose their crossed fingers. I did it back. "And then of course, yours."

I grinned as I looked down at my hand. Stroking my thumb over the silver band on my wedding finger. Brooklyn knocked his against mine, almost giving me a fist bump.

"Where are you leaving to?" Freya asked, leaning across the chair to join the conversation.

"We're flying into Tokyo, spending a few days there then heading to Yamakoshi."

Freya smiled at them, before requesting they bring back some mochi for her.

"Are you ready kids?"

We turned as one, all gasping unanimously. Eliza grinned at us from the doorway. "Sorry, *not* kids, not at all. Look at you fully integrated adults."

"What are you doing here?" Brooklyn laughed.

"I am your chaperone," she gasped. "It's a job for

life." She smiled as she walked towards us. "No, I came to be in the audience. Arden is here too, Tony."

"Our support system." I rose my fist, Brooklyn laughed doing it back.

"On set please," a voice called down the hall. I looked towards the TV that sat in the corner of the dressing room. A clock had appeared on screen, counting down to *obviously* showtime.

"Break a leg," Eliza said. "And you, enjoy your trip," she added, walking towards Quincy. They met her in the middle of the room, hugging her and speaking quietly to her. "You can call anytime, you know that."

Quincy nodded, smiling at her.

"And you're going to need to stay in touch, you can't expect Arden and I to raise this baby without you," she said. I turned fully to her, as she grinned at Quincy.

"No?" they gasped, stepping back from the hug, Eliza nodded, touching her stomach, Quincy rested their hand on top.

"We went for a surrogate, after discussing our options. Twelve weeks."

"Congratulations," Brooklyn gasped, standing from his chair to hug her.

"On set."

We began to move. Eliza following us down the corridor until she diverted to the audience.

"Be smart, kids, but most importantly…"

I turned to her as she smiled at us all in turn.

"Show the world who each and every one of you actually are."

Brooklyn took my hand, pulling me with him onto the set.

It had been a couch set before social distancing, now, everyone sat in individual armchairs, a little round table between each one. Except for the chairs that Brooklyn and I were led to. They were sat arm to arm. Brooklyn decided this was an invitation to poke me in the arm, I guess because he could reach.

We'd all been offered a drink of our choice. I'd gotten a vodka coke, Brooklyn had whined because he couldn't mix alcohol with his Ritalin - and if he wanted to get through this interview without saying something he probably shouldn't, he needed his Ritalin. He'd ended up drinking a lemonade.

The presenter came onto set, talking to the camera people, being fitted for his microphone.

"Scandal on set, rumours ripe, tonight we have the stars of the *biggest* show on TV, *Adolescent Summers*, here to tell us what happened and where they are now." He turned to us, introducing us one by one. We waved on cue.

He came and sat on his chair, smiling at us all, easing us in with small talk.

"So, Oz..."

I took a drink.

"Tell us how this all started, when you returned from lockdown as Oz..."

I nodded, taking a deep breath then I smiled at him.

"Stay with me here..." I began. "It's kind of a long story, and it jumps around a bit, there's things you need to know, so other things have context." I looked to Brooklyn as he nodded, smiling, encouraging me to continue. "Have you ever heard that song from *Sunset Boulevard*?"

The interviewer very openly frowned.

"That song struck me on our first day back in set, because it didn't matter how much I changed, *that* set never did."

Author's note

I started writing *Adolescent Summers* back in 2021, the later end, not the lockdown end as I wanted to write a story about fame – fun fact: this led to multiple books about famous people, but that's for later! – this one specifically was always Oz's story and came from the idea of transitioning during a season break. Simple, right? Throw in lockdown, and some outdated views, and suddenly the *Adolescent Summers* crew was born. It was simple, and Oz, Brooklyn, and Quincy made it so easy to write about them.

Fast forward to the Spring of 2022 and *Heartstopper* is released, and fast forward a little more to November 2022 and the 'fan base' had forced Kit Connor out through Twitter, after him being accused for 'queerbaiting', just FYI real people can't queerbait.

Queerbaiting is a marketing technique for fiction and entertainment in which creators hint at, but do not depict, same-sex romance or other LGBTQ+ representation.

Real people cannot do that and we, as a fan base, are not entitled to this information about anyone, celebrity or not. At this point *Adolescent Summers* was written and sitting in the editing pile waiting for its moment to shine and I suddenly realised just how important this book was.

There is a point, very early in Oz's transition where

he feels overwhelmed by everything, and to top it all off fans begin speculating about his gender, sending him trans flags and other trans merchandise as fan mail. All this before he's come out himself. Luckily for Oz he's been doing this whole 'fame' thing a while, he has Brooklyn to incept his fan mail, and he takes his time with coming out, with feeling comfortable opening his own fan mail, and accepting his identity. Some of us, Kit Connor included, don't have that privilege.

I remember being heartbroken the day it happened, how could a group of people who claimed to love him, love the show, love the series, attack and accuse an eighteen-year-old so much that he was forced to come out – and don't get me started on how those 'fans' missed the entire point of *Heartstopper* as it was, but the fact that this isn't even a rare occurrence, this type of thing happens all the time.

How often do you see speculation? How often do you see people asking, 'are you gay?' How often do people Google search someone's sexuality, or someone's partner? And how often are these things whispered in real life, about real people? It's 2024, get over it!

Some people are queer, and you are not entitled to this information.

This book is about Oz, but this book is also about Quincy, Brooklyn, and AJ. This book is about society standards and the need to hide. The span of this book is just over 10 years, starting in 2011 and ending around 2022. These characters start their journeys as children, the eldest being twelve, the youngest nine, and they grow and develop as the series goes on. They enter into relationships, they break up, they discover their sexualities, they explore their gender, they fall in love just like every teenager around the world does, the only difference is these kids do it on an international stage and everyone feels entitled to knowing every damn thing about them. At every point in this book, they deserved better (although shout out for Eliza who looked after those kids as if they were her own) and that is mostly what I want people to take from this story.

Oz, Quincy, Brooklyn, and AJ are all just people. They're teenagers for the most part, who are doing a job, whilst also navigating hormones and their parents, and adults' expectations just like the celebrities or TV stars we see on our screens. They give a huge part of themselves to us, the viewers, the fans, they give their souls, their passion.

There is a line in the song *Alive* by the Scarlet Opera, '*I've given it all away but some things are mine*'. When I heard this song for the first time, I knew this song would belong to *Adolescent Summers*, belong to Oz because like those on our screen, he gives so much to his fans, but there are some things that he wished just belonged to him, like his relationship with Brooklyn, like his transition.

This book touches upon this in more than just a gender and sexuality way. It touches upon neurodiversity and culture, it touches upon never escaping the limelight and losing people because of it, but it also explores the dangers of fame, the dangers of everyone knowing things about you (referring to Brookyln's car!) and of course the fear, the fear Dakota and Freya feel about exposing a well-known and well-respected director, so they don't ruin their own careers, their own futures.

The system is messed up, and teenagers and children in the system deserve so much better than they are getting. We, as fans, can take the first step and stop demanding the entire lives of people we see on our screens.

And stop assuming the sexuality or gender of people

you don't know – *actually* stop assuming the sexuality or gender of people you *do* know. Stop demanding people share their neurodiversity, or their culture.

Stop demanding, stop accusing, and start listening to their voices.

If you got this far, thank you for reading both *Adolescent Summers*, and this authors note. Thank you for joining Oz on his journey and I hope you take something from it. This isn't the last of the *Adolescent Summers* cast, so I won't give you a glimpse into their futures but know it all turns out okay, and one day hopefully soon, Japan will legalise gay marriage and Quincy and AJ will be able to get married as they have planned but for now, they're happy and thriving!

On a real note, thank you to my partner Lottie for not only loving Oz and Brooklyn as much as I do, but also willingly listening to me talking non-stop about them, helping me with any hard decisions and getting me through the last few months!

SRL Publishing don't just publish books, we also do our best in keeping this world sustainable. In the UK alone, over 77 million books are destroyed each year, unsold and unread, due to overproduction and bigger profit margins.

Our business model is inherently sustainable by only printing what we sell. While this means our cost price is much higher, it means we have minimum waste and zero returns. We made a public promise in 2020 to never overprint our books for the sake of profit.

We give back to our planet by calculating the number of trees used for our products so we can then replace them. We also calculate our carbon emissions and support projects which reduce CO_2. These same projects also support the United Nations Sustainable Development Goals.

The way we operate means we knowingly waive our profit margins for the sake of the environment. Every book sold via the SRL website plants at least one tree.

To find out more, please visit
www.srlpublishing.co.uk/responsibility